One Thing and Another

With thanks to …

Jan Cooper, David Cutler, Tony Ellis, Les Elvin, Jill Jenkins, John Miles, Barry Purdell, Linda Whyte, Irene Wright for their help during the past four years reading various drafts with a critical eye, editing and generally keeping me sane.

Former Woolworths Hastings branch staff: Debbie Baldock, Betty Ellwood and Gill Ward for their time and giving me a good sense about life on the shop floor at Woolies. Local studies at Hastings Library, Hastings & St Leonards Observer, Jess Steele – Deptford Forum Publishing, Hastings Pier & White Rock Trust (www.hpwrt.co.uk), Fiona Pienkowska – artist/printmaker, Jude Keen – designer, Jonathan Maine – Bookseller Crow on the hill (www.booksellercrow.co.uk), The Hastings Trawler, Hastings Own, Ian & Elaine Dixon – Winchelsea Beach, The Ship – Winchelsea Beach, Steve Peak's '*Mugsborough Revisited*'. Finally, Robert Tressell's '*The Ragged Trousered Philanthropists*' that led me to Hastings many years ago.

Mel Wright, July 2012

*   *   *

The author, Mel Wright is a community worker and a musician. He has written two previous novels: *Be Lucky!* and *Eva's Waltz* (Deptford Forum Publishing). He lives in London but also spends time in his caravan on Winchelsea Beach where most of this current novel was written.

Chris & Claire

One Thing and Another
a seaside caper

Mel Wright

All best wishes

Mel

25/2/13

Deptford Forum Publishing

Deptford Forum Publishing

One Thing and Another
©Mel Wright, 2012
First edition

First published in UK 2012
All rights reserved

Front cover illustration: *Watching The Girls Go By*
Fiona Pienkowska – artist/printmaker: info@fionapienkowska.com
www.fionapienkowska.com
Typesetting and layout by Jude Keen Ltd, 020 8355 4541
Printed and bound by **imprint**digital.net

www.melwright.co.uk

Deptford Forum Publishing www.dfpbooks.co.uk

ISBN 978-1-898536-18-5

For Isabella and a new generation

"Never trust a man who wears white shoes and has a moustache."
– someone's mum

∽ One ∽

Hastings – 2008

An unseasonably cold wind ripped across the lonely seafront and drove sheets of rain up into the town. It was early summer but you could have the fooled the day trippers. The loose ropes on flag poles feverishly clanked out a hypnotic rhythm, while the crazy golf course flooded. Beach clad visitors were forced to fork out more than they bargained for inside flashing amusement arcades, whilst some huddled in steamed-up cafes nursing mugs of tea. Others sheltered in rain lashed shop doorways clutching bags of vinegary chips or loitered uncomfortably in trinket shops with their dank hair dripping wet onto comic postcards. The local gulls had the right idea. Some of them sensibly conserved their energy by sheltering under the rusty rafters of the abandoned Victorian pier. The more hungry creatures high up, noisily circled the town's ancient narrow lanes and backdoor kitchens in the hope of easy pickings.

* * *

Bill

At the Job Centre high up the hill in St Leonards, a young adviser hovered around Bill as he laid down his drenched umbrella and stood self consciously in front of the newly

11

installed job search computer. He made him feel awkward. Bill could just see him over his left shoulder and he froze about what to do next.

"All right, sir?" the man spoke, friendly enough.

"Aye, yes. I was just … "

"You do it like this." He leaned forward, taking over, pressing the large button.

"See? Easy."

"Aye, thanks," but Bill was irritated already. 'Does he think I'm thick or something?' Bill trawled through different work categories: professional, skilled, catering, funeral services etc.

'Driver wanted with own van and clean license. Must be willing to be on call. Average £400 per week.'

'Office Assistant. Must have computer and administrative skills. Good prospects. Local. £12,000 pa.'

Bill scrolled down the list of jobs. They were not at all what he wanted, but after a long spell of looking for work, he was desperate to find something. During the past year he had applied for countless vacancies, been to umpteen interviews, endlessly re-jigged his CV, lowered his sights and following job centre advice had 'seriously revised his employment expectations'. With the pile of rejection letters and e-mails that said 'we regret to inform you' or promised to 'keep his details in case … ', Bill had come to the cold realisation that he was seen as a dinosaur in the job market.

Bill hit the key for 'Bar/Hotel,' studied the jobs and flipped back to one vacancy that he had spotted:

'Doorman/ Night Porter. Smart, reliable. Duties include: security of premises, checking in, cleaning, setting up breakfast, 40 hours. Shift work, local hotel. Uniform supplied. Good communication skills essential.'

'Hotel porter.' That might just do me. There could be canny tips and maybe you'd get your meals provided.' He thought about The Grand in his home town, Newcastle Upon Tyne. Two months ago Bill would have dismissed this job completely but now, what had he got to lose?

He noted the job vacancy number and looked around at the morning's gathering at the Centre. Quieter than usual, but it was a wet Wednesday.

A few people were awaiting appointments – some going through the motions and others perhaps on a last chance. Despite his conversion to being more flexible over job opportunities, Bill was still seething underneath, feeling betrayal and outrage. The light engineering trade that he had given his all for these last forty years had given him the push. And now for the first time in his life, redundant.

'Fuck!'

Just five years before his retirement.

'Fuck, fuck, almighty fuck.'

He'd been ripped off. His work pension in tatters after a Maxwell type bust and his state pension still a good swim away, he had to rely on his dwindling savings.

Bill stepped up to the desk. An adviser was on a computer and she made no sign that she had noticed him. He waited a while but felt sure that he was being ignored. He coughed gently to no avail.

"Excuse me."

There was still no response and she continued, glued to her screen.

"*Excuse me,*" Bill repeated, exasperation showing in his voice.

The middle aged woman cleared her throat and turned to Bill,

"Yes *SIR*, can I help?"

They looked at each other with an equal measure of snooty disrespect.

"I'm enquiring about the job as a hotel porter. Can you give me anymore details?"

She looked it up on the computer and then with a sudden spark, her manner became helpful.

"It's at The Cambridge, but I've got no more information. Are you interested in an interview?" She even smiled. Bill was stunned by this instant transformation and wondered if she was on a bonus whenever she clinched a job.

"Interested?" Bill looked at her almost accusingly, "I've no choice, pet. What with the way things are going with the crunch."

Her eyes narrowed again. "Any experience of hotel work?" Her disinterested tone was on the verge of being reinstated.

Bill shook his head. "I was an engineer by trade … " she hastily interrupted him.

"Well let's see, shall we." She phoned the hotel and booked an interview.

"Appointment at 10.30 am tomorrow, OK?"

"Aye that's fine." She handed Bill a print out confirming the details.

"Thanks."

"Don't be late will you?"

"I'm never late, me, pet."

Abi

By night time the rain had stopped. In a first floor council flat up town towards the station and in a bedroom femininely decorated with soft colours and cushions, Abi was entertaining. She liked being on top. It was her favourite position. She didn't mind being underneath her lover but she preferred to be more in charge of the rhythm and besides she could avoid all that bad breath.

Tonight things were hotting up. Gerry, a double glazing fitter who she'd been seeing for a couple of weeks, was coming to the boil and Abi rode him gently. She half opened her eyes as his hands reached up and gently squeezed her nipples through her new lacy black bra. Catching her breath, she unfastened herself and released her breasts invitingly for her new man.

"Oh yesss," he cried admiringly, cupping them, moaning with delight.

Abi skilfully slowed the pace so as he didn't get too excited.

"umm, oh … umm, yes … umm, ahhh."

Abi was enjoying this. She liked showing off a bit during love making.

'Still my biggest asset', she thought to herself, that and her liking for the slinky Ann Summers lingerie which she could hardly afford. Removing garments at the most crucial time – teasing and tantalising, as it said on the blurb:

'It's so sexy you just can't resist a shimmy.'

"umm, oh … umm, yes … umm, ahhh." Gerry was in heaven too.

Abi closed her eyes, moving in harmony.

"Oh yes, that's *nice*," she gasped.

He responded eagerly concentrating on her left breast, circling the tip of his tongue around her hardening nipple.

"Oooo," she purred with delight at the sharpness of his touch.

Their lovemaking was reaching a climax with Abi rocking up and down, one hand gripping on to the bed board, Gerry underneath with his eyes closed – ooing and ahhing.

"Who's this then?" a detached, rather squeaky voice suddenly hung over them.

Their intimacy was abruptly caught off guard as Gerry, startled, jolted out of his trance, seeing an elderly woman peering down at him. She had on a pink nightdress and a matching headband. The bedside lamp threw her eerie shadow across the ceiling. She had no teeth, making her face look rubbery and scary. With her eyes tightly closed, still in ecstasy, oblivious to this interruption, Abi continued to thrust and reaching a climax, huskily cried out in desperation, *"Don't stop … "*

But Gerry had frozen, looking at the old woman standing there, his erection duly folded.

"Ere, what's he doing in our house?" the old woman cried out, crabbily.

Abi's eyes shot open and immediately loosened her grip on

the bed board as she felt Gerry's limp cock smoothly pop out of her vagina like a train leaving a tunnel.

"What are you doing in here?" Abi cried. "Get back to bed."

"I don't like the look of him," the old woman sneered accusingly, pointing to Gerry, looking horrified and trying desperately to cover himself up. Abi quickly got off the bed, wrapped a dressing gown around herself and led the woman out of the room, speaking to her in a hushed tone.

"Come on auntie, you know that you should be in your own bed don't you?"

"I want my breakfast," the old woman retorted.

"But it's two o'clock in the morning."

Rita

The early morning sun had made a promise and by midday the seaside town was basking in a glowing yellow light that felt more like a dusty Mediterranean resort. Hastings was thriving; the Old Town under the eye of surrounding cliff tops and its quirky lean-to buildings, galleries, bric-a-brac shops and fishing huts backdrop. You could also spot some of the town's more bohemian characters with their craggy sunburnt faces. Some looking like they had come down for the day in the seventies and just stayed on. Almost on the sea front, Woolworths, bridging the old and the new, was busy with customers browsing around the bedding, gardening and paint section. The bright and breezy tannoy greeted them: "Don't forget this week's special offer on our very own Pick 'n' Mix selection."

Alone in the upstairs office the young woman's milky voice echoed across the store, dreamily. Unbeknown to all she had her feet up on the desk and was skilfully juggling the microphone, drawing on a cigarette by an open window; her face basking in the sunlight.

Downstairs on the shop floor a few day trippers were buying soft drinks and one little girl, standing shivering in her wet swimwear straight from the beach, was bought a cheap change of clothes by mum. Nearby, an elderly lady, always in a heavy coat and the same canvas slip-ons despite the warmer climes, was inspecting some potted plants. She had done this everyday for no one knew how long; muttering to herself about the prices and chatting to the staff, never buying a thing.

Rita had caught her knee on the checkout stool and winced with pain. She ducked down to rub it with one hand, but continued to scan the shopping items, her head almost peering above the counter. Beep – beep, the scanner sounded, competing as loudly as the gulls squawking on the pavement outside.

"What's wrong, luv?" her young mum customer asked and Rita found herself eye to eye with the woman's infant daughter staring up at her from the other side of the counter. The large woman, with a second infant in a buggy, had a heavy gold chain around her neck and a tattoo on her bare shoulder – *Darren's*.

Rita smiled through the pain, stood up and straightened her uniform.

"Oh just me knee."

"Arthritis?"

The question stung Rita more than her injured knee but before she could answer, the woman was packing away her shopping.

"My gran gets that. She's in agony, she is."

"No it's not arthrit … "

"Tracy, leave those sweets alone. You can't have any, right!" she barked for all the store to hear.

The girl and Rita looked at each other forlornly then the infant let out a low pitch moan that steadily picked up like an air raid siren.

"Nine pounds, forty, please," said Rita above the din.

The mum pulled out a crumpled twenty pound note from the back pocket of her jeans and paid. She picked up the change and left, dragging her bawling daughter along behind her.

On her morning break with her knee still aching, Rita half limped upstairs to the staff room and noticed how cracked her fingernails were as she reached inside her uniform and checked for texts on her mobile.

One from Colin. 'Out tonite save me dinner'

Another from her daughter Gayle. 'Need 20 for food.'

There were only a couple of others in the room. Rita went to her locker to get her handbag. Pasted on the inside of the door was a picture of a young Tom Jones from his '*Not Unusual*' days. She made herself a coffee, sat down and inspected her grazed knee. She touched it gently and then removed her shoes to put her feet up on another chair. Rita took two scratch cards out from her handbag and ran her thumbnail along them until the numbers appeared – no luck on either. She had been fired up by winning ten pounds last week. Rita pulled out a fresh Lotto slip and filled it in. 5 Gayle's birthday, 14 Little Dean's, 19 Colin's, 25 Dad's, 27 her own, 30 Mum's. God rest her soul.

Leo

It was a balmy evening and the sea was calm, glittering with patches of silvery light that spread right out to the horizon. A good time for walking across the beaten tracks of Hastings Country Park from East Hill, catching the sounds of skylarks ascending from ground to air with their rippling chirr-rr-up call echoing across the cliffs.

Leo was late in collecting his post from the communal hallway. Putting aside a depressingly familiar Inland Revenue manila envelope, he turned to another. 'That's the second this month,' he thought to himself as he scrutinised the pale green envelope. The same spindly handwriting, posted second class. Opening it up it contained two tickets for The Stables Theatre in Hastings; an Alan Ayckbourn play. For a while he had wondered if the local postmark may have been a decoy but he reckoned that these mystery gifts he had been getting for a year now were from someone local. Worryingly for him, whoever it was, knew his home address.

Leo had even thought about going to the police but it was hardly a crime being sent complimentary tickets, discount coupons for toothpaste, pizzas – two for one deals at a local restaurant, plus, the odd dusty looking potted plant left on the doorstep. He had even got an unsigned birthday card, so it must be someone who knew him well.

There was never any clue about the sender and Leo had always put these gifts straight in the bin. Who was it that sent them, one of his exes, a female admirer? Leo liked to think that it was the latter. For a while when he first started receiving them he was quite flattered, believing that it was from an acquaintance; perhaps someone whom he had danced with at The Regal. He had quietly eyed the regulars, speculating if any of them might be the mystery sender. A lonely divorcee, unhappy wife or an oversexed pensioner on a desperate do-or-bust mission? The possibilities were becoming bizarre but as time went by Leo's initial curiosity and flattery was replaced by irritation and a more ominous view of being watched – even stalked. It was making him feel quite paranoid. What next, dog poo?

In his small flat, Leo preened himself in front of his bedroom mirror. A Frank Sinatra CD was playing, '*Fly Me To The Moon*' and he swung along to the rhythm. He carefully combed his gelled, thick black hair and then stood admiring his profile. He'd come a long way since being jeered at school for being an 'Eyetie' but as he always said, that was something else that he and Frank had in common.

It was dance night and he wanted to look his best. The first outing for his new M&S suit, cream shirt, dark tie and stylish patent shoes. Mostly purchased with the aid of Payday loans.

The Regal Ballroom in town was still a popular venue and the singles nights attracted quite a variety of punters. Leo was a popular dance partner to many a divorcee whom he charmed with his foxtrots, waltzes, jive, quick-step and tangos which he had learnt as a kid at The Hastings School of Dancing. The ballroom was exquisite, a left over from the 1950's with glittering chandeliers, ornate fittings and gently fading plush scarlet and gilt Viennese-style décor.

As Leo strutted across the dance floor familiar female eyes darted his way – all eager to catch his gaze. He smiled and nodded. Mike the DJ had astutely spotted his promenading and struck up a Billy Fury hit … '*It's all over my jealousy …* '

The tango beat bounced and the strings plucked. Leo smiled, clicked his heels and vainly tipped his head toward Mike for acknowledging his arrival. Just as he reached the side bar a woman stepped out in front of him blocking his way.

"Hello Leo."

Leo's smile remained intact but he was not pleased to see her.

She was an attractive woman in her mid fifties wearing a black dress and pearl necklace. She had dark brown eyes.

"Remember me?" she teased him, slightly rolling her head to one side.

"Jane, darling," he said, taking her hand.

"Come and have a drink."

He led her through to the bar which was empty apart from a young barmaid behind the counter and a man on a stool who was chatting to her.

"Sit down, I'll bring it over," Leo beckoned her to a corner table.

"What are you having?"

"Oh you know, my usual."

"Yes of course."

Leo pulled out a note from his wallet and walked casually over to the bar.

While she got herself settled he glanced back at her. She smiled and he waved the tenner.

The barmaid broke off her conversation to serve him.

"Two gin and tonics, please."

"Ice and lemon?"

"What?" Leo was still preoccupied with looking at his unexpected companion.

"Ice & lemon?"

"Yes, thank you."

He paid, brought the drinks over and sat down at the table.

"Well this is nice seeing you again." Leo raised his glass and smiled.

"Yes, isn't it?" Her voice had subtly turned a little frosty, he noticed.

"But it might have been nicer if you had remembered that my usual drink was Bacardi and coke." Behind the smile Leo froze for a moment then he leant forward patting her arm. "Oh Jane, my dear, I'm so sorry, you know me … " he chuckled.

"Yes, I know you all right, Leo. Too bloody well!" She hissed, looking at him quite angrily.

Her voice rose above the sound of 'La Bamba' coming from the dance floor. Leo drew back slightly from her rebuke, frowning and placing his forefinger over his lips in a gesture to try and quieten her down.

"And what about my money, Leo? Five hundred pounds. When am I going to see that?" Leo's face had turned quite pale.

"Now, darling, please, relax. You know that I was going to get in touch."

"Did I?" she asked and jerkily poured the rest of the tonic right up to the top of her glass.

"Of course. What sort of person do you take me for?" Wisely, Leo didn't give her time to answer. "Look, to tell you the truth my business has gone belly up lately what with the financial situation. And well, it's not been easy. Leo sighed and looked rather sorry for himself.

"It's over three months, Leo. Not a word from you," she rebuked sharply. Leo tried another oily grin.

"You never answer my calls or texts. Nothing," she continued.

Leo shook his head and reached over to hold her hand but she quickly drew back. "Leo, you are a fucking liar!"

He quickly looked behind him but thankfully the couple at the bar were still chatting. When he turned back Jane was standing over him, poised with her full glass of G&T ready to give him a soaking. His face was full of horror. She looked scary.

"Look I know you're upset but … ," he threw his hands up

in defence, closed his eyes, wincing and fearing the worst for the new suit.

Then feeling only a small spattering of the drink, he squeezed his eyes open, shocked to see that she had poured both their drinks over herself.

"Argh, you sod, you horrible sod!" she screamed. Jane was standing slightly hunched, her hair drenched and glistening, the G&T running down her face and already blotching her eye shadow and dripping onto her dress.

Leo couldn't believe it. He automatically got up and brushed some droplets off his suit.

"What are you doing, you stupid woman?" He reached out to comfort her.

"Don't touch me!" she squealed. "Don't you dare touch me!" holding her hand up and stepping aside.

"What?"

"You heard me."

Moving towards the bar, a small crowd, hearing the commotion had gathered by the door. "Look what he did!"

Leo became agitated, following her and gesturing with his hands wide open.

"Jane, please don't." He tried to pacify her, but she lurched forward, almost frenzied and when she turned round sharply he was showered by her soaking hair. The barmaid rushed over with a small towel.

"He did this!" Pointing at Leo, dagger-like. "He's gone mad."

"Me, mad? "Leo tried to laugh it off but he could see a number of accusing eyes lining up.

"I'll call the police," the barmaid said, rather excitedly.

"No, no, I don't want them involved. Just get him out of here." The barmaid tried to help dry her hair.

"What are you doing, you silly woman?" Leo implored. The barmaid gave him a steely look and put her hand reassuringly on Jane's arm as a gesture of solidarity.

"I didn't do this," Leo pointed looking mortified and grinning awkwardly.

"Jane, look, let's just sit down quietly and try and sort this out. There's no need for all this, really."

Leo was standing, shaking his head in disbelief when he felt the heavy hand of one of the ballroom bouncers firmly on his shoulder.

"Right you, we don't want anymore trouble. You're barred."

"You've got it all wrong, she's nuts, mad as a hatter," Leo pleaded as he was marched off across the ballroom, followed by suspicious looks that only a little earlier had been full of evening promise.

"And I hadn't even had a dance," he muttered as he was left on the front steps and was warned not to come back.

∼ Two ∼

The Cambridge Hotel, until recently had been a long term residence for elderly gentlefolk living in declining grandeur. The building had recently been spruced up and now boasted a spa. Bill, dressed in his only suit, dark blue and wearing ill matched grey shoes, stepped up to the reception. The palatial Victorian lobby was quite splendid with its chandelier, ornate brass table lamps and oak panelled walls. The young woman at the counter chatting to one of her colleagues, broke off and beamed up at him.

"Good morning how can I help you?"

Bill detected an East European accent although her English sounded excellent.

"I've come about the vacancy as a doorman." He showed her the details from the Job Centre. She glanced at his paper and picked up the phone.

"Please take a seat, Mr Shields, someone will be with you very shortly."

Bill smiled at her. There was just one other person in the lobby, a man, sitting in an armchair reading The Daily Mail. He lowered the paper slightly, looked at Bill over the rim of his glasses and then continued reading. Bill sat on the plush leather sofa opposite, sinking down much lower than he expected to. He heard a quiet chuckling from behind the newspaper which moved in time with the reader's laughter. Bill thought for a moment that he was laughing at him. The man's long legs were crossed and Bill noticed that he was wearing expensive Italian looking shoes.

As Bill began admiring the decorative ceiling, the clatter of footsteps across the marble floor broke his concentration. A rather stout looking man in his early forties carrying a folder stood slightly back from the sofa so Bill had to crane his neck round to look up at him.

"Gentlemen, I'm afraid you have both had a wasted journey."

The man with the newspaper revealed himself and put it aside.

"What do you mean?"

"The vacancy has been filled I'm afraid. We took somebody on as a doorman yesterday. I had e-mailed the Job Centre but obviously the message hadn't got through to you both."

"Typical!" Bill tutted, raising his eyebrows, looking over to the other candidate who frowned and said, "This really is a disgrace."

The hotel manager shrugged his shoulders and tried to dismiss the matter but he could see that they both looked upset.

"I'm very sorry, gentlemen, but it's just one of those things." He wavered rather apologetically then asked, "Perhaps you would like a cup of coffee before you leave?"

"Something stronger would be more welcome," The Daily Mail reader jumped in quickly. The hotel manager raised his eyebrows, forcing a smile.

"A scotch?" the man suggested.

"And for you, sir?" the manager turned to Bill.

"Oh, a cup of coffee will be fine."

"Very good, gentlemen, I'll see to it."

"With ice please," added the man as the manager walked away.

"What a cock up," Bill remarked.

"Well to be honest it's a relief."

"What do you mean?" Bill asked.

Looking a bit shifty he leant forward, whispering. "That the job's gone!"

"You mean, you weren't interested?" Bill asked.

"Of course not," he sniggered, putting the newspaper aside, "I only came so as to get the Job Centre off my back. This is the third one this month. I wish they'd leave me alone. A doorman, I ask you. Me? Standing outside in all weathers. I'd never live it down."

The drinks arrived and they nodded to the waiter.

"By the way, Leo's the name." He held out his hand and they shook.

"Mine's Bill."

"What's your line then, Bill?" Leo enquired, swigging his scotch and ice.

"It *was* light engineering in Newcastle," Bill said rather forlornly, "forty year until they went bust."

"You mean you worked for the same company for all that time?" Leo asked with a look of disbelief.

"Aye, more or less, yes."

"I see," Leo said as he watched Bill drink his coffee.

"What about yourself?" Bill asked.

"Me?" Leo gestured as though he had a long tale to tell. He sipped his scotch and relaxed back in the armchair looking very much at home.

"Well I've never really fitted in the world of nine to five. I'm more your entrepreneur, if you get my meaning."

"Wheeler dealer?" Bill smiled.

"Well no, not really. More your Richard Branson," Leo suggested.

"Oh aye?" Bill's eyes widened.

"I'm in property development."

Bill sipped his coffee not looking very impressed. "Well you must have taken a pasting. The whole market's collapsing, man."

"It's just a down turn. Things'll spring back, you'll see."

"Well they're talking about house prices dropping even more before they pick up again – the boom's over. Mind you," Bill continued, leaning forward, balancing his cup and saucer carefully in his hand, "I'm glad it is. What chance have young people got in finding a place they can afford, these days?"

Leo laughed at him. "Well you're forgetting, matey, if it weren't for people like me buying and doing places up for rent then they'd really be stuck. When things crashed I was converting a rambling, eight bedroom house up on The Ridge that I'd bought at auction. But what now?" Leo averted looking at Bill in the eye as if he had something to hide and took another swig of whisky.

"I've seen that Sarah Beeny programme, '*Property Ladder*' on the telly about people buying places and doing them up to sell," Bill said chirpily.

"Some of them do OK but it seems a risky business, mind. You can come unstuck and go over budget. Sarah says … "

"They're all amateurs," Leo jumped in sharply, leaning over to Bill, his face beginning to flush. "Look I run a property business. I'm a professional. I've done conversions all over Hastings – top quality. You can't compare it with these part timers." He sat back again, looking rather rattled with Bill.

There was an uneasy silence and Bill wondered if he had hit a nerve.

"Well what you dooin here then?" Bill's melodious Geordie accent rose higher.

"That's the thing with business. It's all about cash flow. And what with the credit crunch I've had to suspend operations."

"Shut up shop, like?"

"In a manner of speaking, yes. Only temporary just until, you know, things pick up."

"You must be gutted, man. Signing on at the Job Centre when you've got your own business. Could you not have diversified into other areas to keep things going?"

Leo gave him a condescending look and shook his head but Bill continued.

"Why aye, it must be a come down for ya? You an entrepreneur chasing a job as a hotel doorman. It's like we're back to the days of Maggie Thatcher, man."

Leo grinned. "To tell you the truth I'm quite enjoying the

break from running my own business for a while. All that responsibility can wear you down, being your own boss."

"Well, I think it's outrageous. I'm a highly skilled engineer, me. Been working since I was an apprentice at sixteen. And now nothing. They want me to forget about all my expertise and learn new skills. Lower me sights and just earn a pittance. I said, 'Look here, pet, you canna expect me to start a new career at my time of life'."

"Well if there aren't any jobs, I suppose you've got no choice, matey," Leo said, flatly.

"Aye well that's as maybe but I reckon it's my trade union activities over the years that's marked my card. They've had their eye on me. That's what I think."

"Who?"

"You know, MI5 or whoever – surveillance."

Leo looked at Bill as though he were deranged.

"So, you've been a trouble maker!"

"No, no just defending rights in the workplace. It goes against the grain nowadays with all this deregulation and short term contracts. Young people haven't got any job security ya know?"

"Sod the young un's. They're a lazy bunch these days. Some of 'em who work for me. I tell you they don't know what work is. And as for job security and health and safety – don't get me started on that. I wish that Maggie Thatcher was back in power!"

Bill looked at Leo stony faced, realising that they really were on different sides of the fence.

"She murdered the north east, that woman," Bill spat out. "Closed all the pits, impoverished all the mining communities. They've never recovered you know?"

"Oh come on, mining was on its last legs here. And it's dangerous, unhealthy work. I'm pleased to see it gone."

"Well it kept this country going for years and now we have to import the stuff from Poland."

The two men realised that they weren't going to agree on this and so they finished their drinks quietly.

"You're a long way from Geordie land. How did you end up down here?"

"I've always liked Hastings and I thought – a new start."

"Well you couldn't have picked a worse place. Things aren't too clever around here."

"We'll see. Anyway I needed to get away."

"MI5?" Leo smiled, mischievously.

Bill looked serious, "No, lots of things. I needed me own space."

"You've got that down here all right. You can certainly lose yourself. I know I have." The men left the hotel, wishing each other good luck and went their separate ways.

∼ Three ∼

"Come on auntie, eat up your cornflakes." Abi's plea was slipping into more of a demand. Sitting opposite each other in their dressing gowns at the breakfast table in the small kitchen of their flat, auntie Millie stared at her cereal wondering for a while who she was.

"Auntie did you hear me?" Abi immediately regretted the sharpness of her tone, noticing how preoccupied the old lady seemed to be.

"Auntie?" she asked more gently as she sipped her black coffee and drew on her Silk Cut.

"Do you want some more sugar?"

The old woman looked up, smiled and in a second she reached over to the bowl. Before Abi could stop her she had scooped up a handful of sugar and the granules showered down like silver rain across the table, floor and on to the cat who quickly scarpered into the bedroom.

"Oh no, look what you've done, you silly mare." Abi screeched but immediately seeing the funny side, yelped with joy and auntie's eyes twinkled with delight as they both bellowed with laughter.

After breakfast, in the bedroom, Abi carefully laid out Millie's clothes on the bed while her aunt sat at the other end watching her.

"What about this nice green dress?" Abi said, holding it up.

"That's not green," Millie laughed. "It's wotsit, yer know," pulling a face.

"What colour is it then?" Abi hovered on the brink of teasing her.

"Yellow, I like yellow."

"It's not yellow. Look, this is yellow," Abi held up a bright vase from her dressing room table.

"I'll have my yellow dress," Millie persisted.

"You haven't got one," Abi was beginning to feel exasperated.

"Look, just put this one on and I'll try and get a yellow dress for you, OK?" Millie looked at her sullenly, "I'm feeling done in today."

Abi gently eased Millie out of her dressing gown. The room had an apple flavour scent. It was what Millie liked. It reminded Abi of scrumping for apples with her friend Rita, on a farm over Winchelsea way when they were kids. Millie stood naked and silent for a moment looking quite vulnerable against the dressing room mirror. Her diminutive frame and sparrow like legs were cast in the warm sunlight streaming through the window. Surprisingly, Abi thought in comparison, that her auntie's small breasts seemed very well preserved. She also noticed her drooping shoulders and how bowed Millie's back had become in recent years. She now towered over her aunt like a giant. Abi had to sometimes remind herself that this was still the Millie who showed her a good sense of humour and how kindness itself can change almost anything. Abi was ashamed to admit that she didn't follow her example. She knew that she had a very different, more volatile temperament but Millie had always given her a great sense of belonging. She realised that at least.

The real auntie was still there of course but in the morning it just took her longer to fire herself up and get going. When she did, Millie could be as lively and funny as she always was. Whenever Abi thought about her own possible future dotage she immediately dismissed it, instead she paid as much attention to her appearance as possible – applying facial creams, doing exercises and dreaming about various out of reach cosmetic surgery procedures which professed to hold back the ageing process.

During the sixties Abi's mum and Millie ran a B&B in Hastings. Auntie enjoyed being a seaside landlady and was more front-of-house than Abi's mum who cooked the breakfasts and handled the business side of things. Millie was never much good with money, that was definitely something she and Abi had in common. In the post-war heyday of British holidays, Abi recalled that the house was full every summer with families on their annual holidays. As she got older Abi helped out to earn some extra pocket money. She enjoyed the atmosphere of the place and clientele – entertained by Millie's breezy early morning singsong serving of full English breakfasts – "Red hot plates coming through. Okey doke!"

Then later Abi's mum became ill and the advent of foreign package holidays put paid to the traditional B&B. In Hastings the holiday trade suffered. Millie blamed it solely on Freddie Laker, famous for his cheap air travel. For a woman without a harsh word to say about anyone, she let loose venomously whenever the plight of B&Bs came up. Freddie Laker was the devil! But what with Abi's mum dying from lung cancer when her daughter was in her early twenties things started to go from bad to worse. During the recession in the seventies, their vacancy sign seemed to be permanently on display. Being stony broke, Millie had to eventually sell up and move into a council flat. Much later, Abi moved in to look after her.

"Come on then," Abi sighed, trying to coax her as they began their morning routine:

"OK auntie, stand up. Nightdress off."

Over the head, panic, struggle, and loud scream from Millie inside the garment. "Where am I?"

Done.

"Knickers on." Lift left foot, then the right. Stand up. "They're on!"

"Bra." Right arm, left arm. Fasten up.

Done.

"Sit down, auntie."

"Tights." Roll them up, get on left foot. Millie wriggled it around.

Chase it, lose it.

They tried once more.

Abi rolled them up again. Millie wriggled even more.

"It's impossible!"

Abi screamed.

Even bigger scream from auntie.

Abi gave up on tights and threw them across the room and continued.

Dress on over head (repeat nightdress procedure in reverse).

Auntie screamed again, "Where am I?"

Finished.

Relax!

Abi collapsed in a heap on the bed and auntie looked down at her.

"Where's my yellow dress?" Millie began mooching around in her wardrobe.

"What?" Abi had her eyes closed. She was already feeling completely exhausted and it was only half past ten.

"I'll just get ready for work then," auntie said casually.

"Yeah, sure, whatever," Abi agreed, lazily. "Have a good day at the shop."

Just as Abi was dozing off her phone buzzed from inside her dressing gown pocket. She felt for it without opening her eyes or losing her drowsy bliss. She peeked at the message.

"Thanx 4 hot romp. Auntie could join us nxt time! G x"

Abi automatically deleted the message and then her one-off lover's number from her mobile altogether.

"No next time for you, darling." She rolled over on her side and buried herself under auntie's duvet. Abi's mind quickly drifted afar as the warmth of the bed soaked through her body and Millie's moving around the flat became muffled. Closing her eyes, colourful puffy clouds appeared dancing across a bright blue sky. Abi floated away in the expanse, as she dozed and dozed.

She wanted to stay there forever.

∼ Four ∼

At Woolworths Bill was looking at the household cleaning materials high on the shelves, but decided that he could buy them cheaper in Tesco's. All the same Woolies drew him in just as it did as a child in Newcastle going with mum to buy sweets and later in his early teens for budget Embassy record versions of pop songs.

On the upper floor Bill picked up some J cloths and hooks for hanging cups. He then looked at a set of plates, picking one up and wondering if he should splash out in the unlikely event that he might invite anyone around to his flat for dinner. He considered what to get; white rimmed, Denby Imperial or Country Cottage – it was all very confusing. He held one up to the light but suddenly his hand slipped. Reacting jerkily, almost juggling the plate, he lost his grip on his heavy Poundland carrier bag and a bottle of tomato sauce hopped out and hit the floor with such force, splattering a streaky ketchuppy pattern that was reminiscent of a Jackson Pollock painting.

"Oh no!" Bill squirmed with embarrassment, looking at the broken glass. People already began shuffling around him and stepping over the gooey mess.

Almost immediately, over the shop's tannoy came: "Staff announcement. Michael, can you go to aisle four to clear a spillage please."

Bill was a little spooked by this and while he was looking up, he heard another voice behind him.

"Hello matey, been having fun?"

It was Leo from the hotel interview looking just as smug and dapper like before.

"Oh, hi," smiled Bill, still feeling upset. Then a young assistant arrived with a mop and bucket to clear it up.

"Sorry," Bill gestured to him.

"No problem, it happens all the time."

Bill and Leo headed for the checkout downstairs. Whilst they queued up to pay, Leo complained about never being able to find anything he wanted in Woolworths. Bill began championing the good value at Poundland, but Leo didn't look impressed, especially when Bill proudly showed off his bargain hunting cache, including an end-of-the-line dented can of minestrone soup.

"You'd be better off making your own you know, much healthier, probably cheaper too in the long run."

"Well, I'm more of a boil-in-the-bag-man, me!" Bill retorted, trying to strike a note of irony.

"I see," said Leo, looking at him over the rim of his glasses.

Rita was at the check out and without looking up at Bill she began scanning his purchases. She stopped at a bar of milk chocolate that he had picked up.

"Do you know these are buy one, get one free?"

This really cheered Bill up and Rita asked an assistant to collect another one for him. While they waited, she asked him "What have you done to your hand, is that blood?"

Bill hadn't noticed that he had caught some of the spilt ketchup on the sleeve of his jacket.

"Oh I've just had an accident with a bottle of tomato sauce."

"Now he's very saucy!" Leo piped up, from behind, chuckling.

"Oh is he?" Rita grinned and could see Bill trying to dab it off with a tissue.

"Look at this, I'll have to get it dry cleaned now," he moaned under his breath.

"When you get home, just get your wife to dab it off with some stain remover, that should do the trick," suggested Rita.

"I think I can manage, thanks."

"That'll be three pounds sixty please."

While Bill searched for a tenner, Leo, now standing beside him, stuck his oar in again.

"Quite frankly I think he could do with some help with his dry cleaning," Leo winked.

"Give it a rest, can't you," Bill snapped.

Rita began scanning Leo's shopping, gazing at the two of them with mild amusement.

Leo moved forward, spotting her name badge. "As for me, Rita Edwards, I wouldn't say no to a helping hand from a good lady like yourself."

Rita smiled, "Down Romeo, or you'll have my manager on my back for fraternising with the customers."

"Lovely word, fraternise, don't you think – you'll have to show me what it means sometime," he grinned.

Rita glanced over at Bill and they both raised their eyebrows.

As Leo finished packing his purchases they walked to the door.

"Are you always like this?" Bill asked, tetchily, still dabbing at the sauce stain on his jacket.

"Like what?"

"You know, with women."

"What's the matter with you?" Leo shrugged. "We both had a bit of a laugh, didn't we, and we made her day," Leo said, nodding towards Rita. Bill shook his head in disbelief as they left the store.

Just by the exit Leo noticed on the community notice board:
'Dance and Social. Cliff End Community Centre. Saturday 17th May. 8pm. Plus Grand Draw, prize £100. Admission £5.'

"That looks good, how about going, Bill?"

"I canna' dance," Bill moaned.

"Of course you can."

"I've got two left feet, man."

"Look, I'll teach you, it's easy. Listen matey, it'll be fine and there's a chance of winning some dosh. I could do with that at the moment. Come on, you'll enjoy it."

∼ Five ∼

The Cliff End Community Centre was heaving. The Saturday night dance had attracted a big crowd. By the time Bill and Leo had arrived there were only a few tables left. They ambled up to the makeshift bar and while Leo looked around to see if there was anyone he knew or should be avoiding, Bill bought some drinks.

"Cheers, matey," said Leo, supping the cold lager.

"Urgh!" Bill winced, "this beer's foul. And plastic glasses!"

"You should stick to the lager."

The flashing disco lights showed up the signs of the hall's regular use as a youth club and sports centre. The dancing had already begun and a slow number got some women up together in a circle. 'When you are in love with a beautiful woman … '

"Anyone you fancy?" asked Leo.

"I told you, I'm just here for a pint and the draw."

"Cor that one's got a big future in front of her," Leo ogled a rather plump young blonde woman with high heels and a skimpy top swinging herself around.

"You're old enough to be her grandfather."

"Let's go and join the dancing," suggested Leo.

"No way, man," Bill hurriedly looked round for a seat to retreat to.

They carried on drinking, standing by the bar, gazing at the dancers moving around on the floor to '*Don't Leave Me This Way*', '*Le Freak*' and '*Blame It On The Boogie*'.

Suddenly the disco mood was changed by '*Agadoo.*' A larger group converged on to the floor in a circle and did all the hand movements.

'*Ag – a – doo, doo doo push pineapple to the tree …* '

Young women, mothers, grandmothers, nieces, aunties and children all bounded around to the sound of Black Lace. One of the older women took the lead and shouted out the lyrics. Leo laughed at the fun.

By now Bill and Leo had spotted a vacant table near the bar.

"What's your lucky draw number, Leo?"

"Forty seven," he replied, pulling it out of his jacket pocket to check.

"Yours?"

"Fifty. That was the year my wife was born," Bill remarked.

Leo looked curious. "Oh yeah. So, where's she tonight then?"

"She died," Bill stated quite matter of fact, glancing at the dancers and taking a drink of his beer.

"Oh I see, I'm sorry to hear that."

Bill shrugged his shoulders.

"How long ago?"

"A couple of year now."

"Was it … ?"

Bill looked Leo straight in the eye as though he knew what he was going to say, "Cancer, aye."

"Oh!" Feeling awkward and at a loss to say anything more, Leo suddenly jumped to his feet and had another swig of his lager.

"I'm going to have a dance."

With '*Brown Girl In The Ring*' rousing the crowd, he went into the middle of the dance floor. Bill remained rooted to his seat and looked at Leo dancing away as the music blared out. Swiftly finishing his drink, he decided to take Leo's advice and go on to lager. He reckoned he could afford to buy a couple more drinks during the evening and so he went up to the bar while it wasn't crowded. As he was served, a woman joined him at the counter and he instinctively looked over. It was Rita, the checkout woman from Woolworths.

He caught her eye and she acknowledged him with a smile.

"Oh, hello, did you get your dry cleaning done OK then?"

Bill smiled,

"Oh aye, it wasn't that bad, mind."

"You're a Geordie aren't you. Where are you from?"

"Newcastle originally but I've been living doon south for a while now. Almost lost my accent! "

"I love the Geordie dialect."

"A lot of people canna understand it," Bill remarked as he paid for his pint and Rita got in her order of several drinks.

"Do you , er … ?"

"Come here often," Rita swiftly joked above the loud music.

"Oh, no," Bill laughed. "I meant do you like working at Woolies?"

Rita nodded. "It's OK, the money's not great but I like my mates there and you meet all sorts."

"How's your flirty mate?" she asked but Bill misheard her.

"Me what, dirty mate?"

"Flirty," Rita laughed.

"Oh him," he smiled. "Well he's hardly me mate but there he is," and he pointed to the middle of the crowd where Leo was dancing with a group of women to '*Hold On To Your Love!*'

"He looks like he's enjoying himself," Rita grinned, picking up her tray of drinks.

"Yes he knows how to do that all right."

"Well I'd better get these back to my lot," and nodded over to the table where there was a large group of her work mates.

A little while later Leo returned to the table looking quite exhausted. He took his jacket off and slumped down in the chair. Running the back of his hand over his hot and sweaty forehead, he took a long drink of lager.

"Ahhh … " he sighed with relief, "that's better. They're an energetic bunch, I can tell you, matey, especially that red head I've been dancing with."

They both looked over towards the tall woman still dancing away.

"Did you get her name?" asked Bill, still having to shout over the music.

'When you're in love with a beautiful woman … '

"Abi, and she can certainly dance that bird," Leo left Bill and went back to the dance floor.

∼ Six ∼

Two weeks later Bill and Leo arranged to meet at Rosa's cafe on the seafront. The place had opened in 1953, the year of the Queen's Coronation. Rosa's family came from Italy. Her parents were socialists and they arrived in Britain in the late forties and settled in Hastings. On the wall behind the counter, there was a framed, faded, black and white photograph of Palmiro Togliatti, an Italian wartime communist leader next to a small Italian flag and a faded black and white photo of Rosa's late mother. During the war her family had fought the fascists. Bill, being a staunch trade unionist himself, had taken a shine to the place and Rosa's father now quite elderly, sometimes still helped out in the cafe with washing and clearing up. Rosa was rather plump, late fifties, a cheery matriarch with a deep cockney accent even though she had only ever been to London twice in her life. Perhaps her regular banter with south London day trippers had rubbed off.

The cafe, open all year round still had a classic fifties look about it, with rather creaking formica tables, strawberry red and cream walls, oblong mirrors and chairs with worn leather seating. It was a welcoming place and the menu was cheap and cheerful, which is another reason Bill liked it. The all day breakfast – combinations of eggs, bacon, baked beans, bubble and squeak, black pudding – the marathon Porky Buster included three sausages. Rosa's warming afters consisted of apple crumble or steam pudding and custard were a popular delight.

"Hello darling, how are you?" Rosa greeted Bill as he fell into the cafe, buffeted by a strong gale, struggling to close the door behind him. He ordered a mug of tea and sat by the window observing the grey sky, shredded by menacing inky black clouds. Up towards the pier, surging waves slammed hard against the shingle and shot over the sea wall on to the pavement. A few solitary figures cautiously snaked around it along the promenade. The cafe was normally a magnet for day trippers during the summer but on a chilly day like today, it was quiet. Rosa's daughter brought over Bill's tea.

Bill opened his Guardian and began reading. In a short while he got so engrossed in the crossword that he didn't notice that Rita and Abi from the dance had slipped in and were sitting on the other side of the cafe.

Windblown, Abi removed her raincoat, tried to straighten out her tangled hair and squeezed her long legs under the fixed table opposite Rita.

Their drinks arrived and she cradled her milky coffee in both hands after their brisk walk along the front.

"So, how's your Colin?" Abi asked.

"Well you know, the usual," Rita muttered putting some sugar into her cup.

"Pissing you about you mean!"

Rita raised her eyebrows and quietly sipped her coffee.

Abi sighed, "I tell you Rita, you're daft to stay with him the way he treats you. He's a bully." Rita looked at her blankly.

"Honestly love, I worry about you with him. He's been getting worse since your Gayle's moved out."

"Don't worry about me, I can look after myself. We're not in the school playground now you know," she laughed.

Abi got her cigarettes out of her coat pocket and placed the packet on the table, deciding to get warm before venturing outside for a drag. She yawned.

"Tired?"

"A bit, yeah," she stretched out her arms.

"And how is auntie?" Rita assumed that Abi had had another restless night with her.

"Oh don't ask. I just had to get out this morning before I went dotty. I caught her trying to clean the kitchen windows with washing up liquid. She had soap suds up her arms, down her clothes and all over the windows. It was like a bubble bath. I had to change her dress again. It was a nightmare!"

Abi put her head in her hands in mock desperation. Rita began to chuckle at the thought of the bubbly chaos.

"It's not funny, Rita. She's gonna be the death of me, that old cow."

"Now, come on, you don't mean that. She's been like a mother to you. And she was always good to me when we were young."

"Well you look after her then! You move in with her and I'll come and stay with Colin. How's that?" Abi's face lit up.

"Oh, he'd like that," Rita grinned.

"I bet he would until I put some arsenic in his cornflakes!"

"Don't be wicked!"

The women laughed and began to feel much warmer now that the coffee was doing the trick.

"So how's the new boyfriend, Gerry?"

"Don't ask." Abi rolled her eyes. "He got very clingy so I dumped him," she said rather offhand.

"Oh, that was quick wasn't it? I didn't even meet him," Rita sounded disappointed.

"He wasn't much to write home about," Abi began fiddling with her cigarette lighter lying on the table, dying to have a drag.

"I liked Dave with the tattoo, he was funny. What happened there?" Rita enquired.

"Oh him!" Abi thought for a moment how best to explain. "He was funny all over, that one. Just didn't know when to stop."

"Oh I see," Rita nodded.

"Well I don't think you do, Rita, he was weird. He used to like doing Tommy Cooper impressions. You know even while we were at it." Rita moved closer.

"After we'd made love and were lying there, you know romantic like, he'd say, "'Just like that!'" Abi mimicked.

Rita bellowed with laughter.

"Honest, he did!"

"And what about Felix who reckoned he had a Lambada?" Rita said.

"Don't be daft, that's a dance. It was meant to be a Lamborghini," Abi corrected her. "Well he was just a bit a too old in the tooth for me. He just didn't have the oomph. Shame really."

Rita smiled and drank her coffee.

"Perhaps this Gerry was after making a commitment," Rita suggested.

"Well he can do that with someone else. All I want is to have a bit of fun and not get trapped by some possessive bloke."

"Abi, you have to remember, you're no spring chicken yourself."

She gave Rita a look.

"Well what I mean is, you might not always be able to pick and choose, you know."

Abi sat up straight and looked at her reflection in the cafe window, drawing her stomach in and lifting her head up.

"Do you think I've got a double chin?"

"Well not double exactly," Rita tried to be diplomatic.

"What do you mean, 'not exactly'?"

"Well, more rounded, I'd say."

"Rounded?" Abi looked startled. "You cow!" she spat.

Rita sniggered at her friend's vanity.

"You're just a jealous old drudge."

"And you're a sagging old tart." Rita replied, getting into the banter.

"Do you really think I'm dropping?" Abi looked quite concerned.

"We all are aren't we?"

"Speak for yourself."

Just then Leo breezed in, his hair also standing up on end from the rough weather.

He greeted Rosa with a hug.

"Buon giorno. Come sta?"

"All the better for seeing you, my sweetheart," replied Leo and they kissed each other on the cheek. Hearing Leo's loud entrance, Bill looked up from his crossword. Abi and Rita also recognised Leo from the dance and then Rita and Bill spotted each other and they waved. Leo went over to their table.

"Well hello ladies, what a lovely surprise," taking off his coat, putting it on the back of a chair and making himself comfortable. He called Bill over and he joined them.

"Another coffee?" Leo asked.

"Oh yes please!" Abi replied.

Leo looked at Bill, standing, holding his newspaper and mug of tea.

"Can you do the honours, matey. I seem to have come out without much cash?"

Bill sighed, placed his mug on the table and went over to the counter to order.

When he came back, he overheard Leo telling Abi about Bill's bottle of ketchup episode in Woolies when they first met Rita. Abi was laughing aloud.

"It wasn't that funny," Bill remarked. "It cost me a fiver to get my jacket cleaned."

When they all got their drinks, Abi studied Leo with some curiosity.

"We've seen you around town a lot. You used to put groups on at the pier didn't you, back in the sixties?"

Leo shot back a look of being caught out. "I might have done. Who's asking?" he chuckled, realising that these may have been kiss-me-quick Hastings girls.

"Just me! We used to go, didn't we, Rita? Is there a problem?"

Abi dropped a sugar cube in her coffee and stirred it slowly whilst looking at Leo.

"Oh no, well you can't be too careful can you? All sorts of

people come out the woodwork still expecting some pay off after forty years."

"My friend Georgina used to go out with you," Rita piped up looking rather smug. Leo looked even more nervous as his mind ticked over to former girlfriend – name check mode. He shook his head, a natural reaction.

"What was her last name?"

"Morrison."

Leo pursed his lips, still shaking his head. "No, sorry. The name doesn't ring a bell. Sure it was me?"

"Double sure," Rita nodded confidently, sipping her coffee.

"When, exactly?"

"Sixty seven I think."

"Ah the Summer of love," Leo's eyes almost popped as though he had hit a modern history button and '*Sergeant Pepper's Lonely Hearts Club Band*' had rolled out.

"Well she had quite a thing about you, I remember her saying."

"What did she look like, this Georgina?"

"Brunette, quite small like me and nice figure in those days."

Leo looked none the wiser. It was impossible to recall the many girls he had on the go during the sixties.

"The thing is," he explained diplomatically, "as I was involved in the music scene, I met tons of girls and to be honest without meaning to sound big headed, that period is a bit of a blur now. Not that I'm saying that this friend of yours was a hanger on."

"Groupie?" Rita jumped in.

"No, not one of those. But things were moving fast." Nevertheless Rita had raised Leo's curiosity. "So what happened to her? Does she still live local?"

"Oh she moved over to Brighton. Last I heard she had become a great grandmother."

"Really, Christ!" Leo suddenly went rather pale, contemplating that a possible ex could now be a great grandmother.

"Don't seem possible does it? One minute you're listening to

Pink Floyd on Hastings Pier and the next you've got grand-children in tow. Where does the time go?"

He looked out at the sea. The weather was still blowing a gale.

"So, have you two lived in Hastings since you were kids?" Leo asked.

"Yeah. You?"

Leo nodded, "Man and boy. I was a mod in the sixties. Were you?"

"Sort of, yeah." They gave each other a sidelong glance.

"I bet you weren't in the Bank Holiday bust up with the rockers in Sixty Four? You look a bit too young."

"I was," Abi trumped up, "I was still at school but we used to hang around with a mod gang, didn't we Rita?"

"Yeah, it was a laugh but that Bank Holiday got a bit serious."

"It was great!" Leo grinned, "giving those rockers from Brighton a pasting."

Bill looked on feeling rather left out of the conversation.

"But you know Pete Townsend was right," Leo said, "we should all die before we get old. Why don't we? There's still time. All that stuff we did in the sixties – all that drive and energy, even working class kids like me could make it.

I can still see The Who playing now at The Pier, sweating and pumping out '*My Generation* 'and us mods spinning around town on our Lambrettas on uppers and downers. Who'd have thought that we'd still be here nearly fifty years on, sitting in deckchairs on the Hastings beach just like our parents.

I tell you, it makes you think.

Leo's phone buzzed and he put his glasses on to check a text. Frowning, he sighed and muttered to himself, "Well they can sing for that," putting the phone back in his pocket.

"That raffle at the dance on Saturday was a right fix," Abi complained.

"I know what you mean," Rita agreed. "The hundred quid prize would have been very handy. Even the scratch cards are letting me down lately."

"Well I think it's a mugs game," Bill piped up. "They all take you to the cleaners, the Lotto and all. It's sheer exploitation, pet."

Rita looked a bit nonplussed by his remark, and Bill immediately felt he'd gone too far. "Well I know they can be a bit of fun, like."

"Exactly," Leo agreed. "A bit of fun and that's what we all want isn't it, at the end of the day? But I reckon you have to make your own luck in this world."

"How d'ya mean?" Abi asked.

"You have to grab opportunities to make a bit of extra cash."

"I wish I could change my name and get out of paying off my credit cards," Abi moaned, twirling her finger through her hair and wondering how much longer they could manage on the paltry carers allowance and her aunt's state pension.

"Well all I know is, it cost me nearly forty quid on Saturday night. The time I paid for the drinks, draw, raffle, cab home. And," Rita said begrudgingly, "my Gayle is always on the scrounge. 'Mum,'" she mimicked her high pitched voice, "'can I borrow twenty till Friday? Dean needs some new shoes'. I know I'll never see it again."

Leo grinned, "Look I've got just the thing that'll make us all some readies." He went to his inside jacket pocket and pulled out a piece of paper which he carefully unfolded and laid flat on the table for all to see. It was a picture of a dog, a greyhound.

"Meet Fly By Knight, with a 'K,'" Leo exclaimed.

Abi and Rita peered at the coloured photocopy. Standing next to the dog, was a man in grey trousers and a blue bomber jacket.

"What's this then?" Rita asked.

"It could be our passport to a regular pot of cash," Leo said confidently.

"What, you mean we put a bet on it?" Abi asked.

"More than that," Leo smiled, looking self assured, "We'd buy a share in him. Form a syndicate!"

"Buy a greyhound, where would we keep it?" Rita blurted out and looked perplexed.

Leo shook his head, smiling. "We wouldn't have to. My mate Terry is the owner and trainer. He looks after him and prepares him for the races. He'd still have a share in him and carry on arranging the kennels and vet checks. Fly's a winner all right: Poole last week, Crayford, you name it. The dog's got great form. Look at this write up in the Racing Post

Bill put his glasses on and studied the picture more closely. '*Fly by name, fly by nature. Watch this one take off*'.

"Look," Leo quietly explained to them, "I've known Terry for quite a while, he's a good sort. He just wants to downsize his investments."

"Is that Terry in the picture?" Abi asked.

Leo nodded and Abi turned to Rita, "He hasn't got much dress style has he?"

"The dog or Terry?" Rita quipped and they both giggled.

Leo was slightly irritated by their asides and in a mildly patronising tone, he asked. "Do you know anything about greyhound racing, ladies?" Before they could answer he said, "I can tell you that this little beauty is a dead cert. He'll make us a regular packet." They all studied the picture a bit more seriously.

"So what do you say about coming in on the action? We could earn up to a grand a month, I reckon."

"Each?" Rita almost screamed.

"No," Leo replied, astonished at her naivety, "between us."

"Well, it sounds good to me."

"What's the catch?" Bill asked.

"No catch," Leo laughed, drinking his coffee.

"Well it would certainly suit me at the moment," Abi told Rita. "I could pay my debts and buy some new clobber. Maybe have a pamper day too!"

"Oh yes a pamper day," Rita nodded dreamily, "that would be lovely."

"It all sounds very nice but there's bound to be a catch," Bill repeated.

"No catch, honest," said Leo trying hard to be reassuring,

"but," he added, "you would of course all have to put some cash in to own a share."

There was an awkward silence.

"Oh, aye?" Bill's eyes lit up.

"Well you'd be a share holder in the syndicate. You can't expect it for nothing." Leo looked at him blankly.

"How much?" Bill enquired with a hint of doubt on his face.

"It's not a lot, as I say just a small contribution to be equal partners," Leo explained.

"How much?" Bill persisted.

"You have to see it as a long term … "

"How much?" Bill was getting impatient and the two women stayed silent eyeing the men's ping pong conversation.

"Two hundred quid," said Leo, finally and then added swiftly for clarification, "each!"

"I can't lay my hands on that much," Abi declared.

"Nor me," Rita agreed, "can't we pay in instalments?"

Bill sat back and raised his eyebrows with a told-you-so look on his face.

"Hang on," Leo remonstrated. "Hear me out." He spoke quietly as the cafe was beginning to fill with lunchtime diners.

"Look here, think about it. Eight hundred pounds stake between us and it could pay out between two hundred and fifty pounds *each* a month."

He spoke slowly and deliberately to try and ensure they completely understood.

"Surely you can find a way of raising the money? You've all just said that you're fed up being skint. Don't you see? This is a way out."

"I could sell my body," Abi giggled.

"That should bring in a tenner," Rita joked.

"Oh, very funny."

"You must all have something to hock," suggested Leo.

"What about doing a boot sale?" Rita chimed.

Leo sighed and looked doubtful. This wasn't going to bring in enough cash in his view.

"That's a great idea, Rita," said Abi. "I've got loads of stuff to get rid of.

"But we'll need a car!" said Rita and she looked straight at Bill. "Have you got wheels?"

Bill looked a little uneasy, "Well, aye, yes," he admitted, tentatively, "but it's only a little motor."

"Come on," Rita smiled encouragingly, "It'll be fun." She reached over and touched his arm.

"I'm not sure," Bill screwed up his face. "Don't you think we should go and see this dog first?"

"Oh please, Bill," Abi urged him, "strike while the iron's hot, eh?"

"OK then," Bill agreed reluctantly.

"That's settled it then, thanks Bill. Next Sunday at St Leonard's. We'll have to get going early and it'll cost a tenner for the pitch." Abi was already scheming in her mind what she could get rid of. Those pumps from last year's sales and that foot spa she'd bought for Millie but she'd never got on with.

"Just think," Abi's eyes glazed over, "this time next year we could have a few grand between us."

~ Seven ~

On Sunday Bill turned up at 6.45 am outside Rita's house as arranged; it was a chilly grey morning. She lived in an Edwardian terrace not far from Hastings Museum. Her road was full with parked cars so Bill had to double park. She was all ready for him at the door and he helped her carry three bursting black rubbish sacks of jumble for the boot sale.

"They're pretty heavy. You don't know you've got so much stuff, do you?"

As he crammed it all into the boot of his old car, Bill looked up and saw the curtains of the upstairs bedroom flicker. He wondered if it was her husband.

"Chilly isn't it?" said Rita as she hopped into the front seat. Strapping on her seat belt, Bill started up the car which croaked, shuddered and then roared. Rita wondered whether it was unusual for such a small car to be so noisy before feeling the sudden blast of the heater scorching her ankles.

"Do you normally have a lie in on a Sunday, Bill?" she asked trying to adjust her legs out of range of the heater.

"Me? Oh no, not really. I like to get up early, habit I suppose. What about you, pet?"

"Yeah, usually, especially if I've been on earlies during the week. But at least doing this today gets me out of the chores at home for a while!"

"Doesn't your husband mind?"

"No, he won't notice. He'll be out on the golf course this morning I expect. I'm a golfing widow," she laughed. The car suddenly lurched down the hill and Rita was surprised at the speed Bill was driving. Approaching a sharp bend, inside her head she was shouting – '*brake, brake, brake!*'

The car screeched and Rita disconcertingly felt her door clatter. She wondered if it had anything to do with the rust she noticed as she got in.

"What does your husband do?"

"Um, he works for the council in the environment department. But don't ask me what," she blabbered. "*Left here!* All I know is that he hates his job. He's always moaning about it."

"I wish I had a job to complain about," Bill said with a resigned tone as he stamped hard on the brake and swung left tipping a half full Coke bottle on to Rita's lap making her jump. "Has he been there long?"

Rita didn't reply immediately as she was gritting her teeth and had decided not to look at the road but try and take her mind off it by looking up at the passing shop signs.

"Over thirty years," she gulped, beginning to feel more than queasy. "*Now right – not this one, the next.*" Bill noticed there was a slight shrill in her voice.

"That's good," he said.

"What?"

"About him working for the Council. More secure."

"I don't know about that. They're always talking about cut backs," she said, breathlessly

"*MIND, this is one way!*" Rita gripped Bill's arm and had to stop herself from grabbing the steering wheel.

"I know that, Rita. Are you OK?"

She thought Bill sounded very calm under the circumstances.

"Yes, sorry, it's just that … Ah, we're almost there."

They had arrived at St Leonards Station car park and began queuing to get into the boot sale. Bill's car was full to the brim with Leo dropping stuff round and having collected things from Abi the day before. They were coming over later and had agreed to arrive after Bill and Rita had set up the stall.

The sale was already underway while people were unloading their vehicles; boxes, bin bags being emptied on tables. Bill and Rita set up the stall with Bill's trestle table and began to unpack. Things were not separated very well: clothes in with books, old vinyl records, CDs, videos, DVDs, jewellery etc. Rita unpacked them and Bill began putting them on the table and on the ground where they had been allocated. Rita was curious about what Abi had contributed and held up a risqué scarlet basque and smiled to herself about what saucy escapades she had participated in. Bill began putting Leo's CDs on a table including the Bee Gees, Rod Stewart, George Michael, Elton John and Abba.

Even before they had finished setting up, there were a few people poking around interested in their wares.

"How much d'yer want for this mate?" holding up a model car.

They hadn't had a chance to confer over prices and it was one of Rita's.

"Fifty pence," she said.

"It's worth more than that," Bill whispered to her.

But the man walked away with the car at her price and Bill shook his head.

"Look," said Bill. "I really think we should price our things properly," and pulled out some post-it notes from his pocket.

"OK, if you like, that's a good idea," Rita agreed.

Without consulting her, Bill began pricing things up.

"That's a bit steep isn't it?" Rita remarked, seeing him put £2 on DVDs.

"Well if we want to make this cash we've got to get a fair price," he said, wondering how much to mark up some chest expanders Leo had put in the sale.

It was still feeling cold and Rita shuffled from one foot to the other to keep warm. She opened a coffee flask she had brought along and offered Bill a cup.

"That's lovely, pet," and he wound his hands around it, holding it near his face. The steam misted up his glasses and Rita laughed at his temporary loss of vision.

Eight thirty came round and after initial interest the sale was going slowly.

A few people wandered over to their stall, enquired about pieces and offered much lower prices. Bill was adamant they couldn't take anything less and they walked off.

"Don't you think we should try and you know, haggle a bit?" Rita suggested, adjusting her scarf to keep the cold out.

Bill looked at her in amazement. "Haggle? No, I don't. These prices are very fair and I know because I do a lot of shopping around."

"Do you?" Rita didn't look impressed.

"Oh aye." Bill said surveying the table. "Believe me, these are fair prices."

Nine thirty and the sale was getting busier but they had only sold one CD, The Beatles' '*A Hard Days Night.*' Rita was beginning to lose patience with Bill over his rigid stand on the prices and frustrated that neither Abi nor Leo had yet turned up.

"They said that they'd be here by eight o'clock." Bill looked rather peeved too.

"You know, it's funny," said Rita looking around the boot sale. "There's some pretty poor people living round here. Some of the stalls are just complete rubbish. It's sad really. These cast offs say something about peoples lives don't you think?" Bill nodded.

As it was still quiet, they each took turns to have a mosey round the other stalls. Bill went first and was attracted by the piles of CD's and books nearby. He picked up a vintage Howlin' Wolf vinyl album although he did not have a record player any longer. The stalls were quite mixed including more commercial household goods, greetings cards, plants. Others where people were having a clear out at home of ornaments, tools and toys which people had tired of or had no further use for. Bill didn't want to clutter his flat but he knew he couldn't resist a bargain. He was pleased to find some packets of quality soap for half the price that he would normally have paid in town. Rita's look around was much shorter than Bill's, she had no real interest in buying anything second hand but she came back with a colouring-in book for her grandson, Dean. "This will keep him quiet for a while!"

"How old is he?" Bill enquired.

"Seven."

"Do you see much of him?"

"Oh yes, my daughter, Gayle lives up the road and she's around all the time. He's a lovely little boy. Mad on Dr Who at the moment."

Bill smiled.

They each had another drink of coffee from the flask.

"What about your family back home, Bill?"

"Well Helen my wife died a couple of year ago. She had lung cancer," he said, rather matter of fact.

"Oh, I'm sorry to hear that, Bill." Rita felt that she had put her foot in it.

"That must have been terrible."

"Aye, it was. We found out in the September and she was gone by January."

Rita looked at Bill's sad face.

"So it was all pretty sudden. It must have been really hard." He nodded, "It was all over in no time. Nearly forty year we were together.

"Got children?"

"Two boys."

Bill sipped his coffee as he eyed the crowd.

"They don't keep in touch much, but then neither do I really."

"Do you get on?"

"Well they've got their own lives. One of them's turned out to be a bit of a Tory," Bill laughed limply. "So we don't always see eye to eye. The other one's never really settled down."

"What was she like, your wife?"

Bill thought for a moment.

"Oh, I don't know … You live with someone for so long, you take them for granted. I thought we'd go on forever or at least into our retirement. She was my rock, she kept me going. But then … I tell you, it's the hardest thing I've had to deal with in my life, her going." There was a moments silence between them.

"Do you still think it was a good idea moving down here to Hastings? Hasn't it felt a bit lonely?"

Bill looked back at Rita and shook his head. "No, not really. Things were going from bad to worse in Newcastle. Shortly after Helen died, I lost my job – made redundant. A double whammy you might say. I couldn't bear it at home any longer. Everything was closing in on me. Hastings somehow seemed the right place for a new start. I had only ever been here once before," he chuckled. "Madness really."

"So you just upped sticks and left?"

"Aye, there was nothing to keep me there."

"What about your friends?"

"Helen was always more sociable than me."

"But you must miss the north surely – it's your roots."

"Oh aye, it's not easy. Just the lingo for a start!" Bill grinned. "I now see why people think of us up there as a foreign country. But no, I'm OK here. I'm more anonymous in Hastings. I can be me own man."

"Is that what you want?"

"Yeah, I think so. It'll do for now anyway."

"Ok campers, how's it going?" Suddenly there was Leo grinning and wearing a stylish raincoat and scarf with a large cappuccino from the station cafe in his hand. Almost immediately he was selling to passing punters. Much to Bill's annoyance, he completely ignored his pricing and used it to bargain with as soon as anyone started to show any interest at all.

"DVD's, three for two fifty, matey, OK? Yes we've got change for twenty. That's a lovely photo isn't it? The Tyne Bridge – family heirloom I dare say. And we've got our resident Geordie here," nodding to Bill who was suddenly having to scramble for change for Leo.

The crowd gathered as Leo's enticing patter attracted more and more people.

"Collectable vinyl. Dire Straits, The Beatles, ladies and gents," even though he had no idea what was in the pile of records.

"You do know that I marked up the prices!" Bill protested.

"Don't stop me now, Geordie. I'm on a roll." Leo swept up more sales, totally absorbed.

Bill couldn't deny that the table was beginning to empty and that their coffers were mounting. Rita was very impressed with Leo's sales patter and cheekiness. As Bill stood quietly at the end of the table watching her laughing at his jokes, he felt a bit put out. Within a couple hours, the table was almost clear and Leo was declaring, 'A special price for last knockings."

"How much please?"

A little girl held up a red purse to Bill.

He had originally marked it up for £1.

"Fifty pence, pet."

"I've only got thirty," she said.

"Oh, away then, pet, that'll do," Bill quickly caved in.

"Thanks mister."

By noon they surprised themselves about how much they had sold. The dull weather had turned sunny which made the bitter morning more bearable. And there was a whiff of fried onions trailing across the site from the nearby hot dog stall.

"Time for a cuppa. Anyone want one?" asked Bill.

"Not for me," said Rita, "I'll need to go to the loo."

"Well where's Abi then? I thought she'd promised to be here to help," Leo complained, glancing at his watch.

"Aye, she's late all right," Bill said, returning and handing a tea to Leo.

"Honestly, you can't rely on some people," Leo began to tut and Bill nodded.

"Now hang on!" Rita sprang sharply to Abi's defence. "She has a difficult enough job looking after her elderly aunt. That's why she's not turned up. How would you like it, caring for someone who is incontinent and doesn't know the time of day."

The two men were taken aback by Rita's outburst and looked rather sheepish.

"Aye, you're right, Rita," Bill apologised and Leo conceded an "Ummm, suppose so."

With lunchtime beckoning, they decided to call it a day and packed up the remainders of the sale in the back of Bill's car. They slowly wound their way out of the car park as a trail of other vehicles also left the site.

Sitting in the back seat of Bill's car with the remaining bin bags of left over jumble, Rita felt less stressed about his driving as they set off. Her mobile buzzed.

"It's Abi," Rita said, reading the message to herself; *'Sorry! Held up. Last night's hot date A x '*

"Well, what does she say?" Bill asked, looking at Rita in the car mirror.

"Oh, you know," she replied, "she's been up all night."

Bill shook his head. "It must be murder caring for someone, day in day out with no time for yourself."

Leo agreed. "I couldn't do it, matey. I know that. I've got to hand it to her, she deserves a medal that girl."

Rita smiled to herself and began counting the money.

"How much have we made?" Leo asked.

"Hang on a minute. One hundred and sixty seven pounds, fifty six pence."

"It's a start I suppose," said Leo.

As they neared the exit, Bill noticed Leo sink down in his seat and shield his face.

"What's wrong, man?"

"There's someone I don't want to see, that's all. Just keep going."

They decided to go to The Eagle for a drink. The pub was near Hastings Station and was struggling not to become one of the country's fifty or so pub closures a week. The half cocked pictures hanging on the walls and the ancient plastic pot plants dotted around the place were hardly its saving grace. There had been a series of landlords – some of them locals, some were bussed in by the brewery. They all started out with a burst of breezy enthusiasm to make a go of it. However after a couple of months of limp quiz nights, karaoke specials and curry evenings, customers were still thin on the ground. The landlords' gusto swiftly turned to grim determination. Even so, with the pull of cheap beer, a steady gaggle of regulars – although not spending enough to keep the place afloat, gave it an attractive quirky atmosphere.

The group walked in and whilst Rita and Leo found a window seat, Bill went to the bar and bought some drinks. The current landlord was at the grim determination stage of managing the pub and seemed to have a fixed grin as he served his customers.

"Well that wasn't a bad morning's work," Rita said, as Bill placed their drinks on the table.

Bill nodded agreement but Leo frowned at the shortfall.

"We still need another six hundred odd quid or else the deal's off."

"Well don't look at me," Bill said, "I'm as broke as everyone else."

"I've got an idea how to bump it up," Rita chipped in, "but you'll have to allow me a tenner from our takings."

"What for?"

"Just a minute," she said eagerly, "trust me!"

While the men drank, Rita disappeared around the other side of the bar.

"What's she up to?" Bill asked Leo.

"Dunno but she seems determined."

Ten minutes later she returned with a smile on her face and sat down opposite them.

"You look pleased with yourself," Leo said, slightly preoccupied with sending a text.

"I am," Rita agreed, her face flushed with excitement as she pulled out of her coat pocket a pile of pound coins which she lined up on the table.

"Fifty one quid," she calculated.

"We've even got money for another drink," Bill chipped in.

"That's fantastic," Leo congratulated her. Like the pub's fruit machine that Rita had struck gold with, his eyes lit up at the sight of the cash.

"You're a little angel, isn't she Bill?" Leo said and gave her a peck on her cheek. Bill nodded.

"But we've still got to raise another six hundred quid between us. So we'll have to get thinking fast," Leo added. "Anyway here's to Fly by Knight, he's gonna' be a winner," Leo raised his glass. Rita and Bill joined him.

"I'd still like to see him though before we leap into this," Bill said.

"So you will, matey, so you will," Leo replied.

~ Eight ~

Millie smiled at the waiter, a rather plump older man, his red braided, black waistcoat a little too tight, the buttons straining to pop. He smiled back at her as he waited with his notepad in hand. Millie couldn't take her eyes off him. He had a nice face and she thought it reminded her of someone who had been very kind to her before. It was the way he was standing and looking down at Abi whilst she made her mind up about something. She always took her time. That was it! He had a lot of patience, this man. He hadn't become irritated or excused himself because he needed to go to the loo. He just stood there with his pencil and thingy and he wasn't annoyed. Not like that woman with the dog in the park the other day when Millie had called it, "Hello, Rover," and tried to stroke him.

"Don't call him that!" the woman spat out. The dog suddenly lurched towards her, straining on its heavy studded lead. Auntie was fearless and continued to reach out to touch the beast even though it was snarling at her.

"What's his name?" she asked the owner. The woman swore at her, jerked violently at the lead and walked off.

'How rude' she thought.

But this nice man was very different. He was Indian or something and perhaps didn't speak much English.

Millie was enjoying this trip out. She'd got herself smartened up, wearing her favourite frock and pearl necklace. She suddenly remembered, Mr Patel, her neighbour, when she lived back in London for a while in that lodging house. There he was standing on the doorstep holding a tray of sweets and a big smile just like this waiter. It was to celebrate some festival. His daughter, what was her name? Standing in front of him, wearing a lovely sarong – all these colours, lighting up the street. They were good to Millie who had just arrived from Hastings and the Patels from goodness knows where. They clicked all right. They didn't know anybody in the street and neither did she. They were all in the same boat – feeling a bit lost kind of thing. Those sweets were an opening, of sorts. The start of something but Millie couldn't quite remember what. Now she'd fired herself up about it all, it was downright disappointing not to be able to recall what happened next. Disappointing and you know …

Millie noticed now that as the waiter spoke to Abi, he bent over to make sure he understood what she was saying. That was a sign of a good person, in her opinion. Showed respect and although she couldn't quite hear what they were saying herself, he was nodding his head and writing things down in his thingy. Now Abi was nodding too as he was speaking, explaining something. His voice was definitely foreign sounding. He waved his pencil around as though he was drawing in the air. Abi was laughing and he was laughing too. Millie also began laughing although she wasn't sure why. Finally they both looked at her and the man called her 'Madam.' She liked that and she straightened herself up.

Abi asked her, "Poppadom, auntie?"

Millie shook her head, wondering if her hearing was playing up again.

"Pompadoo?" she queried.

The man laughed and auntie enjoyed that. He had a hearty laugh and she always liked to fill people with fun.

"President Pompidou!" she added. Abi began screeching with laughter and the people sitting at the next table heard the banter, stopped eating their meal and chuckled.

"Yes please a President Pompidou on toast!"

A minute later he returned with some relish. Auntie watched as Abi snapped a piece of poppadom and dipped it in the mango chutney and gently munched it. She didn't say a word to Millie. It was another test – would she copy her? Auntie looked over at the next table and watched them eating. She carefully picked up a whole poppadom with both hands. She felt the rough texture with her fingers and studied its wavy lines. For some reason it reminded her of the seaside, a child paddling and looking for crabs in the rock pools. Without realising what she was doing she snapped the poppadom in half and she stared at the broken pieces and different shapes scattered on the plate.

"That's lovely," Abi said.

Millie struggled to dip the larger piece into the relish and Abi leant over and helped by breaking off a smaller piece for her. Auntie put it into her mouth. The tang of lime gave her a nice feeling and she screwed her face up in joy. Abi leaned over and put her hand fondly on her arm.

"Nice?"

"Yes, it's very … you know."

"Yes I do."

*   *   *

Later that week, Rita and Abi met for a coffee and chatted about Millie.

"Shouldn't you be taking her to see a doctor or talking to them about how she's been? This confusion that she has, it might be something more serious."

Rita looked worried.

"Well, what are they going to do? You know she's always been a bit dotty."

"Yeah but this forgetfulness and everything, it needs looking into. They might be able to help and you're always complaining about her."

"I don't see how they can help. What I need is a break now and then, that's all, just to keep myself from going loopy."

"Exactly, they've got places where she can go – respite care, give you some time out."

"No, I don't want her going away somewhere; that wouldn't help. She needs someone to come in and stay with her for a while, keep an eye on her when I go out."

"Like me you mean?"

"Well yeah but you're working. I just need to have a night out without worrying about her."

"Has she had any accidents when you have been out?"

"No, not really except when she's been round to the Turkish shop and left the front door open. Luckily they know her and because she didn't have any money with her they brought her back. That's why I've put that big note on the inside of the front door: *Don't go out on your own*."

"Does it help?"

"Millie thinks it's for me," Abi laughed. "She asked me why I can't go out by myself at my age!"

"Well I still think that you should have a word with a social worker or somebody. Pat at work – her nan gets people coming in to care for her."

"Does she live on her own?"

"I think so."

"Well there you are you see. They consider her in some danger. Anyway they'll want to know all about how much money we've got and they'll be nosing around."

"Millie may have Alzheimer's, Abi, and need specialist help."

"Well even if she has they can't do much for her. There's no cure is there? And I'll tell you what, Rita, she isn't going to end up in some home where they all sit round staring at the telly all day long. Not if I've got anything to do with it."

∽ Nine ∽

There had just been a heavy summer shower, followed almost immediately by brilliant sunshine, producing a colourful rainbow over East Hill. Leo didn't notice because he had things on his mind and strode briskly along leafy Croft Road trying to make up for being late. He also neglected to see the glazed effect the morning light had on the soaked paving stones and gravel, or the glistening wet trees, the grass, the weeds and the overgrown ivy, imbedded in the stone walls. As he cut through the Old Town alleyways, he had little time to lose if he was to catch the bus to Rye. He even remembered his bus pass to save himself some money.

The bus sped into Ore, high up towards Fairlight, opening up glimpses through the trees of the Brede Valley. It then rattled down to Pett Level and Winchelsea Beach where the earlier rainfall had flooded the sea road. The uneven road caused the bus to bump and spray jets of water as it passed by, with the blinding sun reflecting on the window, now obscuring a view of the windmill across at Ickelsham.

Leo never felt fully at ease in Rye; its ancient cobbled streets and winding lanes leading to the top of the hill and overlooking Romney Marsh were a magnet for tourists but it had always left him cold. He had always felt that the people in the town thought they were a cut above. When the bus arrived at the railway station it had become overcast again. The place was busy with visitors with their umbrellas half cocked, milling around waiting at bus stops or decamping to the local cafes for fish and chips.

Leo was on a mission and earnestly made his way up to the high street, stopping half way to catch his breath. Side-stepping day trippers pottering around the narrow street, Leo honed in on a row of antique and bric a brac shops. He sauntered into a couple of them but groups of tourists were also mooching. The final shop along the way was empty and Leo was attracted by a sign in the window: '*Old Jewellery and Valuables always wanted for cash.*' Leo pushed at the door hard. It was stiff and as it creaked open, the owner, a man perhaps in his early seventies, glanced over. Leo went straight up to him at the counter and took out a package from his jacket pocket.

"I wonder if you would be interested in this?" Leo undid a small M&S carrier and carefully handed him an object wrapped up in newspaper. Without a word the antique dealer opened it up and inspected it whilst Leo gazed around at the shop's ordered clutter from bygone years – mainly jewellery, vases and pictures. The musty smell turned Leo's stomach, it felt like a mausoleum.

The dealer closely examined markings on the silver cigarette case which Leo had given him. Despite his optimism for a sale, Leo had already sized him and his shop up and wasn't very impressed. Old style public school, inherited wealth. Leo was beginning to regret not taking the case to one of the second hand traders in Hastings. Rye, he thought, would be a better prospect and besides he knew a lot of them in the Old Town shops in Hastings and he might feel obliged to repay some favours. He also wondered if he should have gone to Brighton or even London which might have been better still.

"Well," said the dealer, screwing up his nose, running his fingers across the case and looking over the rim of his glasses in a snooty way, "have you got a figure in mind?" Leo really didn't like his manner.

He leant forward slightly with his hand resting on the glass counter, ignoring the notice, saying: '*Please do not lean on the counter. It might break!*'

"It's a family heirloom, early 1930's – Deco," Leo said with an air of authority. "I've been told it's worth a hundred and fifty!"

The man gave a little burp, shook his head and smiled wryly at Leo, placing the case gently back down on top of the crumpled newspaper.

"I'm sorry, we won't be able to do business at that sort of price, sir."

Leo's heart sank. The invitation for cash purchases in the window looked so promising.

"I'm afraid it's not an original Art Deco which I think you have been led to believe. It's in fact a replica. Quite a nice one I grant you, but more nineteen seventies than thirties."

"What you mean it's not pucka?" Leo looked genuinely aghast.

"No sir, not pucka at all, I'm afraid," he replied rather mockingly and removed his glasses. Leo noticed that the man had big saucer-like eyes.

"Well I don't understand it, my uncle left it to me in his will and, you know, I thought it was from way back."

The man gave him another knowing smile. Leo was now feeling quite frustrated by bothering to come to Rye at all and wondered if he could still make Brighton.

"Well," Leo asked grudgingly, "what do you think its worth?"

"Oh, I don't know," the proprietor said, raising his sagging shoulders, showing little enthusiasm, holding the case in his hands again and opening it up. "It's not in bad condition I suppose."

"No, that's right," Leo agreed, instantly brightening and thinking that he might still win him round yet, to get a decent enough price.

"I suppose I could offer you twenty-five."

"Twenty five quid?" Leo sputtered in disgust, but quickly pulled himself round.

"What about thirty?"

"I'm sorry sir, but twenty five really is our best offer – for a replica like this."

"I'd get much more on e-bay," Leo chipped in but quickly saw that this was not making any impression on the dealer who was already beginning to wrap the case back in the newspaper.

"Ok, you win, I'll take twenty five for it."

"Are you sure, sir? You don't want to try selling it on *e-bay*?"

"No," Leo shook his head. Anyway my computer's on the blink and well, if you say it's a copy," Leo shrugged his shoulders casually, trying to hide his disappointment.

The deal was quickly concluded, Leo signed a declaration that he owned the item and he then signed another receipt for receiving the cash. Glancing at his watch, he dashed out of the shop. If he was lucky he would just make the bookies in time for the one-fifteen at Kempton Park. Then he might double his money and raise his share to buy into the greyhound.

∼ Ten ∼

"Hello Angel pie ... " Bill was startled by the woman's booming voice sitting just behind him upstairs on the bus. He'd been day dreaming looking out of the window on his way home from Glyne Gap. Her accent was unusual for around here. South African perhaps? It had a ring and as the bus trundled along towards Hastings, passing the ship-shaped Marine Court and The White Rock Hotel she became more animated.

"Vat's dat woman cooking for you today den?Ah no, man, dat ain't right."

Bill found himself sucked into her mobile phone conversation.

"Dat ain't right," she repeated. Her conversation filled the upper deck. Bill became part mesmerised and part irritated by her rasping voice.

"I tell you, my darling, you have got to put your foot down, hard. Do you know vat I mean?" Bill was sitting near enough to also hear the tinny, distant voice of her male caller. The woman drew a deep breath, "Do you?" and continued excitedly, "It isn't right. She's treating you like *dirt,* really," her voice raised higher. But suddenly she switched to a more intimate tone.

"Ok, look, calm down den. I'm just trying to point out to you, yeah, vot she's doing, OK? It's not right de vey she is, my love. You're a good man and people take advantage – you said so yourself."

There was a long pause whilst the woman listened and repeated, "um, um, um, um." Finally Bill heard her shuffle and move to get off the bus, still chattering as she went downstairs.

"Get her to do somtin' nutritious, something tasty, my love. You know you like that nice creamy tagliatelle, don't you? Could she manage that do you think?"

Bill saw her disappear into a shop in Queens Road, mobile still on ear.

By the time he got back home it was late afternoon and he felt hot from the stuffy bus ride. Bill lived in a ground floor flat in a Victorian house by Alexandra Park. He picked up the post from the doormat, leaving the upstairs mail on the table and taking his post and shopping into the kitchen. Before he began to put his groceries away he selected a CD from a shelf and the spiky sounds of Lightnin' Hopkins suddenly tore out and brightened Bill's mood.

He had been renting this accommodation for a couple of years. It was the first time that he had lived on his own, having been married to Helen since his mid-twenties. Before that he lived at home with his parents. As an engineer, Bill was a practical sort and he kept the place tidy. On the mantelpiece was a photo of his wife and himself on holiday in Spain with their two sons. That would have been 1990.

His flat was quite spacious, despite being just one bedroom with a kitchen, living room and bathroom. The old fashioned long sash windows at the front, overlooked the park and bookshelves which he had made himself lined the walls. At the back, the garden rose up steeply in an awkward fashion. Uneven stone steps were overgrown with nettles and bindweed that led to a wilderness of brambles which neither the landlord nor tenants, including Bill, showed any interest in clearing. Bill had never ventured to the end of the garden seeing it as unchartered territory. It was a haven for small birds and the odd cat that occasionally emerged from its jungle.

Bill threw open a window and inspected his morning post. He tore up the junk mail without opening it including an envelope declaring '*You may have won £250, 000,*' and then squirmed at the gas bill for £108.46p. There was also a road tax renewal and he wondered how much longer he could afford to keep his old car running. Opening up his lap top, preparing himself for another job search, a new message popped up from his union. '*Ben Walters – Sad to Announce.*'

It was a circular to all union members about the death of a colleague and a close associate of Bill's. He had died suddenly from a heart attack.

Bill gasped at the news and with echoes of Helen, his wife's recent death, still on his mind, his legs suddenly felt like lead. He switched on the kettle to make some coffee. Bill thought that Ben was quite a healthy lad too. Worked out, did running and competed in the Great North Run, he remembered. As he spooned coffee and sugar into a mug, he recalled first meeting Ben following a union event in Newcastle. Ben had encouraged Bill to become a shop steward during the early seventies. Ben was quite an orator and had fellow workers captivated by his speeches about workers rights and fair pay. He had also introduced Bill to Robert Tressell's '*The Ragged Trousered Philanthropists,*' the classic English socialist novel. Bill reckoned that the book changed his life, being set against the background of hard working conditions of painters and decorators living in an Edwardian town, Mugsborough, based on Hastings. This vivid portrayal of hope and struggle against injustice inspired Bill. He often pondered now as to why all these ideals had turned sour. Socialism these days seemed old hat to the younger generation and Bill despised New Labour. Maybe, he thought, as the cuts were bound to take hold, things would perhaps change politically for the better.

Bill changed the CD to bluesman Magic Sam and re-reading the e-mail he discovered that Ben's funeral was to be at Gateshead in a week's time. He decided there and then that apart from the expense of the rail fare, he could not face going back home. He would send a card to pay his respects to Ben's family. If he went it would mean meeting up with his old colleagues and his cover would be blown about getting a job as an engineer in a traffic systems company in Hastings. Bill never found it easy, all these lies about his new life on the coast. His kids only knew the bare bones because apart from sending birthday and Christmas cards he hadn't been in touch with them for over a year since he had left the north east. The anger and disappointment of both losing his wife to cancer and his job in Newcastle had all been too much for him.

Thinking about Ben, Bill reached up and grabbed 'The Ragged Trousered Philanthropists' from a shelf and sat down in an armchair. A welcome cool breeze flickered into the living room as he opened the book to one of his favourite chapters, 'The Great Money Trick.' This is where the main character, Frank Owen a painter and decorator – based on the author himself, is requested, rather tongue in cheek by his fellow workers, to give them an impromptu lunchtime talk. He does so, on the rules of capitalism, by cutting up small pieces of bread to represent the raw materials and money.

Despite their trying to poke fun at him, he demonstrates how the bosses always make a profit from the working man – even though his workmates remain sceptical. Bill fondly recalled his discussions in the pub with Ben about the book after union meetings. Ben said that the novel was one of the factors in the Labour Party winning the General Election after the Second World War. Also that Tresell's simple explanation condensed the very point that Karl Marx had made in 'Das Capital,' about the proletariat's relationship to the means of production which had gone over Bill's head.

Bill smiled as he remembered these times with Ben and his thoughts were tinged with sadness and self pity. Living alone had its compensations but at times like this he felt very down. He hated to admit he was lonely. This was his new life, even if a solitary one. Was this impetuous decision to move to Hastings such a good idea? To escape to the south coast where he didn't know anyone? Bill had to make it work.

His eyes grew heavy and he began drifting off to sleep in the chair.

When he awoke he had a stiff neck. It was evening, half light and still very warm. He leaned over lazily to switch on a table lamp. This languid stretch brought on a long yawn and the novel slid from his lap and fell to the floor with a thud. Bill sat quietly wondering whether to continue reading or make himself some tea. Through the thin wall adjoining next door, he heard the high pitch buzz of a hairdryer and the long and short bursts were interspersed by a phone-in radio programme, distorted voices clattering as if down a tube. Bill remained still for a while longer. The hairdryer stopped but the radio continued. He heard feet on the staircase running up and down. A door slammed hard. A young woman's voice barked, "You do it!" And then there was complete silence just before his mobile beeped. It was a text from Rita, asking if there was any news about raising the money to buy the greyhound.

She said that she had been promised some overtime at work but it had fallen through. Bill replied that he had seen an advert for people to deliver free newspapers door to door. It didn't pay much but it might help.

*   *   *

So, despite his misgivings about Leo's syndicate, Bill took on the newspaper delivery round and was given an area nearby to where he lived. It included the other side of Alexandra Park. He got himself a shopping trolley to haul the papers round with, but he had to climb up high garden paths and steps, puffing himself out. When it rained he was careful not to deliver sodden newspapers. He hated it but at least he raised some cash.

∾ Eleven ∾

Millie was having a late breakfast. She stood transfixed, impatiently holding her plate, peering at the red glow inside the toaster until a slice of white bread popped out and landed on the worktop. She stared down at it for a moment, its burnt sooty edges smelling of smoke. Just the way she liked it, nice and crisp. Picking it up carefully, she began very gently to spread some margarine with a knife feeling it crackle and creak – at anytime likely to snap. This had happened before often enough, toast broken in two or more, some of it shattering on to the floor.

Hearing the letter box rattle, Millie went out to the hall and found a manila envelope. It was for her – Ms M. Purbright; it looked rather official. Munching her toast, Millie picked it up and stood by the doormat staring at it for a while. Abi glanced sidelong at her as she slid swiftly by into the bathroom.

"Anything for me?" she rang out.

"No, nothing. No love letters today!" Millie chuckled.

"OK," and Abi closed the door.

Millie heard the boiler fire up for her shower and Abi singing. She wandered back into the kitchen, still staring at the envelope marked with her name, sat down at the table, picked up the table knife with spread still on it and sliced it open.

Dear Ms Purbright. Someone has contacted this agency who believes they may be related to you, if you wish to know more contact this number …

Millie gasped. It was like a punch in the stomach. Her past had come hurtling back after all these years to haunt her. She knew exactly who that 'someone' was. She wondered what she should do but her concentration was interrupted by the sound of the hissing shower and the water running away. Above it all, Abi was singing aloud, "*I've Got You Under My Skin*." She had a nice voice, Mille thought, sounds a bit like Cilla Black.

～ Twelve ～

Inside Leo's flat, Radio 2 blared out Crosby, Stills & Nash's *'Marekesh Express'* while he ran his fingers along the knife edge crease of his dark blue linen trousers. He placed them on the back of a chair and got to work on ironing his Jermyn Street shirt. Carefully laying it out and smoothing it with the palm of his hand, he very gently guided the iron lightly across the shirt before placing it on a hanger. Next, his favourite Gucci black leather shoes. He stood and admired the mirror-like gleam from his earlier polish.

Sipping his morning coffee, he was in jubilant mood. Having had no luck on the horses, Leo believed that he had found a way of raising his share of the greyhound stake – he had a job interview! Leo looked at the advert again in The Hastings Observer spread out on the living room table. *'Male and female life models required for art classes. Must be available for daytime and evening sessions. No experience necessary. £6.50 per hour.'* Leo smiled to himself as he thought about the class. Baring his all in front of strangers. He didn't mind one bit. He could certainly do with some extra cash and the woman on the phone at the college said that for the successful applicants, there could be several bookings a week.

The interview, as it turned out, was rather informal. Leo saw Anne Vaux, a young tutor at Hastings College of Art, near Burton

St Leonards, who was friendly enough. She was quite casual, asking him what he had done work wise and how available he was to do the sittings. She showed him the art class room with several easels stacked in the corner and examples of students work up on the walls. Leo thought that some of it was rather good. Still life and life drawings.

"Have you done any modelling before?" she enquired.

"Me? No, never." Leo grinned. "I imagine that you can get a bit cold in the winter," he said, pointing to one of the drawings of a nude woman and looking more closely to see if it was someone he knew in Hastings.

"We have an electric heater, it's usually warm enough."

"And are all the sittings without clothes on?"

"Mostly, are you OK with that?"

"Oh yes, I'm not bashful."

"The teacher will give you an idea of what pose they're looking for."

"I see," said Leo, admiring a sketch of another female form reclining on a mattress.

The tutor looked at Leo with interest. "We don't get many older gentlemen apply for this sort of thing." Leo suddenly realised that she was referring to him and chuckled at the thought of being referred to as an 'older gentleman'. He looked her in the eye rather flirtingly. "I like to think of myself as more mature," he said coolly.

"Yes, of course," she replied. "Well, if you're available and happy with the fee, after we take up references we can offer you some work very soon."

"Really?" Leo was delighted and surprised at this on the spot decision. He looked thoughtful. "But don't you want to see the goods first of all as it were? I can assure you it's all there."

She frowned, not understanding quite what he meant but then suddenly realised and Leo noticed that she blushed slightly.

"No, no that's not necessary at all," she laughed it off. "We like all shapes and sizes."

Leo nodded, "Yes of course."

Not long after Leo was asked to model for a class on a Tuesday afternoon. He arrived early and met the art teacher. He was expecting a woman but it turned out to be a man, in his mid-thirties, Trevor.

He told Leo that most of the students were on an access course, hoping to apply to university. He was shown the stockroom where he could change.

Leo began to undress, put his dressing gown on and waited to be called in. He looked around at the shelves, cluttered with different types of paints – oils, acrylics, jars containing brushes, pencils and charcoal. Half hidden lying on the floor, were students' paintings gathering dust. Leo picked up a few including a life drawing of a woman who looked like she was in her seventies. He thought the student had caught the model's face very well. Partly sad but the world weary look in her eyes, Leo thought, were brilliant. He wondered how he would turn out on paper.

Leo heard the clatter and babble of young people arriving in the classroom. The teacher beckoned him in and told him that he wanted the class to do several quick drawings to help them warm up. Leo suddenly felt a little nervous and still in his dressing gown he gazed at the crowded art room of young students chatting away. They all seemed about eighteen years old and as he whisked off his gown he noticed that the room went quiet. He also saw that some of the girls blushed and covered their mouths but it didn't bother him at all.

Trevor took control, "OK everybody, let's focus now on what we learnt last time about getting the perspective right. I want you to do a five minute drawing of our model." Meanwhile he had ushered Leo to the middle of the circle of easels and into a standing position with his hands on his hips. The class complied. The five minute pose was followed by two minutes, then a minute and finally a thirty-second pose. As he changed position, Leo started to feel more confident and began modelling by his own initiative. His arms outstretched and hands behind his head. Even one on one leg which proved very uncomfortable as he nearly toppled over. During the rest period he put his dressing gown back on and wandered about while the teacher talked to the students about their work; he was curious to see some of their efforts.

"I'm not that fat am I?" Leo asked one boy with a baseball cap who had portrayed him as quite rotund.

"It's just an impression," the boy said sulkily, taking it as a criticism of his work. But the next one really caught Leo off guard. It was quite abstract and the girl with a pony tail was still working on it while Leo stood behind her.

"Is that me?" Leo said chuckling.

"Yeah," she said, not taking her eye off the picture which portrayed him with only one eye and a small body.

"It's in the style of Dali, yeah?" she smiled mischievously.

"Oh, I see," Leo was rather bemused and winked at her.

The teacher rallied them back together for some longer drawings. When the class had finished and after Leo had got dressed, Trevor came over to sign his time sheet.

"You're a natural, that was great!" Leo was rather chuffed.

"At their age," Trevor explained, "they can get a bit embarrassed but you were fine about talking to them. It helped put them at their ease. Well done."

Leo felt good about it all and asked, "Same time next week?"

"Absolutely!"

A few days later, Leo was phoned by another art teacher at the college to attend a morning class for an older group of students. Leo arrived early and waited whilst the students set up their easels. The woman teacher asked Leo to sit on a stool facing the door with one hand resting over his leg. The group seemed quite middle class and were mixed, male and female. Some were quite elderly and others about Leo's age group in their late fifties, early sixties. They all seemed to know each other well and he wondered if he knew any of them. Different to the young students, Leo felt a bit self conscious, perhaps as they were more his peers. As the group began drawing and painting, Leo settled into the pose, looking straight ahead at the door. After a little while he was feeling more comfortable about the job. He was also managing to discipline himself, not fidgeting or being distracted – trying to stay calm and relaxed.

Five minutes into the pose, the classroom door swung open loudly and a late- comer arrived. Leo, still concentrating on the pose, managed not to be distracted but as the woman stepped into the classroom, she drew back on seeing him and tripped on an easel, causing a drawing board to fall on the floor with a shattering din. They suddenly caught each other's eye. Leo gasped. It was his ex, Jane, from the recent ballroom escapade.

Although shaken, Leo took a deep breath and somehow, perhaps through shock, managed to maintain his pose. Jane gathered up the contents of her bag – paint brushes, pencils sprawled across the floor. Whilst the teacher helped remount the drawing board on to the easel, Leo feared that she might cause another scene and he'd lose his job.

During the break, Leo hastily donned his dressing gown and decided to stay well clear of Jane and chatted to one of the other students about her drawing. The session seemed to drag on forever. At the end of the lesson, still anxious to avoid his former girlfriend, Leo slipped swiftly into the stockroom and changed back into his clothes double quick. Forgetting to get his time sheet signed, he scuttled down the corridor not looking behind him. In the mid day heat he darted down to a small café opposite the promenade, sat down rather breathless with other lunchtime diners, ordered scrambled egg and coffee and checked to see if he had received any texts. Picking up a newspaper from the rack, he buried himself in it and tried his best to forget the whole sorry business with Jane.

Leo's lunch soon arrived and he tucked into his food, reading the newspaper.

"Are you avoiding me?"

It was Jane. Leo looked up and gave a faint smile but then instinctively held on to his mug of coffee in case she had any more ideas of a repeat performance.

"Oh hello," Leo tried to sound as casual as he could.

"May I?" she was already pulling back an empty chair.

Leo was at a loss as to know what to say and just nodded at her as she placed her bags under the table and sat opposite him.

Leo hesitated, "I 'erm think I owe you an apology. That money I owe you … " he blurted out rather embarrassed. Jane looked at him sheepishly.

"I'm the one who should be saying sorry about how I behaved at that dance."

Leo felt a great sense of relief.

"It did give me a shock."

"Well I was *very* angry at the time. It wasn't just the money it was the thought of you two timing me."

"Two timing?" Leo looked bewildered.

"Don't deny it." Leo felt another spat coming on.

"The way you'd been dancing with that French woman the other week," she said accusingly.

"What French woman?" Leo implored.

"The one with the funny eye."

"Funny eye?" Leo queried, stunned at the accusation. "I don't know who you mean. Look, I didn't want to upset you, honestly, and I will pay you back soon. That's why I got this job," he lied. Jane looked at him thinking, 'as if butter wouldn't melt!'

"Can I get you a tea or a coffee or something?" Leo offered.

"No, sorry, I've got to be going," she glanced at her watch.

"I, umm just wanted to say though," she hesitated; a smile crept on her face. "We did have some fun together, didn't we?"

Leo nodded, taken aback and looking rather confused.

"Oh yes, lots."

"You being in the classroom today rather startled me," she added. "I wasn't expecting … , particularly," she went on, "seeing you in the all together!"

Leo smiled, "Oh, yes I see."

She looked at him rather bashfully.

"Does that mean," he began gingerly, "you'd like to meet up again some time?"

"I'm not sure about that," she suddenly looked rather startled at the thought.

"Oh, OK, of course."

Jane got up to go. She looked down at him and his plate of now lukewarm scrambled egg.

"Well I dare say I'll be seeing more of you anyway," and raised her eyebrows.

"Oh, yes, of course, in the classroom," as he laughed, he felt a sudden pain in his chest.

"What's up with you?"

"Oh just a touch of heartburn. I've had it for a while now."

"Why don't you see a doctor?"

"No, no. I don't believe in 'em," he grinned, "once they get their claws into you you've had it."

"But it might be more serious than you think."

"I've got my own home cures, thanks."

"Brandy?" Jane grinned.

"Peppermint tea, if you don't mind," Leo feigned being insulted by her remark. "Then a brandy," he laughed.

As Jane turned to go, Leo drew himself up in his chair and said,

"By the way, you haven't been sending me cards and things have you?"

"Why on earth would I do that?" she frowned and giggled slightly.

"No, quite," Leo smiled, "sorry to mention it. See you soon."

∼ Thirteen ∼

At home, Rita held on to the kitchen work top as her head spun. It took her breath away and her knees felt weak as she broke into a sweat. She closed her eyes, but it gave her little relief from the queasy feeling. Rita knew by recent experience that it usually passed over in a little while. Opening her eyes she reached for the tap and poured herself a glass of water. It helped to calm her almost immediately and she sat down at the kitchen table, panting. She took some deep breaths, keeping her eyes closed. Gradually the intensity of the dizziness subsided.

Eventually standing up, Rita still felt a bit wobbly as she stepped from the kitchen into the back room. She thought that she might topple and collapse in a heap. She steadied herself by standing with her back to the wall. Rita wondered what Colin would do if he returned and found her sprawled out face down on the carpet. He would probably just step over her without noticing, she thought.

She dismissed the idea and wondered what could be causing these dizzy spells. She tried to quell her darkest thoughts that it was early signs of an incurable disease – Parkinsons, M.S, Motor Neurone. Rita quickly broke out of this mindset, gave in to her unsteadiness and laid down on the sofa, drifting off into a dream, finally escaping from everything.

The following week Rita went to see her doctor. At the bright refurbished health centre, Rita casually eyed the notice board whist she waited for her appointment. *'Tea Dance for the Over 50's,' 'Diabetes – Act now,' 'Carers Group meetings.'* The surgery was beginning to fill up and Rita was pleased that she had arrived early, so that she wouldn't be late for work. She was also glad she had changed GPs from her previous male doctor who usually stared at his computer screen throughout the consultation with her, breaking only to use medical jargon she didn't understand. When she had mentioned about feeling tired and lack of energy, he gave her a 'pull yourself together' mantra. Rita had been struggling for some time with feeling low, but she had not spoken to anybody about it. She told herself she could manage and she usually did. Her job kept her going and although the pay was not up to much, she really enjoyed the company and banter with her mates. But sitting in the surgery now staring at the notice board she knew she had to do something about the panic attacks she was having. They gripped her, got her pulse beating ten to a dozen and made her feel so dizzy she had to hold on to something to steady herself. Sometimes it happened at home when she was on her own and was able to sit down, but at work it was a different story – more public and scary. Rita always thought of herself as resilient and strong. Why was this happening? It frightened the shit out of her.

Suddenly the electronic board pinged and her name appeared like a train departure. *'Mrs Rita Edwards Room 10.'* She quickly got up and went to the consulting room. Dr Tong sat at her desk, a young Chinese looking woman, probably in her early thirties, Rita thought. She beamed at Rita and gestured her to sit down.

The room was tidy and on her desk was a photo of a young child.

"Hello, what can I do for you?"

Rita was apprehensive, the woman looked younger than her daughter, Gayle, and she thought she could hardly have much experience as a doctor.

"Well," Rita began quite dead pan, "I've been having these turns."

The doctor listened thoughtfully.

"I've been feeling dizzy and breathless," and she added tentatively, "it's making me feel very nervous." She looked at the GP who was nodding whilst Rita spoke. The doctor asked how often the episodes occurred and a little about Rita's family situation, work and general health. Whether she was sleeping well or if she was worrying about anything in particular. She took Rita's blood pressure whilst they talked and Rita told her about the recent incident at work when she nearly collapsed.

Rita's blood pressure was a little high and the GP said she should have a blood test.

"We'll have to see if there is anything physically wrong with you, Mrs Edwards. But in the meantime I can prescribe something that may help the anxiety you are feeling."

Rita was grateful and relieved that she was being listened to. She also wondered if it might be one of those mystery viruses that might go on for years. Pat at work had one of those.

"Of course," the doctor said in a kindly manner, "you may have a touch of depression."

Rita was taken aback to hear this.

"How do you mean?" she asked.

"Well, panic attacks and not sleeping can be signs of low depression," she said but could see that Rita looked rather alarmed at the thought.

"Look, don't worry" she tried to reassure her, "it's quite a common condition and if it is then there are ways to help sort it out."

"I'm not a mental case!"

The young woman smiled. "Many very active people in their lives can have a bout of depression from time to time. It's not always clear why it happens. I'm just saying that it *might* be a cause of why you are sometimes experiencing these attacks."

"I see."

"What I suggest is that you come and see me again in a week when we get the blood test results back and we can have another chat then, OK?"

Rita got up and smiled nervously as she put her coat back on, still wondering if this GP was qualified enough to really help her with the suggestion of depression running through her mind.

*   *   *

Later on, while Rita was relaxing at home with her feet up on the sofa watching the local news, her mobile buzzed. She knew who it was before she looked. Her daughter Gayle contacted her several times a day, mostly to have a moan: 'Dean's playing up again,' 'Not eating his food,' 'Won't sleep.' But also simply asking for money, 'Can I pop over for a tenner? Pay back Friday?' Sometimes Gayle cut to the chase and just waited for Rita after work. Rita always responded by giving her the money. Gayle's flat was just two streets away and for Rita it was sometimes too close for comfort. 'She's always on the cadge,' Rita's husband complained about his daughter but he didn't know the half of it. Rita, bent down, plucked the phone from her handbag and read the text: 'Mum phone me urgent'.

"What is it, love?"

"They've got me down to go on a money management course," Gayle blurted out angrily. "They say that if I don't go, they will cut my benefit!" Rita listened patiently as her daughter ranted on about the Benefits Office trying to get her to manage her finances better and to start thinking about a job for herself as Dean was now at school. Gayle had hardly ever done any work, unless you counted the three days she did at McDonald's and another short spell at a local bakers. Rita listened to her patiently. "Look love, you know that you don't manage your money very well do you? Maybe this will help."

"You're on their side are you?" Gayle hit back.

"No," Rita said quietly, "I'm just saying that maybe it's not a bad thing. It might help you."

There was a silence.

Rita heard her daughter snuffling, a usual sign when things

weren't going her way. Many phone calls usually involved her daughter turning on the waterworks. "Come on Gayle, don't upset yourself. That won't solve anything. When I see you tomorrow I'll have a look at the letter."

There was another silence.

"Gayle?" but she had gone.

On a rather sultry afternoon about a week later, Rita went with Gayle to the money management seminar. They arrived at the Job Centre and were directed to a pokey meeting room where two other people had already arrived: a teenager listening to her ipod and busy texting and a woman who looked about a similar age to Rita, reading a copy of The Sun. They sat down. Nobody looked at one another. Rita spoke to Gayle in a whisper.

"Not many here are there?"

"I told you it would be a waste of time didn't I?" Gayle said, belligerently.

Another teenager, a boy, swaggered in and recognised the girl with the ipod and sat down next to her, putting his feet up on the back of the chair in front.

"Right?" he mumbled.

"Yeah," she replied without looking up at him.

She then removed her earplugs and whispered something to the boy who looked over at Gayle and they both started giggling.

Gayle stiffened as if about to retaliate when the door swung open and the trainer, a woman in her early thirties, dressed in a dark blue suit with her ID hanging from around her neck, entered with a pile of papers and a lap top. She didn't acknowledge the group and hurriedly set up her computer for power point. She located the file and tried to raise the presentation on the screen but at each attempt a message was displayed indicating a failed connection. After several attempts accompanied by deep sighs it was still not working.

"It's broken ain't it, shall we all go home?" asked the boy, grinning.

The trainer ignored him and continued fiddling with the

machine. Finally, she gave up, left and returned with a new lap top. Within a few minutes her presentation was up and running: '*Managing Your Finances*'. The boy whistled and the girl giggled again. The trainer stared at him coldly and asked him to take his feet off the chair in front. He complied sullenly and in slow motion.

"Hello, my name is Veena Rahman," she grinned widely, tapping her ID card, "and I would like to welcome you to this seminar about managing your money."

"What money?" asked the older woman, and the boy sniggered. The trainer overlooked the remark and continued.

"We all have to keep to a budget. Can anyone tell me what a budget is, please?" There was an uneasy silence. Nobody answered.

"A budget, what is it?" she repeated, smiling as though she might give someone a sweet for the correct answer.

"It's what the government do every year, ain't it?" said the boy.

"It's what we can each afford to spend and what amount we should try to keep to," she stated.

There were blank faces in the room.

She shuffled some papers on the table in front of her and cleared her throat.

"What about when you receive your benefit. What's the first thing that you should do?" Her eyes scanned the small group but again everyone remained silent. Just as she turned back to look at the screen, Rita put her hand up.

"Excuse me, is it working out what you need to pay out for?"

The trainer smiled, "Yes, yes, that's it!" relieved at this welcome breakthrough.

Gayle looked at her mother, angry but also embarrassed. The trainer continued. "We should make a list of what we need to pay for – the essentials. I imagine you are all on housing benefit?" There were a few nods.

"So let's see. What are the essentials?"

"Budweiser!" the boy called out. She shook her head in dismay and caught Rita's eye in the hope of her providing another sensible contribution. "Food," Rita said on cue.

"Exactly – food, heating, clothes. Money you put away for bills" the trainer added to help move things along.

"If I paid off my debts," the older woman spoke up, "I'd have nothing left." The teenagers burst out laughing.

"Yes, well that's where debt counselling comes in to see if they can help to renegotiate your payments in order to keep your creditors happy and allow you enough to live on."

"Not my money-lenders, they won't, love," the woman replied. "They're not that kosher. And the debt's getting bigger every week."

"Well, OK," the instructor sidestepped this, "let's look at some tips shall we, to see how to make the most of our money?"

The boy's mobile rang out a rap call tune and the trainer gave him another stern look. "Turn mobiles off please!"

'Do's & Don'ts' sprang up on the screen.

"Do's: Set yourself a budget and keep to it. Make sure that you don't go over," she emphasised.

"You mean be stingy with yourself," the older woman called out."

Rita chuckled.

"Go for a whole week without spending much at all. Think: stop!" The trainer put up her hand to demonstrate the point, "Do I need to buy that?"

"Yeah!" the boy cried out and the girl giggled some more.

"Why not have left overs and what you have in the cupboard?"

"Left overs?" Gayle mumbled to her mother. "She's gotta be joking, ain't she?"

"Don'ts " the instructor continued.

"Don't be tempted to buy things that you really don't need. Take aways for example. They can be expensive. Don't buy on impulse. You know, we see something we like, we buy it, but do we really need it?"

"Yeah," the boy quipped again.

"Instead, it's always better to bargain hunt. If you really need something look around for better prices. Make your money go further." She smiled at the audience. Her message complete.

*　*　*

After the session, Rita took Gayle for a coffee nearby. The cafe was busy and there was loud music playing. They managed to find a table with a single occupant, a young man with a fashionable black woollen hat who was eating a burger and reading The Daily Mirror. The waitress came over promptly to see to their order. She was in her mid-twenties and very polite and attentive which immediately put Gayle's back up. Gayle studied the menu, Rita smiled at the waitress.

"A coffee for me please," Rita said. "Gayle?"

"Yeah, OK, same here."

"Anything to eat?" the young woman asked. They shook their heads and the she smiled, "perfect." She scribbled out the bill, placed it on the table and went to get their drinks.

Conscious of the boy sitting opposite, Rita wasn't able to have the heart to heart chat with her daughter she had hoped.

"Well that talk was helpful wasn't it? Some useful tips," Rita said positively.

Gayle was still in a strop and she ignored her while she looked at the menu.

"Well I've learnt a few things myself about spending," Rita continued.

There was still no response from Gayle who was biting her nails and Rita looked at the boy who had finished his burger and still had his head down in the newspaper.

Their coffees arrived and Rita smiled at the waitress.

"Perfect," she beamed back.

Gayle put two sugars in hers and Rita added a sweetner from her bag.

They both stirred their drinks in silence. The boy lifted his head up, glanced at Gayle and then put his hand in his trouser pocket for money to pay the bill. At the same time his mobile phone rang loudly, The Simpsons theme tune …

"Greg, hiya man, how are you doing?" Rita noticed that as he smiled, his teeth were very brown. A smoker, she thought, like she used to be until she gave up last New Year, well almost.

"The other night, yeah, yeah, it was a blast, man. You should have come … "

The conversation faded as the boy went up to pay his bill and leave.

The two women continued to sip their coffee in silence then Rita tried again.

"Well Gayle, did you think it was helpful?"

"What?" her daughter asked truculently. Rita thought; a twenty-eight year old going on thirteen.

"The seminar whatsit," Rita said, irritated by her manner.

Gayle stretched and yawned. "Waste of time if you ask me."

"But you do need some help managing your money don't you? You won't take any advice from me or your dad."

"It's easy for you," Gayle retorted, "there's two of you. I've got Dean and it ain't easy managing on what they give me."

"I know it's not much, Gayle, but you get regular help from me, don't you?"

"No, I'm not saying *that*. It's just that everybody's on at me – get a fucking job, look after Dean, pay the bills and it just don't stop, mum. I've had it up to here." Her face reddened as she raised her voice.

Rita watched as Gayle played around nervously with the bowl of sugar packs.

Rita well knew the signs with Gayle. Like her husband they were two of a kind. Moody and self centred.

"What if," Rita tried again, "I go through your finances with you to try and help you sort out a budget like the lady said?"

"Mum, give it a fucking rest!" Gayle exploded as customers looked up startled. She put her head in her hands and spoke more quietly through gritted teeth.

"For the last time, I don't need your help making a fucking

budget. I just need a bit more cash – that's all."

Rita retreated and stared at the ceiling for a while then tried again.

"Well, how are you managing this week?"

Gayle shrugged her shoulders, still holding her face in her hands. As she lifted them Rita saw that her eyes were red with tears.

"Oh, Gayle darling. What is it? I'm your mum."

"I just need twenty quid to get through this week, that's all."

Rita frowned, inside she wanted to say 'No, enough is enough. Ten pounds last week, fifteen the week before. Thirty last month to help pay off her gas bill.' But as her head began spinning with the calculations she found herself automatically dipping into her purse and pulling out a twenty pound note. She folded it tightly and passed it across the table to Gayle.

Gayle took the note, wiped her eyes and finished her coffee.

Without a further word between them, they got up, Rita paid the bill at the cash desk and they left. Outside the cafe Rita kissed Gayle on the cheek.

"I've got to get back to work. Give my love to Dean," she said.

"Bye," Gayle replied, hurrying off and not looking back.

Rita wished she had a packet of fags with her. She couldn't wait for the odd crafty one from Abi.

*   *   *

The next evening after finishing her shift at Woolies, Rita was still wondering how she could raise her share in the greyhound. She checked with the office but there was still no overtime available. On her way out, she began chatting to Michael, one of the young trainees. He was a nice lad, pleasant and respectful; the son of one of the sales assistants. He came in for quite a lot of ribbing from some of the girls who were often teasing him about girlfriends and asking when he was going to take one of them out. Rita smiled at their shenanigans but was pleased that the boy seemed to take it all in his stride. Not many eighteen year olds could. Rita thought that he seemed quite old fashioned in his manner, almost too gentlemanly for this day and age.

"Have the girls been behaving themselves today, Michael?" Rita asked him.

"Oh yes," he replied rather matter of fact.

"Well, I don't know how you stand for it sometimes. They take liberties and I've told them so. Not that they listen to me," she laughed.

"They're not a bad crowd, Rita. I'm getting to know them now," he said in a quiet, worldy way.

"Are you?" Rita looked at him thoughtfully. "Michael. I hope you don't mind me asking but are you a Christian?"

He smiled at her and looked a bit dumbfounded. "No, not at all. Why do you ask?"

"Oh nothing," Rita replied, "I just wondered."

～ Fourteen ～

Abi was standing, looking in the window of CashIn. A second hand electric guitar, Dyson vacuum cleaner, mobile phones, cameras, all displayed at knock down prices. *'We can buy for cash so you can pay your bills.'* Inside, the place was busy with buyers and sellers. Most of them were men but a young couple with their daughter of about nine were looking at a keyboard and the girl enthusiastically nodded at her mum as she bent over her. "If we get it for you, make sure you look after it carefully."

Abi stepped up to the counter and took a necklace carefully out of her handbag. The young woman assistant smiled as Abi laid it out on the glass top.

"Oh, they're nice – pearls! My nan's got something like this." She held it up to the light and checked the clasp. Abi was surprised at the womans cheeriness as she found these places quite depressing. A magnet for people hard up, needing to get by – not at all how she saw herself. For some people they were a last ditch attempt to pay the rent, she thought. Abi could hardly bear to speak. Her throat had dried up. "How much can I get for it?" she finally croaked, almost a whisper.

"Hang on a minute," the young woman slipped into a side room and Abi glimpsed through the opening at an older man sitting at a desk. He looked like he was the manager. The assistant soon returned.

"We can offer you twenty exchange or fifteen cash on this," and she placed the necklace back on the counter top. For a moment they both stood opposite each other, silently, just looking at it. Abi felt numb, then she coughed and glanced furtively around the shop in case anyone was there that she knew.

"OK," she said at last, gently moving the necklace towards the assistant.

The young woman carefully turned to a computer nearby and began to log the details of the sale. Sellers name, postcode and street number. As Abi produced some ID, she feared that the next question would be: 'Who does this necklace really belong to?' The assistant printed the sheet and then rattled off in a mechanical tone, the shop's standard declaration to sellers that she must have done a hundred times before and their conditions of purchase. Abi was hardly listening. Then when the woman had finished, she handed Abi a pen and asked her to sign her name. Abi lingered a little; her hand hovered lightly over the form and she felt that she was going to be sick.

"I'm sorry ... " she suddenly snapped, "I can't do this." Quickly snatching the necklace back, Abi turned and swiftly edged her way through the queue that had formed behind her, gasping for air as she opened the door. Outside a cool breeze and some gentle spots of rain speckled her face and helped calm her. Standing by the kerbside for a moment, the sudden wave of guilt that had almost throttled her inside the shop began to ease. Abi took a deep breath and hurried away clutching the necklace, intent on returning it before Millie noticed it was missing. As her feet padded along the pavement which was already glistening from the drizzle, she felt like a child again, arriving home late.

∼ Fifteen ∼

Millie originally came from Bethnal Green in London's east end. In 1940 when she was ten years old, the family house, a little terrace block off Cambridge Road was flattened by a bomb. Her sister, Flora aged seven, was killed outright but Millie, her mum and the cat were unscathed; buried in the rubble for hours before the rescue team could get them out. Not long after Flora's funeral, they went to live with an aunt in Hastings which could hardly be considered a safe haven with the threat of invasion looming. Millie's dad who was in the army had been taken prisoner at Dunkirk. Millie and her mum were on their own. However the move to Hastings was a good one for Millie and she quickly settled into a new school. Some of the kids ribbed her because she was a Londoner but her good humour always saw her through. It wasn't an easy time though. Her mother put on a brave face leaving London, deeply regretting not evacuating the children earlier, grieving the loss of Flora and fretting about the fate of her husband now locked up in Germany. She was on the verge of a mental breakdown. She couldn't sleep and wouldn't eat. The couple lived with Millie's aunt, Grace, above a shop in Clive Vale. Grace went to the doctor to get some help for her sister in law. Eventually she was admitted to a psychiatric hospital. Gradually Millie's mum recovered but it was touch and go for a while.

After the war, her dad returned from Germany and the family went back to London to live but Millie wasn't happy. She had made many friends in Hastings and loved living by the sea and she vowed to herself that she would return. After she left school, she started work in a candle factory in the East End and for a while she lived in lodgings but she hated it. Things went a bit haywire soon after. She then moved back down to Hastings and stayed with her aunt again. She began working at Plummer's a department store in town, which sold hats, ladies clothes, stationery and toys. She liked the toy department best, especially at Christmas time. She loved the look on the kids' faces when they visited Santa's grotto.

Millie plodded through life. She always seemed to be happy in her work, made friends and had a few boyfriends although she never married. She liked going to the pictures and watching all those old American films. She still fondly remembered seeing '*The Big Sleep*' and '*The Maltese Falcon*' starring her favourite, Humphrey Bogart and she also saw Robert Mitchum in '*Build My Gallows High.*' Cheery Millie they called her.

In the early sixties, she became very good mates with Abi's mum, Barbara. She was a rather quiet and reserved woman in her late thirties who was divorced. Barbara brought Abi into the store occasionally and Millie made a fuss of her which made the poor girl blush, but she loved it at the same time. Millie would play jokes on her and take her around the store, introducing her as her own daughter to the staff. Soon after, Barbara and Millie decided to start a B&B in Hastings. Their lives blossomed.

～ Sixteen ～

Rita's husband, Colin, had left for work and Rita stood in front of the bathroom mirror. This new tooth paste was far too minty for her liking. The taste reminded her of the cornetto ice cream that Gayle loved as a child. She quickly rinsed her mouth to get rid of the taste and while looking at her reflection she ran her small finger across her slightly uneven teeth. The way they looked had always troubled her. In recent years even more so, as perfect looking teeth, according to the media, seemed to be what everyone was after these days. Rita had vaguely thought about having cosmetic dentistry but whether she could get over her fear of treatment, was another matter and perhaps more importantly whether she could afford it. Abi had encouraged her to take out a loan and get it done. But then she was always going on about cosmetic this and that: face lifts, nips, tucks and breast implants. Rita studied her face, feeling rather dispirited that ageing seemed to be taking its toll on her. The thin lines were now permanent fixtures. She recalled people saying that you turn into your own mother and Rita dreaded the thought. She gently touched her face, massaging the skin, drawing it back, temporarily hiding the little wrinkles that had dug themselves a home. She tilted her head backwards to hide her emerging double chin.

Even though she wasn't very happy with how she looked, could she really be bothered to do anything about it?

*   *   *

As things turned out, a few days later Rita had a bit of luck.

On the way to work, she bought herself a scratch card and standing inside the crowded bus she leant against a seat to stabilise herself and started scratching the symbols off with her work's locker key. A winning line began to appear. She rubbed quicker – a jackpot prize £1,000!

Rita gasped and almost squealed with delight. She clambered off at the next bus stop, standing on the pavement for a moment, her head reeling, needing to get some air. She thought that she may have another turn again but waltzing into work, she was dying to tell somebody about it.

During the morning break in the staff room Rita felt light headed. The win had taken her mind off Gayle phoning last night to say she needed help in paying a final demand electricity bill. Something had snapped in Rita as her daughter droned on about a wrong meter reading and having a row with the utility company.

"I'm sorry love," Rita feigned, "you're breaking up. I can't hear you … "

Now at work Rita turned her phone off and placed it on the shelf of her locker. Despite a surge of guilt, she decided that she wouldn't tell Gayle or Colin about her win. As she headed for the checkout, Kate, the manager, was circling and demanding why certain display stands weren't ready. At lunch time Rita sent a text to Abi asking to meet her for a drink at The Eagle. She would explode if she didn't tell someone the news.

After work at the pub, Abi was late as usual, but when she arrived Rita was grinning from ear to ear but before she could blurt out to her, 'Guess what?'

Abi collapsed down in the chair, looking all-in.

"What a day!" Abi complained.

"Five o'clock this morning Millie comes into my room with a cereal bowl. I'm still half asleep and she stands over me. 'When's the milkman coming?' I told her that we've got milk in the fridge and to make herself some cornflakes. I can hear some clattering in the kitchen and then she's back again. 'When's the milkman coming?'" Rita, despite giving her usual sympathetic ear, was still on the edge of her seat, dying to tell Abi about her win.

"So," Abi continued, "this goes on for about twenty minutes, to-ing and fro-ing. 'The milkman, the milkman.' Under the duvet I'm pulling my hair out and the day's not even begun."

"Poor old you," Rita squeezed her arm in support.

"Then there's this almighty crash and she's dropped the cornflakes and milk all over the kitchen floor." Abi put her head in her hands, shaking in despair with it all. Rita went up to the bar and got Abi a glass of wine.

"I've been telling you that you need to get some help in," said Rita, giving Abi the drink. "Do you want me to come with you to see social services?"

"No, fear. I don't want them around poking around," Abi replied, gulping her wine. Abi looked exasperated, "I just want a decent night's sleep, that's all."

Rita put her hand on her shoulder. "Look I'll come over for a night this week so you can get some sleep, or go out with your new bloke. Craig isn't it?"

"Oh *him*," Abi exploded. Rita had touched a nerve.

"Do you know, he asked me out last Friday to go to the pictures? I arranged for a neighbour to come in for a few hours to look after Millie. Then the bugger phones up half an hour beforehand to cancel. Says he doesn't feel well. Got a dicky tummy or something." Abi took a long drink of wine.

"Well that can be nasty," Rita jumped in.

"Well I think he was pulling a fast one."

"You don't know that for certain, do you?"

"No but I've just got this feeling that's all."

They both finished their drinks and Abi went to the bar and got another round in.

"So, what did you want to see me about?" Abi asked eventually. "You said you had something to tell me."

Rita beamed at Abi.

"I've won on a scratch card!" Abi's eyes lit up.

"How much?"

"One thousand quid," Rita whispered, moving in closer to Abi.

"Fantastic!" Abi screamed, turning a few heads at the bar and hugged her friend with joy.

"So, what are you going to do with it?"

"Well, for a start, it means that I can pay my share for the greyhound. And I thought that I could pay yours too. I know that you're short of cash."

Abi was delighted and flung her arms around her again, "Oh Rita, you're such a pal." She nearly blurted out about almost selling Millie's necklace, but was still feeling too ashamed. "You're a star. I'll pay you back when we have a win! What does Colin think?"

"I haven't told him or Gayle. If they get suspicious I'll tell them that I've been awarded some Woolies gift vouchers for being employee of the month, or something. I've also had some ideas about spending the rest," Rita said, drawing breath and feeling great relief in telling Abi. She didn't quite know how to say it, putting her glass on the table. "I'm going to pamper myself. You know massages, saunas, manicure, and facials – the works."

"About time!" Abi cheered. "You devil! What's got into you?"

"Well it must be fate. I was just thinking the other day, Abi. I'm really looking ancient. I want to get some of my looks back. I don't want to end up an old bag. Not yet anyway!"

Abi gave her another hug. "We'll be old bags together, love."

"I'm so pleased for you, Rita. It'll do you the world of good and I'll help you if you like? I love spending other people's money!" The two women chatted for a couple of hours in the pub, until Rita got a text from Colin asking where his dinner was.

"Now Rita," Abi gave her a serious look. "Promise me that you won't change your mind and blow the rest of your winnings on the family. You can spend it on me if you like, but not them. I'm a more deserving case!" she laughed.

"I promise," Rita said putting her coat on ready to go. "And we'll have some fun too, a few nights out. What do you say? I won't forget a good friend."

"Ahh," Abi cooed. "I'm getting all excited now – a Rita makeover!"

"Oh and just one more thing," Rita leant close to Abi, "Don't tell the boys –Leo and Bill. We'll just say we managed to sell a few things. Mum's the word."

∼ Seventeen ∼

A cool Hastings morning and in the sky patchy dark clouds drifted slowly on their way, shielding an eager sun, only allowing it to throw random bursts across the town.

For a change the group had agreed to meet up at a different café near the pier. Unusually, Leo was the first to arrive. He was the only one in the place and the assistant was trying to fix the coffee machine. He was still feeling a bit irritated that he'd had to chivvy Bill up this week about the money for the greyhound syndicate. Leo sat down and thumbed through the Racing Post, looking at yesterday's results including Fly By Knight's 11/1 win at Brighton. He had circled it in red biro. 'This should finally convince Bill, if he needed to,' he thought. The girls had been all right. Abi seemed particularly jubilant and remarkably she said that she had no real trouble raising her share. He was also very relieved to hear that Rita had got her contribution sorted too.

"You've both done very well, you won't regret it," Leo told Abi on the phone. Bill though was a different kettle of fish. Leo had left several messages on his voice mail and he still didn't know if he had raised his share of the money.

In a short while all three of them turned up together and Abi tapped on the window and pulled a face at him before they all trooped into the café.

"Did you get my message?" Leo blurted out, looking up at

Bill, and ignoring Rita and Abi who sat down opposite him. "I've been trying you all week."

"Yes," Bill replied flatly, "but I've been busy doing a paper round to try and pay you. For what good it'll do."

"Don't be like that, Bill," Rita chided him. "I could do with a win. They've just cut back on our staff discount at Woolies."

"Yeah, stop putting the mockers on it," Abi agreed, looking at the menu.

Leo drew himself up, looking at Rita and Abi, then rather self-righteously at Bill.

"You heard the ladies, Bill. Have you got it or not?"

Grudgingly, Bill took out an envelope from his trouser pocket and laid it on the table. Leo's eyes lit up.

"One hundred and fifty pounds. It's all there, go on check it." Bill made it sound like a challenge.

Leo began carefully flicking through the notes, made up of tenners.

"I shall want a receipt," Bill said whilst he removed his jacket and put it on the back of his chair.

"A receipt? Surely there's no need … " Leo looked up from counting.

"I just want to make sure this is all above board in case there's any funny business."

"What funny business?" Leo sneered. "Look Bill, if you don't want to come in with us on this I can always find someone else." There was a moments silence and he started counting from the beginning again, muttering under his breath, "Funny business," shaking his head.

"No need for that," Bill said, more casually, "I've agreed to do it, but I just want it all to be crystal clear, that's all."

"Here's ours too." Rita passed Leo a roll of notes, surreptitiously, causing Leo to stumble over his counting again. When he had finally finished Bill's he began counting theirs.

"That's OK," said Abi, seeing Leo pick up speed, "it's all there. Me and Rita did it together."

Leo put all the money carefully in his wallet and slipped it inside his leather jacket. "Well that's it then," he smiled, "we've got ourselves a racing syndicate!" Still waiting to be served, he went up to the counter to order some coffees. Bill was amazed to see him paying for them, but looked carefully to see if it was coming out of his own money or theirs. Leo soon returned with a tray of drinks.

"I'm afraid the coffees are off. So, four mugs. Tea I meant, not us!" he laughed. Anyway the next drink we have together will be champagne, celebrating a win!"

Leo was oozing with confidence. "Look here," he said, sitting down again and pointing out Fly's most recent success in the racing paper.

I certainly hope that we get a good return soon," groaned Abi.

"You'll see," Leo grinned at her, "we'll all get a nice buzz when Fly does the business."

"So, what happens next?" Rita asked, sipping her tea and checking her watch as she was due to start her shift soon.

"I'm off to see Terry, Fly's trainer tomorrow lunchtime to settle the deal, look at the dog and whatever … "

"I could go with you if you like," Bill broke in, catching Leo's eye.

"Ah, well, Bill, that's not a good idea at this stage. You see Terry's pretty busy and I know him of old. He always likes to sort things out one to one and I might have to negotiate with him." Leo could see that Bill wasn't too impressed with his answer. "You will get to see the dog soon, I promise."

"There will be a contract, I assume?" Bill took a sip of tea.

"Of course, an agreement. That goes without saying."

"Well you haven't mentioned one so far." Bill was still uptight and looked at Abi and Rita for some back up.

"Look, we'll do the paperwork. It will all be legal." Leo had finished his tea first and then checked his mobile for messages.

"Anyway, now we've done what we need to, I better be on my way."

"When will the first race be, Leo? You know, as part of the syndicate?"

Rita asked as Leo stood up and the waitress, having given up on fixing the coffee machine came over and scooped up their empty mugs.

"Very soon. We won't have to wait long. It could even be by the end of the week. Don't worry, I'll give you a bell."

"Receipt for my cash?" Bill reminded Leo with an air of frustration.

"What, right now? I haven't got any paper."

Whilst Leo was fumbling, doing up the zip of his leather jacket, Bill whisked out some paper and a pen. He began writing a receipt for Leo to sign. Leo was getting more agitated as the zip of his jacket was still stuck.

"Come on, Bill. I've got an appointment. I'm going to be late."

"This won't take a minute," he still had his head down writing, but he did seem to be quite slow.

"I don't know why you're bothering, I'll get all the papers when I see Terry tomorrow," Leo grumbled, finally managing to pull the zip on his jacket.

"Aye, well tomorrow's a long way off, anything could happen in between. You might get knocked down by a bus."

Bill handed the paper to Leo for his signature. Without reading it, Leo hurriedly signed it and was about to put the pen in his pocket when he remembered it was Bill's.

"OK then, happy? I'd better shoot off." Leo stepped back towards the door.

"Don't you want a receipt too?" Bill asked Rita and Abi.

Leo's face dropped but suddenly forced a smile at them both.

"No, that's OK, Leo. We know where you live!" Abi grinned

Leo looked aghast. "Do you?" then he realised that she was only joking. In a flurry, he dashed away waving his hand. Abi called out after him, "You mind how you go. Don't spend it on loose women."

"What, like you, you mean?" Rita ribbed her as Leo disappeared. She looked at Bill's face as he peered out the café window, watching Leo dart across the road.

"Don't look so worried, Bill. It'll be all right. I know that

Leo's a bit of a scallywag but he won't do a runner with our cash. Hastings is a small town – he can't get far! Just think of all that prize money we'll be raking in. Your Job Centre days could soon be over."

Bill looked at her warmly and smiled, suddenly feeling more positive about things.

"Why aye, let's enjoy the moment I suppose. It's not everyday that you get to own a racing greyhound."

"Exactly," Abi smiled. "This time next month I could be sunning it somewhere with some nice fella."

"And what about Mille?" asked Rita.

"Oh, yeah, auntie as well – she'll have one too!"

They got up to go. Standing outside the café, Abi lit up a cigarette. The weather seemed to be getting warmer and the redundant pier, framed by the sea was instantly brought to life by a brilliant stream of sunlight hitting the old ballroom .

~ Eighteen ~

It had been a couple of weeks since the group had bought their share in the greyhound. Then one morning Bill got a call from Leo on his mobile. He sounded excited and was walking along somewhere in town. Bill could hear traffic noise in the background.

"Fly By Knight's running at 3.15 today at Newcastle, make sure you put a bet on. And let Rita and Abi know will you?"

"My home town," Bill enthused.

"What?" Leo's voice was breaking up.

"I said it's my home town, maybe it'll bring us luck. Are you going to the betting shop to watch the race?"

"Of course, William Hill, I'll be there by 3 o'clock."

"OK Leo," but the phone had already gone dead.

It was a bright sunny day in Hastings and after lunch Bill took a walk along the sea front before meeting up with Leo. There were plenty of day trippers strolling around. A sweet smell from the donut stall was drawing a crowd next to the fun fair with its rattling ghost train and amusement arcade of flashing lights and pumping out a booming beat and inside, the impossible crane game to lift money out. Bill stopped to gaze at a boy and a girl on the swan pedalo which was probably one of the oldest attractions of the small seaside fun park. He smiled at their uncoordinated efforts on the water to steer as their swan went round in circles. The fair reminded Bill of his childhood visiting the Spanish City at Whitley Bay.

Bill arrived at the betting shop just before 3pm. Leo was already there amongst a group of his cronies, crowded together and looking up at the television screen complaining about a slightly late starting race at Haydock Park.

"Come on Blue Queen, gertcha!" shouted one of them as the race set off across the flat.

The raucous excitement ran around the room infectiously – everyone's eyes popping. Bill followed the race and the front runners bunched up neck to neck. But then a breakthrough which none of Leo's crowd wanted.

"Aaaagh!" they droned before getting the result they feared.

The punters screwed up their receipts and tossed them willy nilly across the floor in disgust.

"He should have walked it, shouldn't he?" cried Barney, one of Leo's pals.

"Never mind," replied Leo, spotting Bill come in. "Our dog's running soon. Put a tenner on it and you'll get some of your money back, and more!"

Barney looked at the stakes. He was not usually a dogs man.

"Honest, really," Leo enthused. "You'll be quids in."

"Oh all right – in for a pound I suppose."

"What's the odds?" Bill asked Leo, coming over.

"Seven to one."

"What's that mean?" Bill asked innocently.

"It means if you don't get a quick move on you'll not get anything back. They'll be in the traps soon!"

Bill hurriedly paid his stake and they both stood in front of the screen with Barney who had just returned from having a quick fag outside.

As the dogs settled in the traps, Leo turned to Bill, "Well this is it, matey, our path to a fortune."

"Here goes," Barney joined in as the electronic hare hurled round, the traps opened and the dogs shot out.

Bill felt a rush of excitement. Number two – Knight was

somewhere lost in the middle. The grouping was too tightly packed for him to pick up a placing as the greyhounds sped along.

"Come on, break loose," Leo ranted, trying to drive the dog on, waving his betting slip at the screen.

"There she goes," Barney observed as number two spurted out in front by a good length.

"Yes, come on, boy," cheered Leo. Bill's eyes widened and he suddenly wished he had upped his stake.

The excitement of the race grew in other parts of the town too.

"Yes, yes, yes!" Abi shouted, leaning close up to her television in their flat with Millie sitting on the sofa beside her trying to dunk a rich tea biscuit in her mug of tea which was spilling over with the thrill of it all. "Number two, number two!" Abi hugged her as Knight darted in first past the post.

"Whoopee!"

"That's it, Fly boy," Rita exploded in the staff room at Woolworths. The tiny portable telly which her friend, Pat had brought in had such poor reception, it looked like the dogs were racing in a snowstorm. A few of them were crowded around the set. "Yes, he's done it," they cheered, jumping with joy.

Back in the betting shop there was much celebration too. Leo slapped Barney on the back and Bill quietly calculated how much he'd won. Leo was drunk with excitement, singing "*Yeah, yeah, yeah,*" doing a little boogaloo dance around the shop. He tried to grab Bill's hand to join him.

"Away man," he protested and went to the toilet while Leo stepped up to collect his winnings.

Buoyant with the win Leo persuaded Bill to go with him to a local bar to celebrate. It was not an ideal place as far as Bill was concerned. Loud music and expensive bottled beer but this didn't bother Leo. He smiled at the young woman serving.

"Two double scotches, my lovely and one for yourself."

She smiled, "Thanks, I'll just have a coke please."

"Have something stronger," Leo insisted.

"Not while I'm working."

"Well what time do you finish? I'll buy you one then!"

The young woman smiled at his cheekiness. "It might be a bit late for you."

"Oh I can take the pace, I'm a night owl, me," Leo replied.

"What did you have to say that for?" Bill frowned as they moved along the bar and sat on some stools.

Leo grinned at him. "She loved it – they all do," he looked over to her again raised his glass and she did too.

"Talking of which," Leo added, "did you hear about this survey in the paper that they carried out on speed dating?"

Bill shook his head.

"They tested out what male aftershave women found most attractive and they came up with the smell of men's perspiration. That's what turns women on most of all!"

"Are you sure?" Bill looked at Leo in disbelief.

"Yes, honest. It's the cave man aroma, see. I'm not surprised really. We're all primitive when it comes down to it."

"Why, that's a load of tosh, man, surely?"

"That's what they found. There must be something in it."

"It's probably a ruse to market a new product."

"What Neanderthal man after shave?"

"Aye, yeah," Bill replied. "They get up to all sorts to get you to buy things."

"Well Bill we've done it. Our first race and we won!"

He clinked his glass against Bill's. "Not a bad start, eh?"

"I must say," Bill declared, "I had me doubts at first but he sailed through, I'll give you that." They both relaxed on the stools looking at the young crowd of drinkers.

"It's great winning, isn't it? It's almost as good as sex." Leo took another swig of his whisky.

"How much did you pick up then, Bill?"

"A few quid, you know."

"Well no I don't, what do you mean, hundreds, thousands?"

"Don't be daft, man."

Leo looked at him a bit harder.

"Surely you must know?"

Bill prevaricated, "Well I don't actually. I haven't collected my winnings yet, as it was busy. I'll do it later on."

Leo looked sceptical and could see that Bill didn't want to tell him.

"OK, another drink?" Leo suggested and pushed his empty glass across the bar towards Bill.

"So, how much will we each get from the syndicate?"

"Difficult to say. I'll have a word with Terry to see what it works out at after his costs have been deducted. Don't worry Bill, I'm sure it'll be a tidy packet.

* * *

A few days later Abi, Rita and Bill were sitting in Rosa's cafe waiting for Leo to turn up and see what they had made from the prize money.

"So, how much did you win on Fly? Abi asked Rita. "Millie and me put a tenner on and we made £70."

"Did Millie enjoy it?"

"Of course she did. She's always likes a flutter on races. And you?" she asked Rita. "I got some of the girls together at work and we made £40 between us. We're putting it towards an evening out. We could do with cheering up. Things are not good at work. Everyone's saying that Woolies are selling up. We're forever having to do stock checks."

"That's capitalism for you," Bill said drinking his tea listening to the pair of them.

"Well Bill how did you do?" Abi asked him, but then her phone buzzed and she pulled it out of her bag. Looking at the text she giggled and showed Rita who looked and smiled. "So, are you seeing that Craig then?"

"I'll text him back later – leave him dangling."

Bill was getting a bit irritated with the interruption when Leo arrived with his usual gregarious bonhomie – hugging Rosa. He strutted over to their table singing, *I'm In The Money,* *still* high from their racing success. The women laughed and Bill looked up and raised a smile.

"Good afternoon, my lovelies." He leant over and gave them both a kiss on the cheek.

"Coffees and liqueurs all round," he called out to Rosa.

"Don't be daft you know that we don't have an alcohol license!" Rosa reminded him, tossing her head back.

"Oh, yes of course. I was just speaking metaphorically."

"You what?" Abi screwed up her face.

"Never mind, just the coffees then," he sat down and relaxed in the chair.

"You're like the cat that got the cream. Isn't he, Abi?" Rita grinned.

"You lucky people," chimed Leo, smiling back. "Do you remember Tommy Trinder? No, you'll be too young. What about you Bill? Anyway, what did I tell you?" he boasted rubbing his finger and thumb together referring to their winnings. The coffees arrived and he lifted up his cup to toast their first win.

"To Fly By Knight."

"Hooray," Abi cheered and they all laughed.

"So is everybody happy with their winnings?" Leo enquired.

"Not half," Rita replied. "When's the next race?" she asked eagerly.

"Tuesday at Romford, I think."

"Come on then, Leo. Tell us how much you made. I bet it was a lot," Rita said rolling her eyes.

Leo looked at her with a twinkle in his eye. "That's strictly between me and my bookmaker," he replied candidly.

"You can tell us, Leo," Abi joined in. "I made £70," and then she paused and looked at Bill as she realised that he still hadn't declared his winnings either.

"That's a point, Bill, how much did you make?"

"Well, erm, Bill looked a little embarrassed, " … .just £14."

"*What?*" Leo shot back. "I thought you were being a bit sheepish the other day. That means you only put two quid on!"

"So what." Bill replied with a 'none-of-your-business' look.

"Well you couldn't have had much confidence in our greyhound, that's all," Leo said looking indignant.

"No, it's not that. Anyway what about you?" Bill hit back instinctively, but wished he hadn't.

"Well if you must know, a few hundred," replied Leo quite coolly.

He sipped his coffee, glancing at the expression on their faces. Rita broke the uneasy silence.

"Anyway what's it matter how much you put on. It's up to you isn't it? We'll all make a packet I expect from the prize money. What you reckon we'll get, Leo?"

Leo shrugged his shoulders. "Don't worry, I'll be speaking to Terry tomorrow. It's difficult to know exactly how much, but as I say, he's always fair."

* * *

Nothing was heard from Leo until a week later when Bill bumped into him shopping in M&S. Leo was looking at some pesto sauces. Bill crept up on him and gently put his hand on his shoulder "Gotcher!" Leo looked at him over the top of his reading glasses as though Bill was a naughty schoolboy.

"Oh it's you," he smiled, "anything in the bargain bin this morning?"

"Got two dented tins of tomato soup for 50p at Poundland," Bill said rather proudly.

Leo shook his head in sad resignation. "M&S is a bit out of your league isn't it, Bill?"

"Oh, I like to see how the other half lives, like. Anyway, what's the news on our share of the prize money?"

"Ah yes," Leo replied, putting the sauce back on the shelf and picking up another.

"The pay out is not quite as much as I had hoped it would be," Leo said rather guardedly.

"Oh aye!" Bill stiffened.

"It's £45."

"Only £45 each? Well that's very disappointing."

"No," Leo interrupted him firmly, smiling. "It's £45 between us."

"But that's just over eleven pounds each, man!" he said looking alarmed, a desperate tone in his voice.

"Yes I know," Leo sighed, "It's £11.25 actually," and without further ado Leo put down his shopping basket and reached into his trouser pocket. "I can give you yours now if you like." And as Bill repeated "£11.25p!" Leo was busy counting out some loose change.

"But what happened to the big bonus that we were supposed to get?"

Leo wasn't listening, "Have you got 5p and I'll give you £11.30p?"

"Leo!" Bill said, firmly, "what's happened to the money that you reckoned we would get?"

Leo held out the cash, but Bill wasn't budging.

"Well Bill, like I told you all earlier, it's the cost of the dog and then there were a few more expenses like vet bills. In fact Terry said that we were lucky to get that."

"Oh, lucky are we, Leo?" Bill said, raising his voice. "Look you said … "

"Yes I know what I said Bill," Leo conceded, getting irritated with this cross- questioning.

"You have to look at this more as a long-term investment." He held out his hand again to Bill with the cash.

Bill shook his head, looking at the derisory amount.

"We've all been done, Leo. And I don't like it. You sold us a pup."

"A pup!" Leo chuckled, "That's very good, Bill." Bill failed to spot his unintended pun as he stepped back, leaving Leo still holding out the money.

"You can keep your pay out, I'm having nothing more to do with it," he walked away furiously.

*　　*　　*

Bill went straight round to see Rita at Woolies. She was on the counter, but fortunately the shop was pretty quiet.

"Oh hello Bill," Rita smiled at him, but could see that he was upset, his face red with fury.

"I've just seen Leo. I knew we shouldn't have listened to him. That bloody cheat."

"Bill," Rita said calmly, "what's happened?"

"He's tricked us Rita. That man's tricked us. He reckons that after expenses we'll only get £11.25p each."

Rita looked confused. "That's not much. How does he work that out then?"

Bill took a deep breath and tried to calm himself down.

"Because Rita, the man's a fraud and a swindler. I reckon that he and his mate planned to cream off our money all along. We've all been taken for mugs."

"Well I don't like the sound of that."

"You ask him. Phone him and see what he has to say for himself. I told you, I was suspicious from the start. And that dog, Fly By Knight, rightly named I reckon, Rita. It suits Leo down to the ground."

Rita laughed at Bill's joke, but saw that he wasn't seeing the funny side of it.

"I'll be in touch Rita," Bill said, picking up his shopping bag to leave.

"He's not getting away with it. He's a crook."

"Take care of yourself love," she said.

She was feeling more bemused than angry and wondered if Bill had got things right.

During her break she phoned Abi.

"Hi Abi, you'll never guess what!"

119

～ Nineteen ～

Millie had looked everywhere but their cat, Tiggy, was not to be found in any of her favourite places, on the bed, curled up on the sofa or looking out of the kitchen window of their second floor flat. Calling her brought no results either and Millie was in a diz. Abi had gone out shopping and she was sure that Tiggy must have dashed out then. She continued looking in the cupboards, boxes, wardrobes, under the bed and behind doors but to no avail.

Millie opened the front door, peered out and stepped cautiously on to the balcony. The mid-day heat hit her. The blazing sun caught the top of her head quite unexpectedly and her slippered feet warmed through like toast. Millie leant gently over the balcony wall, looking down for any sign of Tiggy along the pavement, or in the road leading up to the station.

A young mum came out of her flat with her daughter, she slammed the door and then hurried along, grabbing the child. "Come on Faye, stop dawdling we've got a train to catch." As they breezed past Millie, the girl hesitated at the top of the stairs, smiled and waved at her. "Faye, I won't say it again … "

'That's it, that's where Tiggy had gone,' thought Millie. She turned towards the stairwell and walked down, passing another neighbour, a man puffing and wheezing coming upstairs with his shopping.

"All right, Millie?" he nodded, pausing and moving aside as she quickened her pace, without a word, on a mission. Reaching the road, Millie was undeterred by the Hastings heatwave, as she strode along and up the hill searching as she went. She spotted a cat sitting in the shade under a car on the other side of the road. Without looking, she jumped out in front of an oncoming car which swerved and blasted its horn. The sudden noise disturbed the cat and it darted out from the shade on to a doorstep. Millie called over, "Tiggy, is that you girl?" As she got nearer, it made another leap up the steps and she saw that it was a tabby and not hers. Disappointed, she stood for a moment feeling a bit bewildered and looking at the creature washing itself, she gathered up her strength for the incline; her face clammy and her eyes heavy. Her carpet slippers failed to grip the pavement and began to make her feet feel sore, burning through the soles. Millie paused to take another breath and she wanted to take her slippers off. Her face was now glowing with perspiration and the sun felt like it was blistering the back of her neck. Millie pushed on along the dusty road, reaching the junction crossing near the station approach. A bus roared passed her, momentarily giving her a glimmer of shade. Millie found the road crossing lights confusing. The traffic had now stopped, but she wasn't sure what to do. It was a one-way street and two cars had lined up in front of her; one of them was revving impatiently as though it was about to do a circuit. The sun on their windows blinded her. Putting her hand up to her forehead she peered at the drivers, one young woman and an older man. The woman nearest to Millie was wearing sun glasses and bobbed her head to the music from inside her car – singing along. The side window was open and she looked at herself in the mirror, flicking her hair from her face. Millie stood still on the kerb – it felt like the edge of a cliff. Her head spun with the heat, noise and fumes. She had also completely forgotten why she was there at all, as she looked this way and that. Suddenly the car shrieked off and the thumping music was gone. The lights changed back; it was quieter again. A man beside her walked across the road and Millie hurried after him, her slippers flapping underfoot.

Continuing up the station approach, another bus sped by; its diesel roar heightening the intensity of the summer's day. The cat, now a shelved memory as Millie reached the station's new concourse, hardly recognising a thing. A train had just arrived and people were spilling out like peas through the barriers into the road, picking up taxis, buses and rushing to appointments. Millie just stood – unconnected. Around her, energetic day trippers were making a beeline for the town and meeting up with friends. Millie gazed at the hurly-burly. Why was she here? She could not fathom. She felt lost. Where was that old round station seat with the plants or was she confusing it with Eastbourne? The high modern glass building, shiny tiled floor and steel pillars were unfamiliar; more like a posh place in London. Although the automatic doors swished open, there was hardly any air creeping through; she was craving for a drink, her throat was dry as a bone – lemonade, tea, water, anything would do. She noticed that there were eyes on her too – side glances, sniggering and doleful looks. Millie had wandered into the middle of it all, like a circus clown. She suddenly felt very lonely standing there in her dressing gown.

"Hello, are you lost?"

A young woman cleaner, pushing a trolley of cleaning materials, was beaming at her. She was quite short, wore a high visibility waistcoat, had a bright purple headscarf tied round her fuzzy hair and a nice smile.

Millie looked closely at her trolley.

"Are you the tea lady?"

The woman laughed – a real belly rumble, "No, not really. Why, do you want a cuppa then?"

"Oh yes please. I'm parched."

"What you doing here?" the woman held Millie's arm affectionately.

"I'm looking for someone but I can't quite remember."

"Are they arriving by train?"

"Maybe. I'm not sure." Millie spoke haltingly, noticing that people were still staring at her. She frowned, looking around again "Where is this place?"

"It's the railway station love, Hastings"

"Is it?" Millie chuckled "It don't look a bit like it."

"It's been tarted up – modernised."

"Oh my word what a turn up," Millie chuckled.

"Were you going somewhere?"

Millie looked at the woman quite vacantly.

"OK, look, you come with me," the woman tried to reassure her. "We'll try and sort things out." Millie held on to the side of the trolley with one hand and they both glided slowly across the concourse, a slow shuffle over its shiny surface that suited Millie's carpet slippers a lot better.

"You must be very hot in that night gown. We'll get you a drink."

Millie was sat down at a table beside a mobile café bar and the cleaner had a word with the young woman who ran it.

"Any sugar?" she called over to Millie.

Millie thought for a moment, "Two please." She was given a tea in a paper cup and she noticed that the woman had a tattoo on her arm of a bird.

"Let it cool down first or you'll burn your mouth," the woman said and was now on her mobile phone reporting in. "I've just found this old lady wandering around in her dressing gown … "

Millie sipped her tea. First one today, she thought.

"Nice?" the cleaner asked, still holding the phone to her ear.

"Yes thank you, very nice. Are there any biscuits?"

"You'll get me shot you will. Nico, bung a packet of those biscuits over will you?"

Millie loosened her dressing gown and made herself a little more comfortable.

"Nice colour nightie," the cleaner said, "I like the bows."

"This old thing. I've had it a few years now. Bit too warm in this weather though."

"Well you'd better not strip off here or we really will be in trouble!"

Millie roared.

While Millie sat quite contentedly munching her biscuit, a station official turned up. He didn't speak directly to Millie, but stood nearby, talking to the cleaner and then he made a phone call.

He cast a cursory eye over Millie and then turned again to the cleaner.

"What's her name?" The woman repeated the question to Millie as though she was an interpreter.

"What's your name, love?"

"My name is Miss M. E. Purbright," Millie said slowly and deliberately, brushing some crumbs off her gown.

"Ask her where she lives," he instructed the cleaner with a bored tone in his voice.

Millie grasped the woman's arm lightly, whispering,

"I'm sorry dear, but I can't tell you that information. It's classified." The station man overheard, sighed wearily, and spoke on the phone again,

"No, she hasn't a clue. You'd better get down here pronto."

Turning to the cleaner he said off hand,

"Hang on here for a while, there's help on its way." He then marched briskly off back to his office.

The cleaner sat down next to Millie, "Someone will be over to help you soon love, but it would be good to know where you live and if there's anyone who we can call to tell them you're here. Is there anybody?"

"There's only my niece, Abi, and our cat."

"Is this nearby?"

"Oh, yes."

"How did you get here?"

"Well I walked over," Millie looked at her amazed at the question. "How else?"

"Which road do you live in?"

Millie concentrated "I think it begins with an H."

The woman looked thoughtful and smiled. "Harold? Havelock? What about Hoads Wood?"

"That's miles away," the café woman said while she was serving another customer.

"No, wait a minute, I mean M," Mille said, smiling.

"You're trying to get me going now aren't you?" the cleaner laughed.

The café woman came round and another customer joined in.

"Middle Street? St Margarets? Manor Street?"

It was like a pub quiz. Millie's mind was still blank but she was enjoying it all the same.

"Would you know the way?" the cleaner asked.

Millie supped some more tea, holding half a digestive biscuit in the other hand with more crumbs tumbling down on the table.

"Of course I would. It's only down the road." She seemed suddenly very lucid. "We could walk it, easy."

Just then two uniformed women police officers arrived. One very tall and slim, the other short and stocky. The cleaner explained the circumstances and they nodded sympathetically.

"Miss Purbright, we have got our car and we would like to give you a lift home, can you show us the way?"

Millie was amused at their presence. "You're not going to take me to clink are you?" she laughed.

They smiled and all three of them moved in slow step rhythm across the concourse. Millie waved back at the cleaner who headed for the loos with her trolley to carry on with her duties.

Millie felt quite important getting into the police car. She had not been in one before; inside it smelt of vinegar and chips.

"'Have you just had your lunch in here?"

The tall officer who was driving, smiled, "We've just had a quick bite to eat. Are you hungry?"

"My Abi will be home soon, she'll do me something."

"Who's she then?"

"My niece. She looks after me."

"OK."

It didn't take long to retrace her steps, although with the town's one way system, Millie got mixed up where her road was. Finally they arrived back at the flat. The front door was still open.

"There you are!" Millie cried out with joy as Tiggy the cat jumped down from the window sill and curled herself around her legs.

"So, where's your niece then, Miss Purbright?" The tall PC asked.

"Oh, she'll be out doing her shopping I expect. Would you like a cup of tea?"

"No, we're fine," said the smaller one bending down to stroke the cat.

"She likes you," Millie sat down in the kitchen. "Phew, it's still hot isn't it?" Her nightie was sticking to her like a wet tissue. The tall police officer got a call on her two-way and stepped on to the landing to take it just as Abi arrived. She had seen the policewoman come out of the flat and raced up the stairs; her heart beating hard as she appeared at the doorway.

"What's happened, where's auntie?"

"It's all OK, she's just in there." Millie was making some tea and quietly chatting to the short police officer.

"Ah, there you are, Abi. Do you want a cup too?" asked Millie.

"What have you been up to?" Abi blurted out breathlessly.

"Nothing. I just popped out and these kind ladies brought me back in their police car which smells of chips. Made me feel quite hungry. Did you get some eggs, Abi?" Her niece put the bags down on the table.

"You'll be the death of me," Abi looked seriously at her aunt.

"We'd better be off then. We've just had another call," said the tall one and they made their way to the door. "You look after yourself, Miss Purbright."

"OK, I will." Millie poured the hot water into the teapot. Standing at the front door they explained to Abi that she had been found wandering around the station in her night clothes. Abi shook her head, wondering if she should now lock her in when she went out.

"Do you get any help with caring for her?"

"No, we're OK, I'll keep a closer eye on her."

"Maybe you should take her to see her GP, just to be on the safe side."

"She just forgets things sometimes. Nothing serious."

"Yes but wandering around town in her dressing gown. Anything could happen."

Inside the flat, Abi slumped down at the kitchen table and the cat immediately jumped up on to her lap purring and rubbing her head against her chin. Millie made Abi a mug of tea, brimming over the top and spilling on the table top. Abi lit up a cigarette.

"There you are. They were nice weren't they, them two?" Millie sat down.

"What are we gonna' do with you, auntie?"

~ Twenty ~

A sea mist slowly crept up the beach, chilling everything in its path – a damp shroud instantly dulling the light. Abi, Rita and Millie were sitting in Rosa's cafe having taken refuge there from their walk along the front. They were all still shivering from the cold, having been tricked by the earlier warmth into wearing lighter clothes. Millie stared into her mug. Looking out over the channel, the horizon seemed as if it had been lost forever.

"Drink your coffee auntie, before it gets cold," Rita said, clasping her own tightly so that her finger tips tingled and revived.

Millie nodded to Rita, but she looked a bit thoughtful. Rita's heart went out to her. She recalled when she and Abi were teenagers how interested she was to hear about their new make up fads and clothes. Millie loved the sixties – the music, fashion, everything. She was always telling Abi's mum to be more relaxed when the girls went out for the night. 'They'll look after themselves. You've got to trust them sometime.' Millie was always the one that they each confided in over boyfriends or when they fell out with each other. Many a night Millie would pop into Abi's bedroom while she and Rita were both chatting away listening to records. Often The Stones latest single was blasting away with Abi drooling over Brian Jones. 'He's got nice hair, I'll give him that', Millie said. Abi had pictures of the pop star all over her bedroom wall. Rita preferred Mick Jagger – all that pouting and 'gypsy dancing' as Millie called it.

'Can't get no sat-is-faction, yeah.' She'd sing along and Millie joined in too. They'd all have a laugh. Millie was one of the girls.

Millie stirred her coffee and carefully lifted the full mug up to her lips. Rita smiled as auntie took a long noisy slurp and sighed satisfyingly.

"OK?" Rita asked.

"Mmmm," she purred, "a bit hot though."

Rita was sad to see Millie look so distant at times. "She's in another world," Abi joked.

Abi had just called Bill and put her mobile down on the table.

"Well," she said rather vexed, "that Leo sounds dodgier by the minute. I think you and me have got to find him and have a word. He's not getting away with it!" Abi's eyes narrowed as she began texting furiously.

"What you doing now?" Rita asked.

"I'm trying Leo again. See if he replies this time," she bristled.

"There may be a simple explanation to all of this. Perhaps he's ill," Rita said.

Preoccupied, Abi was only half listening to what Rita was saying.

"Ill?" Abi sneered. "I'll make him ill! Look Rita, I agree with Bill, all this sounds very fishy. He's done a bunk with our money. And do we know where he lives? No. Do we know where this Terry the greyhound trainer lives? No.

I tell you Rita, it's got my goat this has. He's taking us for a ride."

"I just still think he'll turn up and … " Rita began.

"We've been done!" Abi jumped in.

"Would you like another drink, Rita?" Millie suddenly asked and surprisingly they both saw that she had her hand up trying to attract the attention of the waitress.

"I'll get them," Rita offered.

"No, leave her, Rita." Abi said, it's good."

"And do you want one too, Abi a cup of thingy?" Millie asked.

"Yes please, auntie," they both smiled, "a cup of thingy would be nice."

Rosa's daughter attended their table. Millie still had her hand up while she spoke to her.

"Hello dear. Yes, we'll have three cups please of thingy with milk."

Rita sitting beside Millie, mouthed to the waitress 'COFFEE' and nodded. The young woman collected their empty cups and Millie lowered her arm.

"She's nice," Millie remarked, "She reminds me of you when you were young, Abi. You know, when you were watching your figure and would only eat cream crackers because you thought that you wouldn't get a boyfriend."

"I didn't know that," Rita grinned at Abi.

"Umm there's a lot you don't know about me," Abi mused.

"Shall we have some cream crackers too?" said Millie, "I'm feeling a bit peckish."

∽ Twenty One ∽

Millie had received a greetings card from an old friend, Iris, to say that she would visit. She used to run a guest house nearby to hers during the seventies. She was of similar age to Millie and after she and her late husband Freddie, or 'Steady Freddie' as Millie called him, gave up the business, they moved to Bexhill to be nearer their daughter. Once a year Iris visited Hastings by train to see some old friends including Millie. Iris was a tall woman with stout arms and had a deep voice, bellowing out and sometimes frightening the guests when she used to order her husband around their old Hastings B&B.

Iris arrived to see Millie early in the afternoon. The uncertain weather had made her wear a raincoat. It was a little too small for her size. She was holding a pot plant and Abi welcomed her in. Millie was standing just behind nodding and smiling as her friend crossed the threshold. Iris bent down and they hugged.

"Ahh," Millie greeted her, "we've been looking forward all morning haven't we, Abi?"

"Looks like rain," Iris said, almost filling the doorway, handing Abi the plant. She stepped in and removed her coat. "It was spitting just as I left Bexhill, but it seemed to peter out while I was on the train coming here."

They both looked at the heavy sky from the living room window.

131

"I expect we'll have some here before the day's out." Millie nodded. "Not been much of a summer so far, has it?"

The best china was already laid out in the living room. Abi boiled the kettle and brought in a chocolate sponge on a plate with a knife.

"This looks lovely." Iris neatly laid her coat on the back of an armchair and joined Millie, sitting opposite her at the table. "It's always good to be waited on, isn't it Millie? We've done enough of it in our time."

Auntie nodded and smiled in agreement as Iris glanced around the room.

"That's new isn't it?" She pointed to a framed print hanging over where the fireplace used to be.

"Romney Marsh in the winter by a local artist," Abi said as she brought in the teapot from the kitchen. "That mist," Iris got up, holding a napkin close to her lap and leant across to have a closer look. "All mysterious looking, isn't it? I shouldn't like to be there in the winter. It's a bit spooky."

"Oh I love it!" Abi enthused. "Me and Rita used to go there when we werekids. Get the bus over to Rye. It was quite an adventure." Iris sat down again and pulled her chair in, as Millie was quietly admiring the plant that Iris had brought them.

"You not joining us, Abi?" Iris asked.

"No, I'm going to leave you two ladies to it. I've got to pop out. A few things to pick up."

Iris settled down and looked across at Millie.

"You've not got much to say for yourself, Millie. Cat got your tongue?"

Millie laughed. "The cat! She's in the bedroom."

"On the bed I expect. That's what she likes best, isn't it?" Abi had put her jacket on already.

"Anything you need out, auntie?"

"You know me, the usual."

"Your magazine?"

"Yes, that's right. I like the gossip, don't you?"

"Not half," Iris grinned, "as long as it's not about me!"

As Abi prepared to leave, Iris began to pour some milk in the cups. The journey and chatting had made her very thirsty and she could see that Millie was making no move to serve it up.

Hearing the front door close, Iris poured out the tea. "So, how have you been?"

"All right," Millie perked up, "can't complain."

"Mustn't grumble, eh Millie? Who'd listen anyway!" Iris roared, handing Millie her tea.

"That's right, only the cat and I think she's fed up with me bleating."

"So what have you been up to?" Iris asked, picking up two big teaspoonfuls of sugar and gently stirring; the cup pinged.

"Oh this and that. Time just seems to fly when you're doing nothing."

"I know what you mean. I've been retired nearly ten years now. I don't know how we did it in the old days, all those guests coming and going." Iris leant over and picking up a knife, she gently cut the cake into neat slices. Millie looked on contentedly.

"This looks tasty," Millie nodded and held up her plate for Iris to put a piece on it.

"Mmm, that's nice," she glowed and Iris munched away too.

"Have you tried that raspberry sponge, it's very tasty. My Claire picks them up in Eastbourne because they don't seem to have them in Bexhill. I try to get them from Morrison's, they're always a bit cheaper. Where do you go, Millie?"

"Oh, I can't remember now, Tesco's maybe. Somewhere in town. They all seem the same to me. Anyway, Abi gets all the shopping. I just tag along."

As they ate their sponge, the cat joined them to see if there might be some to spare.

"She's a good girl to you, isn't she, your Abi, the way she looks after you?"

Millie nodded and Iris placed her empty plate back down on the table.

"Has she got a fella at the moment?"

Millie raised her eyes to the ceiling with a wry smile on her face. "She's always got some bloke on the go, but she never tells me about it. She's very secretive that way."

Iris nodded but she was still feeling hungry and was wondering if it would appear a bit rude if she took another slice of cake whilst, Millie was still slowly picking away at hers.

"It's funny that she's never settled down with anyone. To tell you the truth, Millie, I was wondering if she might … "

Millie hesitated, taking another bite.

"What?"

"You know, swing both ways."

"Both ways?" Millie held the piece of cake up and looked puzzled.

"Yes, you know – liking women as well as blokes," Iris nodded.

"Bi-sexual you mean?"

Iris was so stunned by Millie's frankness, that in this sudden moment of speculation that seemed to hang in the air, she quickly snatched another piece of sponge and began munching furiously again.

"No, Abi's not like that, but I wouldn't care if she was. There's nothing wrong in it is there? Not if two people care for each other, I mean," Millie continued.

Iris, her mouth now stuffed with cake could only nod in reply before sipping some tea to help ease it down. "Your drink'll get cold, Millie," she spluttered finally. Millie drank a good mouthful and Iris quickly topped her up.

"Do you miss the old B&B game?" Iris asked.

Millie looked thoughtful, pouring herself a drop more milk from the jug.

Before she had a chance to answer, Iris replied to her own question.

"I do sometimes – I must admit. I liked the not knowing who'd turn up for rooms and thinking about what they did for a living."

"Yes, that's right," jumped in Millie.

"There were the regulars, business people stopping over and

134

sales reps with their cars full of clobber."

"Oh yeah, and the odd bloke who'd been thrown out by his missus," Iris chipped in. They both laughed, and the cat jumped up on Millie's lap, her nose sniffing the crumbs on the plate.

"Young couples down for a dirty weekend and the girl blushing at breakfast time. I used to send 'em up rotten," Millie chuckled.

"Holiday makers with their pac a macs, on a budget, who'd want egg and tomato sandwiches for their packed lunch on the beach. My Freddie used to make em up for them."

The two women came alive – sparking off each other with their guest house tales.

"Those were the days, but I don't miss the hard work. I wouldn't have the energy now. I mean we never got a break did we?" Iris complained.

"All those breakfasts and forever changing sheets," Millie added and Iris nodded in agreement having just secured herself another piece of chocolate sponge.

"Well, at Sandbanks, Freddie and I were noted for our lavish Full English and our speciality theme evening meals, but we were always tied to the place. As you know, Millie, we were blessed with winning the award for best guest house in Hastings for two years running – 1978/79. I've still got the citation on my living room wall."

"Yes I remember," Millie put her head to one side. "And wasn't one of the judges your brother in law?"

Iris gave a squeal of laughter. "Don't be daft," with her napkin, she wiped some crumbs from the corners of her mouth. "No dear, Trevor was never one of the judges. Your memory is playing tricks on you. You're thinking of that old dragon, Eydie, at The Grove. She was disqualified one year for watering down the ketchup on the breakfast tables.

"Is she still going?" Millie asked.

Iris leant forward. "Well I heard that she'd found a new bloke. A rich widower from Tunbridge Wells."

"Fancy!"

"Yes, she wooed him with her Brussels sprouts!" Iris said with a twinkle in her eye.

"As long as she doesn't give him any of her steak and kidney pie. It was always more puff than pastry," Millie joked and then looking down noticed that the remaining chocolate sponge had disappeared.

"That went quick. We must have been hungry," Iris loudly burped.

"Excusez-moi"

"Patsy in Priory Road popped off a few weeks back," Millie said rather matter of fact, finishing her cuppa.

"No!" Iris's eyes widened and her fingers nervously played with her necklace.

"Heart," Millie said putting her cup and saucer back on the table. "Dropped down dead on the seafront by the rock shop."

"No!" Iris was still in shock. "But she was only, what … ?

"Seventy-one," Millie jumped in.

"That's no age these days. She always looked so young." Iris finished her tea and stared again at Abi's painting of Romney Marsh on the wall.

Millie picked up the empty teapot and went to the kitchen to refill it but was gone some considerable time. Iris eventually went to see what she was doing and discovered her standing by the sink pouring cold water from the tap into the pot which she was heavily swirling around; there were puddles of water on the kitchen floor and tea bags were floating around the sink like toy boats.

"It's not hot enough is it?" Millie said, "It's gone all queer. I can't seem to get it to work."

"You have to warm it up in the kettle first, silly." Iris giggled rather hysterically and took control of things. "Whatever were you thinking of, love. Here let me do it." Millie stood back. Iris filled the kettle and poured the cold water from the tea pot down the sink.

"You feeling all right, Millie?" Iris put her hand gently on her shoulder.

"OK, yes. I'm OK. Do you want another cup?"

"You go and sit down. I'll bring it in," Iris said.

The two women were more subdued drinking their second round of tea.

Abi returned from shopping and went into the kitchen to make herself a drink. Soon after Iris made moves to leave, putting on her coat.

"Well, my love, I'll see you anon."

Millie got up too, smiling at her old friend.

"Now, don't you over do it. This retirement lark can be a bit overwhelming at times. I'll keep in touch." She gave Millie a peck on the cheek

"Yes, pop round again anytime you're in the area. Good to see you. Bring Freddie next time."

Iris looked aghast.

Millie sat down again and Abi saw Iris to the door.

"Oh good the rain's kept off," Iris clutched her umbrella.

"Thanks for coming to see auntie. She always looks forward to your visits."

Iris stood on the step and said softly, "Is she OK?"

"What do you mean?"

"She didn't seem all there at times this afternoon, and she just mentioned my Freddie as though he was still with us!"

"No, she's OK. She has her off days when she's not quite with it but no, she is bright as a button usually."

"Good, it was nice to see her." Iris called out as she left, "Bye Millie, see you soon."

"Bye," Millie called back.

~ Twenty Two ~

Bill spotted an advert on the vacancies page of The Hastings Observer on Friday whilst he waited to get his haircut in the Old Town.

'Looking For A Challenge – Can You Sell For Us?'

'Earn over £40,000 pa plus car. No previous experience necessary. Extensive training provided for successful applicants.'

Mulling it over, looking in the mirror while his hair was trimmed, Bill wondered if he was up for it. Sales were hardly his forte but he had to try and get out of this rut. *Looking For A Challenge?* Yes, he thought, he was ... kind of.

During the afternoon, Bill phoned the mobile number and the man he spoke to said that they were recruiting a sales team in the area. He invited Bill to meet him in Bexhill on Monday evening.

Bill drove over, but it took some time as the traffic along the A259 was snarled up as usual towards Glyne Gap. On his way over, Bill played some tracks that he had recorded from CD on a cheap homemade cassette. It wavered on the brink of sticking but the bluesy sounds of Otis Spann's singing and piano playing helped to calm his nerves about the interview. If he got this job, Bill thought, he would probably have a CD player in the company car, then he really would enjoy listening to music whilst driving. Arriving early in Bexhill, he parked easily along the seafront, listening to the gulls and taking in the sunset as he strolled to the De la Warr Pavilion, admiring its bright modernist architectural style, recently revamped. The Queen's Hotel where he was meeting was a different story – a grand Victorian building that was now sadly run down. Bill went into the bar which only had one other customer, an elderly woman sitting in an armchair with her nose stuck in a newspaper. Cheesy, soft classical guitar music was playing throughout the foyer. Bill ordered a half-pint of beer and sat at a table by the window. Outside, the street lights had just come on. Bill straightened his tie and patted down his hair that had become ruffled by the sea breeze. Ten minutes later a man with a briefcase arrived; poking his head giraffe-like into the lounge, he looked quite comical. He came over to Bill, all smiles. He looked about forty years of age, quite tall and wore a dark blue suit, although Bill noticed that the trousers were rather short, showing off a pair of green socks that made him look even taller.

"Bill? Derrick … drink?" He reached over the table, shook hands with Bill gripping it very tightly and placed his black leather briefcase on a chair.

"No I'm fine, thanks." Bill lifted up his glass to show that it was still almost full. Derrick quickly picked up his case again and placed it gently on the table. As he clicked it open, the brass locks sprang up like rabbits. He pulled out a glossy brochure and with a wink gave it to Bill before heading for the bar. Looking back, he pointed to Bill's drink, "You sure?"

"No, I'm fine." Bill flipped through the blurb. *'Join our dynamic, go-ahead sales team!'* There were photographs of people sitting around a flip chart in a training room and others of palatial properties in sun drenched locations. Bill gathered that's what the company sold. Derrick returned with a glass of orange juice and ice which rattled as he put it on the table; he smiled at seeing Bill looking at the blurb.

"Sorry I was late, I just had to complete a deal and there were a few adjustments to make on the property. Clients can be so picky, but that's what we're here for; to try and keep them happy." He took a gentle sip from his orange. "Ah, that's better. First sit down I've had all day." He sat back a little in his chair and looked around the lounge. "It's a bit seedy in here isn't it?" he sniggered. "Used to be top notch – high class Bexhill in the old days. It's where you'd come for afternoon tea I expect. You're not from round here are you?"

Bill shook his head, "No, north east, me – Tyneside."

"Oh, really. You know that's one place I've not been. Travelled the world more or less from Oz, Thailand, The States, even Russia but England – Tyneside, missed it somehow," he laughed. "I dare say it's a nice place."

"Oh, aye, it's canny all right."

"Anyway, Bill, down to business." Derrick took out an expensive looking pen from his inside jacket pocket and leant forward. It was then that Bill noticed that his breath smelt of tobacco. "So, tell me about yourself." Bill gave him a résumé of his work career but skated over his reasons for moving to Hastings. Derrick nodded and doodled a bit with his pen, whilst Bill told him about his career. His eyes somehow gave the game away that he wasn't really listening. When Bill had finished talking, Derrick put down his pen, smoothed his tie which he had also been fidgeting with and began to give Bill the full sales pitch.

"It sounds like you're ready for a new challenge." Bill smiled to himself at the patter and hearing that buzzword again. "Let me tell you what we've got to offer." Bill found himself nodding compliantly as if he were a schoolboy. Derrick explained how they operate on a franchise basis. "Hedley Promotions attracts clients with very expensive property abroad to sell." Derrick said that for every place sold, a sales rep could earn a percentage from between £2,000 to £3,000. "Some of my sales team are almost doubling that with bonuses." Bill's eyes lit up at the figures and he wondered when he would get to tell him about the company car with the CD player. There was more to come and Derrick told Bill about other promotions that Bill could participate in after he had received his accredited training.

"So what does the training involve?"

"That's the key to it all," Derrick beamed, taking another sip of orange, "It's your passport, Bill, to a very lucrative income. The courses are held over one week and we take you through selling techniques, client profiles, managing the different stages of deals. You'll come out of it fully briefed, confident and raring to go. All we require from you is the training course fees then we can set you up immediately. And this time next month … "

"Fees?" Bill interrupted.

"Well you see, Bill, you'll be an associate in Hedley Promotions, so naturally we would expect you to pay your way for your training and the expertise."

"How much?"

Derrick's grin widened.

"Just two thousand pounds and you'll be fully certificated." The amount slipped gently off the salesman's tongue and sounded as though you'd be a total fool to refuse the offer.

"Two thousand!! I'd be certified myself if I gave you that amount."

Derrick laughed, "You'll easily get it back in the first month of selling, Bill. Honest."

"I canna' afford that kind of money, man. If you are so certain of my performance can you not deduct it from me sales afterwards, like?"

"No, I'm sorry. It doesn't work like that. We have to see a commitment up front. Company policy I'm afraid. You'll kick yourself if you let this opportunity pass you by, Bill. We are very selective about who we take on but I can see just by talking to you that you've got what it takes."

Ignoring this compliment Bill sighed, "You didn't mention anything on the phone to me about having to pay this kind of money. I wouldn'a bothered to come, me."

Without realising it Bill's Geordie accent was rising in tune with his disappointment and anger.

"You just have to appreciate that this could change your life, Bill."

"It certainly would if I gave you that kind of money, lad." Bill suddenly stood up. "Excuse me I must just go to the loo."

He hurried downstairs to the gents, his head in a whirl.

The bygone splendour of the Victorian lavatory with its original ornate brass fittings and oak panelling somewhat passed Bill by. As he stood alone in the urinal he muttered angrily to himself, "He must think I'm right soft. Two thousand pounds, tuh! Why does everyone seem to want to con you? First Leo, now this. Argh!!!" His voice echoed eerily around the glazed tiled wash room.

Coming back upstairs Bill stormed out of the hotel and sped down the hill – his rage still boiling up about yet another failed job hunt and more angryabout allowing himself to get taken in – "Am I so desperate?"

Bill didn't stop racing until he ended up on the seafront, panting and shaking his fists at the English Channel.

"*Bastards!!!*" he screamed, ignoring the grey night sea, rolling gently in, beating time against the shingle on the beach. An old man appeared, walking a small dog nearby. Fearing Bill was off his head, he stopped, reined in his pet and hurriedly scuttled away in the opposite direction.

Bill spun around, heading back towards his car. He momentarily held on to the bonnet. He then went over, picked up a nearby rubbish bin and hurled it and the overflowing contents like a javelin across the neat promenade lawn straight into the brightly coloured municipal flower arrangement. Pansies and petunias were dramatically flattened and smashed as soil was churned up; fast food containers and plastic drink bottles spilled out and lay in a jumble. Crisp packets fluttered away in the evening breeze. Fortunately for Bill, with the dog walker now a dot in the distance, Bexhill was silent as a grave and nobody seemed to bear witness to his uncharacteristic fury. He just stood staring at the mess hardly believing he had caused it.

"Oh fucking hell."

No time for guilty second thoughts.

Bill got in his car. After the usual hesitation, it started up and slowly moved off. Bill feverishly turned up the cassette player as loud as it would go – Muddy Waters' raunchy '*I'm Ready*' drove him out of town, his mind buzzing with surprised excitement. He suddenly felt more alive than he had done for ages. His wife, Helen, was somewhere in the car with him laughing, calling him a 'stupid bugger,' in amongst the blaring Chicago blues harp and tight shufflebeat drumming. He thought that these old cassette tapes aren't so bad. Beginning to relax, speeding along the sea road towards Hastings, long lines of lights sparkled and bobbed along the shoreline – a welcoming feeling. '*I'm ready, as ready as any man can be.*'

* * *

The following day Bill was back at the Job Centre.

"Retraining," said the adviser.

"What?" asked Bill, looking as downcast as ever, expecting that she might start on about 'skill sets'.

"If you are serious about getting a job, then you'll really have to try a different tack." Bill had not met this young woman who was now reviewing his job situation. Her name badge said Nana Christophedes. She looked Mediterranean, perhaps Cypriot.

She was scanning her computer screen to see what was on offer.

"There are openings in social care. There's plenty of care homes along the south coast."

"Me, changing catheters? I mean I know its worthwhile work, but, well, I don't see me fitting in."

"I see." She continued looking.

"That's not to say I wouldn't do something different." Bill

wanted to show that he was flexible. "You can see from my records how I've tried already but I think it's my age. As soon as they see I'm over fifty I'm done for. And it's not that I'm unwilling, but I just know my limitations." Bill leant forward.

"I reckon, I'm not really a people person," he said rather glumly.

"Well, if you really want to get a job, Mr Shields, then I think you will have to consider some training. I'm sure that you have a lot of transferable skills that will be attractive to a prospective employer. You're clearly reliable, conscientious and hard working."

Bill readily nodded in agreement. Put like that it made him sound as though he would be a good catch for some employer. She handed him some information leaflets on training and opportunities in social care. Bill got up to leave, thanked her and said he would think about it. As he walked out he thought to himself with indignation, 'Transferable skills – shit!'

* * *

Over the next couple of days, Bill thought more about what the young woman at the Job Centre had said and whether he would ever get another job again.

How come middle age had somehow transformed into retirement? He wondered if he would have to accept defeat and take a job that he really didn't want. He was feeling quite low. He looked through the local paper again and nothing seemed right. Then an article caught his eye about the problem that some children have in reading, including dyslexia and what support they need. Bill was interested to read about a scheme for volunteers who go into schools and help children with their reading. Bill recalled that one of his sons had trouble with his reading as a child. He sat with him most evenings to try and help him. After a while his son picked up and as his interest in stories and books grew he began reading well. Despite what he thought about himself not being good with people, Bill liked the idea of helping kids. Also he loved reading himself, mostly history and biographies.

It gave him a lot of enjoyment. Why not pass some of that on?

He phoned the number in the paper and later he was invited to an informal interview. The woman who saw him was a teacher and explained about the scheme and how certain children can get a lot from an adult volunteer spending a little time with them each week. Bill came away from the meeting feeling very good about it all. He agreed to do some training and would have to have a criminal record check. Maybe something at last? Not paid work, but maybe this would help kick start things, he thought.

Bill was able to do some training quite quickly and joined the learning scheme. He attended some sessions where he learnt about the reasons why children have problems reading; how volunteers attending a school regularly listening and encouraging them to read can help to build their confidence. Surprisingly, Bill found that he enjoyed the training. It was very different from anything that he had done before. They also gave him advice about boundaries of contact with the children and that for safety of all concerned, children and volunteers, worked together in an open area. After the police check was completed, he visited a school near where he lived. The special needs teacher was friendly and pleased to see a male volunteer.

Bill was feeling very nervous on his first day, a bit like starting a new job. The teacher invited him to sit in on a class of nine year olds to get an idea about what they were learning. Sitting on a small school chair at a table with a group of kids, Bill felt a little uncomfortable, squatting so low. The children were curious about him as the teacher gave them an exercise to do. They all had a list of words between them and they had to match the word with the meaning that she read out, "What word means to travel?"

At their table they all looked at the list of words on the sheet of paper. One of the girls asked Bill, "Do you know, sir?" Bill wasn't sure if he should be helping or not but tried to be encouraging.

"Well what do you think, sir?" One of the boys pointed to a word. "Is it that one?"

"Yeah," his mate said eagerly, "tick that one." A fair haired girl had taken on responsibility for filling in their answers. She screwed up her face at the boisterous lads, not sure if their answer was right.

"Nah," said a smaller girl, leaning over with her cracked, painted finger nails, "it ain't that one." In turn they all looked at Bill for his help. He scanned the list and saw that the girl's suggestion was correct.

"I think that might be the right one," he said quietly. "*Yes!*" said the girl with the nails, punching the air and the excitable boys sighed.

"Next one is 'accident'," the teacher continued. They all had their eyes pinned to the paper, but Bill noticed that one of the group, a dark haired middle eastern looking boy hadn't yet said anything.

"What do you think?" Bill asked him. The boy shrugged his shoulders and seemed a bit distant. The two other boys energetically piled in again, "Sir, sir," they clambered for his attention. "Is it cat-asphie?"

"Do you mean catastrophe?" Bill asked smiling at their charming mistake. He gently nodded.

"Yeah, that's the one," they exploded. "Put it dahn, Lucy," they instructed her as she shrugged her shoulders and compliantly ticked it. Bill tried again.

"Any ideas?" he gently asked the quiet boy again.

He shook his head and smiled thinly. One of the other boys leant over to Bill.

"He don't say much, cos he comes from abroad see? His English ain't that good – right, Musti?" The boy didn't answer. The teacher kept firing new words and Bill was really getting into the exercise. At break time the teacher asked Bill what he thought.

"Yes, I really liked it. A bit like a pub quiz," he said.

"Good, then we'll be seeing you again shall we?"

"Oh aye," Bill replied enthusiastically. "So, who will I be working with?" he asked.

"Mustafa," she pointed to the quiet boy. "He needs help with his reading and he is rather shy. He came here with his family from Iran."

"So, how does that sound?" she asked Bill, smiling.

"Aye, that's grand by me. I'll see you next week."

∼ Twenty Three ∼

Rita woke up in a good mood and decided that she was going to try and stay that way whatever the day had in store.

Colin had already left for work when she went to have a shower. So, with the house to herself she could have the radio on as loud as she liked. Terry Wogan blasted out from the kitchen.

"And here's one for all you stay-in-beds this morning to get you up and running. With a message to have some breakfast – boost your energy levels, tuck into some cereal or something. Or maybe a fry up if you're that way inclined. There's no doctors listening are there? They don't like that sort of thing do they?" 'Build Me Up Buttercup' sang out while Rita ran her shower. Over the noise of the running water she began humming along and mimicked the singer's voice, 'Why do you build me up baby just to let me down and mess me around? ...' A jet of hot water hit her face and chest immediately, warming her body like a blanket. She rolled her head back, closing her eyes, it took her breath away. She was pleased that Colin had got the shower fixed at last from the luke warm dribble she had put up with for nearly a year of her complaining. Rita turned around to allow the gushing water to run down her back, moving her head round further as it soaked her hair. She could have stood there all day with the steady flow streaming over her – it was great. The power shower had almost eclipsed Terry Wogan, downstairs.

The phone rang and it was only just audible above The Beatles' '*Nowhere Man*.' With her hair dripping wet on the floor and putting a towel around herself, Rita went into the bedroom and picked up her mobile.

"Hello." There was silence at the other end at first.

"Mum, it's me." Rita shut the bedroom door to dull the radio. Gayle sounded distressed and the reception was poor.

"It's Dean," she said, "we're down the hospital waiting to be seen."

Rita felt her heart quickening, "Why, what's up?"

"He's had an accident," Gayle replied, her mobile was breaking up.

"He's got a Tic Tac up his nose."

"A what?" Rita asked.

"A Tic Tac. You know one of those minty chewy things." Rita felt like bursting out laughing but realised it might be serious.

"Mum are you still there?"

Rita took a deep breath and said, more composed, "Can't he blow it down with a tissue?"

"No," said Gayle irritated at her mother, "it's lodged up the back. They say he might need fucking surgery. I'm waiting in A&E. Can you get down here now?"

Half an hour later, Rita arrived to find Gayle and Dean at the children's A&E unit. Gayle was reading a magazine. She looked up. "You took your bleedin' time didn't you?" Rita ignored the remark and sat next to Dean who was looking at a comic. "Sweetie up my nose, Nanny."

"Yes I know, love, they'll soon get you sorted," Rita said. She couldn't resist having a look for herself as she put her arm around him.

"And they're taking their bleedin' time too," Gayle complained. Rita looked around the room. There were several other parents waiting with their children, some playing with toys in the reception area. "Have you seen someone yet?" Rita asked.

"Yeah, a doctor," Gayle said. "She's the one who said that

they might have to do surgery and keep him in."

Gayle was getting quite agitated, complaining to a nurse about the long time they had been there.

Rita was embarrassed by her daughter's behaviour. Dean looked happy enough still looking at the comic.

"I need a fag," Gayle said reaching for her bag.

"Well go on then. Go outside and have one. It might help to calm your nerves but get back soon."

"Mummy won't be long," Gayle reassured Dean. Rita smiled. "I used to have comics when I was a little girl." The little fellow looked up at her, curious that his nan was ever a little girl. "I used to read my brother's Beano," she went on. "There was this boy called Dennis The Menace and he got into trouble just like you!" she teased him as he nestled his head under her arm.

"Dean Edwards," a nurse's voice called out. Rita looked around for Gayle but she was still outside so she took his hand and headed for the cubicle where a nurse was waiting.

"Hello Dean, how are you?" she smiled. He looked at her a little worried.

"Let's just pop you up on here shall we and then we can have a look."

She was an older, black nurse and had a warm kindly manner. She had a younger male nurse assisting her. "I'm just going to have a little look up your nose with my torch. Is that OK?" she smiled and she showed him her slim silver torch which she switched on and off so he could see how it worked. Dean was very impressed and wished he had one. It would be just the thing to explore behind the back of the sofa at home.

"Now," she said, "can you just lean back further for me on the pillow, sweetheart. That's it". She looked up Dean's nostrils with her torch for a moment from different angles and then switched it off. "OK." She turned to Rita. "Are you a relative?"

"I'm his nan," she said feeling a little ashamed that Gayle was absent. "His mum's here. Just popped outside a sec for a cigarette. Shall I go and get her?"

"No that's OK, just stay here with Dean." She had another

look at Dean's nose while Rita held her grandson's hand. "Aha!" She beckoned the male nurse over to have a look and he also peered up Dean's nose.

"I can just see something up your nose. What is it?" she asked Dean.

"One of my mum's Tic Tacs," he replied solemnly.

"Does she want it back?" she joked. He shrugged his shoulders, looking very worried.

"Is it uncomfortable, Dean?"

He nodded.

"Well, we're going to try and get your mum's Tic Tac back for her, OK?"

Dean nodded again. She spoke quietly to her colleague who went away and came back with what looked like long tweezers. The male nurse held the torch and the nurse leant over Dean. "Now, sweetheart, I want you to be a brave boy for me and stay still while I try and get it down, OK?" Rita stood by him and held his hand. As the nurse gently applied the tweezers up his nose, Dean screwed up his eyes and squeezed Rita's hand so tight it hurt.

"Agh!" he complained, his body stiffening like a board.

"You are doing very well, Dean, very brave."

"Just think about Dr Who," Rita said, calmly. The nurse prodded a little more up Dean's nose and then reached over for some tissues. "OK, now I want you to blow your nose very gently into this tissue." The boy sat up, releasing his grip on Rita's hand and blew into the tissue a couple of times. "It feels funny," he said, muffled, from behind the wad of tissues. The nurse had a look and Rita suddenly felt queasy at seeing the tissue covered in blood. But there in the middle, as the nurse moved it round was the offending Tic Tac.

"Hey presto!" she cheered and smiled at their successful effort. Dean's nose was still bleeding, so he held his head back and they applied more tissues. The nurse removed the Tic Tac from the tissue with the tweezers. Rita gave Dean a gentle hug. "You have been brave," she said and she kissed him on top of his head. "Well done Dean, it's all over now. You can go home with your nan."

Rita thanked the nurse.

"It's a pleasure. He should be all right now and the bleeding will stop. But if it continues tomorrow and you are worried contact your GP. And here you are Dean, a souvenir!" She went to give him the Tic Tac now rolled up in a clean tissue. "On second thoughts," she said, "maybe your nan should take charge of it. Now don't do that again will you?" The boy shook his head.

"Say thank you," Rita told him. "Come on little cowboy. Let's find your mum."

Outside A&E, Gayle was still smoking, chatting to someone she knew. Rita was livid with her.

"Where the bloody hell have you been?" Rita startled Gayle. Seeing Dean with a tissue, she bent down. "How are you Dean? Has the doctor made it better?" He still held on to Rita's hand and nodded.

"No thanks to you," Rita spat out.

"Mum!" Gayle protested.

"Don't mum me," she replied. "He needed you in there. They've taken it out and there was lots of blood, the poor fellow," looking down at Dean.

"I'm sorry, all right. You know I've never been good with blood." Gayle held Dean close to her. "Hospitals, doctors. They don't agree with me."

"I know that this lad needs his mum," Rita complained, getting more heated.

"Oh, so I'm fucking neglecting him now, am I?"

Rita looked at her daughter and shook her head in dismay. "I'm off to work."

She bent down and kissed her grandson. "Bye, darling. I'll get you that comic later. Nanny has to go now."

"Mum!" Gayle called out but without turning back Rita walked off.

'Ironic,' thought Rita as she recalled how well the day had

started. She was beginning to get cross with herself about not managing to stay in a good mood. She phoned work and left a message that she was on her way in, but then decided she needed to calm down first. She went into the hospital café for a coffee. She got a cappuccino and sat down at a small table. Looking around she saw an older man in a dressing gown sitting in a wheelchair with a younger man, perhaps his son and a nurse writing some notes. Rita pondered that she had once fancied being a nurse. She was very impressed with the woman who had treated Dean – confident and skilled. She thought that it must be really satisfying at the end of the day to have helped people, maybe even saved lives. Perhaps that's what she should have done – life could have been very different.

Her mobile buzzed but she was reluctant to look, expecting it to be Gayle. Rita left it for a moment but couldn't resist and dipped into her handbag for the phone. It was a text from Abi, 'Can we meet later at The Eagle? Need your help!' Rita smiled, intrigued, wondering what it was about. Boyfriend trouble? Millie trouble? Or just trouble? Rita was in demand.

Back at work Rita had to go and see her manager and explain why she was so late getting in. Her boss, Kate, was temporary and had only been in charge for the past three months. She came from another branch and replaced the much loved, bumbling Dennis who had been sidelined. As soon as she arrived, Rita went up to her office. Kate was in her early thirties and had originally been recruited as a trainee manager but her background did not include membership in a charm school. She was a bit of a bully and the staff hated her. The company liked her because she met all their targets. Rita knocked on the door but she could see that she was on the phone. The woman spotted her and beckoned her in.

"Well that's just not good enough. We were promised delivery by Monday and there is still no sign." She looked sternly at Rita while her caller responded and Rita stood awkwardly by the door.

"What, Friday? That's no good to me," she barked and

ended the call abruptly.

"You wanted to see me, Kate?"

"Yes, Rita" she said with a sigh, looking at some time sheets lying on her desk. "You've been late three times already this month, and now this morning!"

"It's my grandson, Dean, you see," Rita tried to explain, "he's not been well and we had to go to the hospit … "
Before Rita could say anything further, the manager held up her hand for her to stop.

"Rita, I haven't got time for these excuses." She looked straight at her employee. "You don't seem to realise that unless you pull your weight around here you'll be down the Job Centre."

Rita squirmed but remained silent. Dennis would have handled this very differently but 'this cow' she thought, hasn't an inch of humanity.

"You'll have to buckle down or there's no place for you here. We can't afford timewasters."

Rita smarted at the remark, 'timewasters'. She'd been working in this shop for over twenty five years. She felt her hackles rising but quickly remembered what she'd promised herself earlier in the day, to stay calm.

"You know that we have to reach certain targets," Kate told her sharply but Rita, still fuming underneath wasn't listening, "or head office will be on my back. Your job," as if Rita needed reminding, "is to help manage the store by keeping the customers happy and making sure that they can get what they came in for. Is that too much for you?"

Rita was going to ask why certain stock items were taking so long to come in but she just nodded and resigned herself to the humiliating ticking off from this pompous headquarters lackey who had managed to curry favour with the higher ups, becoming their 'golden girl'. Rita looked at the smart suit she was wearing, new hairstyle, immaculate nails. Rita bet that she and her husband lived in a pristine house with clean work tops and no soul. While thinking about this Rita's mind had wandered off and just caught the tail end of her own bollocking.

" ... so, I want better output from you and no more unauthorised time off. Understood?" Rita nodded again and was told to get back to work. By coincidence, on her way down to the shop floor she bumped into their cheery, much loved former manager, Dennis, a man in his mid-fifties. He too looked a little more worn and harassed but was delighted to meet her.

"Rita!" he beamed, "how wonderful to see you." He gave her a hug. She cheered up immediately.

"How are you?" he asked.

"Yes, I'm fine. We don't see much of you these days."

"No, that's true," he agreed. "Head in paperwork or in front of computer screen, I'm afraid."

"But I tell you what, Rita," Dennis whispered, "the firm's really in trouble. They're looking for a buyer."

"So the rumours are true then?

"I'm afraid so," Dennis nodded "but it's been going for almost a hundred years, so I expect we'll get through it."

"We miss you." Rita said and was about to add something catty about his successor but bit her tongue.

"Oh, do you? That's nice to hear. Not like the old days here, is it?"

Rita smiled and shook her head in agreement.

"No, they were great times," Rita agreed. "Those ding dongs after work in the staff room."

"Yes, indeed, indeed," he enthused, "they were great fun."

They both stood there looking at each other, laughing. Rita thought, what a gentleman Dennis was and how much better things were when he was in charge. He got everybody's loyalty, you couldn't buy that.

"Oh well," he looked down the corridor, "I'd better go and see the boss. I'm late!" he said.

"You too. Mind how you go, Dennis. She's on the warpath."

"Oh dear," Dennis frowned. "Some of these young un's eh, Rita? They're no fun when they get so ambitious," and he hurried off.

In a brighter mood having seen Dennis, Rita went back to

the shop floor. She was busy on the checkout over lunchtime and then replenishing the stock of Roses chocolates. With the customers moaning about price rises and complaints about things being out of stock, the rest of the day was uneventful, or 'run of the mill,' as Rita's mate, Pat, said.

"How did you get on with her upstairs?" Pat asked.

"Oh the usual," Rita said, deadpan. "Told me I've got to pull my socks up or else!"

"I hope you told her where to go. She wants to get down here and do some real bloody work."

"Well I just bumped into Dennis. He reckons Woolies is going down the drain."

"They'll get it sorted," Pat shrugged her shoulders. "It's an institution ain't it? Like you Rita!"

"Cheeky mare," Rita laughed.

∼ Twenty Four ∼

Rita had arranged to meet Abi at The Eagle after work and as she had a little time to kill, she decided to walk along the seafront. It had been a very warm day and she even bought an ice cream, but suddenly the temperature dropped with a sea mist closing in. Her light summer jacket was not thick enough to keep the chill from her shoulders and arms. Rita was starting to shiver as she reached the arcades near St Mary in the Castle. Rita watched the mist steadily rolling in, enveloping objects in its path, leaving a damp screen on lamp posts and bollards. People walking on the other side of the road near the toilet block were magically disappearing and then reappearing again further along. Since a child she had always been fascinated by this phenomenon, seeing Hastings spookily made invisible and yet less than a mile inland it was clear as a bell. Cars coming along the sea road had now put their lights on and a bus heading towards the Old Town was lit up and gleaming like a Christmas tree. It faded out of sight into the now eerie silence that had even grounded the gulls.

Up in the town the mist was less apparent. As she walked in the pub she noticed a young man wearing a black leather jacket, sitting at the bar.

"Behave, dog!" He was feeding it a few crisps and the creature, a young Bedlington terrier, was getting excited, his tail wagging wildly, as he stood up against the bar stool hoping for some more. Rita smiled at the dog and the scene of the boy's ineffective effort to calm him.

Rita ordered an orange juice and sat down in a seat away from the bar. She checked her mobile – no messages. She was wondering how Gayle was and if Dean's nose had stopped bleeding. She should phone her but she held off. It would do her daughter good not to have her at her beck and call all the time. But how long would she be able to stop herself speaking to her? The pub was quiet. A couple of older men who looked like they had spent most of the day there were transfixed looking at Sky Sports on the large screen. It reminded Rita that they still hadn't heard a word from Leo about the prize money for their greyhound. At the bar the Bedlington was still vying for attention from its owner and the bag of crisps that he was munching.

Abi arrived a bit late wearing a new lime green jacket that suited her red hair. She caught the men's eyes as she swanned in, but she had a face like thunder. "I'm gonna kill her. Do you know what she's done now?" Taking her handbag off her shoulder, Abi searched for her purse. Rita already knew that this was going to be a one way conversation.

"That woman," she said venomously, "has been driving me crazy all day. She wouldn't let me dress her. I had to fight to get her into the shower and then she threw the soap at me. Look!" she cried, attracting glares from the racing punters for disturbing their sport. Abi pointed to a mark on her cheek where it had hit her. "Also," Abi paused still holding her purse, "while I was having a doze this afternoon, she made herself a sandwich and spread jam all over her clothes and in her hair. She looked like a cream tea!"

"Oh Abi," Rita burst out laughing.

"I blew my top," Abi said, sitting down holding her purse in her lap. "I tell you, I've had it caring for her." Rita gently rubbed her shoulder.

"You've got to get some help, Abi. I've been telling you for months."

"At the moment, I just wish she was in a home," Abi gritted her teeth, her eyes reddening.

"Come on, you don't mean that."

"I do, Rita. She's been really horrible to me all day."

"But she doesn't always know what she's doing, does she?"

"I know that but when you live with her day in day out, it gets to you."

Abi was still clutching her purse and then put it on the table reaching for a tissue from inside her handbag. Rita went to the bar and got her a drink. When she returned Abi seemed to have calmed down.

"Look," said Rita decisively," you need a break."

"But she won't accept anyone else helping her. I have enough trouble myself," she reasoned. "What about when she was in hospital last year after that fall? She led them a right dance."

Rita smiled. "I tell you what. How about you going out this weekend?"

"What do you mean?"

"I'll come and stay over and you have a night out – all night if you like. Millie will be OK. I finish work at five and then you can get your glad rags on and go out on the town with what's his name?" Rita suggested.

"I don't know, Rita." Abi looked sceptical.

"Go on. You haven't had a night out for ages. It'll do you the world of good."

Abi closed her eyes and relaxed back in the chair. "I could sleep for a week, that would set me right." With her eyes still closed she asked Rita,

"Won't Colin mind?"

"What?"

"You staying over."

"He'll have to lump it. He knows where the freezer is. He can warm himself up a lasagne – just about!"

Abi opened one eye. "If you're sure," she said, her voice already becoming more upbeat.

"Yes of course I'm sure. What are mates for?"

Abi leant across and gave her friend a big kiss on the cheek. "Thanks love."

"So, how is what's his name?" Rita asked.

Abi thought for a moment, it had been such a while.

"Craig," Abi sighed," he turned out to be very disappointing. I had high hopes about him. He was a good laugh when we went out for a drink.

"Well?"

"He wasn't very affectionate, you know." Rita raised her eyebrows.

"You mean he wasn't all over you in five minutes like some of your other blokes?"

"No, it's not that. Well it is actually." Abi smiled, "I do have needs!" she said rolling her eyes sipping her drink and staring into space.

"Oh yeah?" Rita grinned playfully.

"Maybe that's why I've never settled down with anyone," Abi mused and then shot back at Rita, "Do you remember those two brothers we used to date, Tom and what'shisname who both worked in the butchers in Queens Road?"

"Clive," Rita reminded her.

"That's it. How old were we then?"

"Sixteen, because I remember that Freddy and the Dreamers were top of the pops." They both broke into "'*You Were Made For Me*' … "

The two old fellows looked over again sternly from their Sports screen – disturbing their race.

"Hey, that's not them is it?" They both laughed.

"Now, they were a lot of fun," Abi recalled enthusiastically, "always out dancing, pictures, the pub."

"Clive wasn't!" Rita complained. "He kept going on about his racing bike. He was dead boring."

"Oh no, Tom was OK, he knew how to give a girl a good time. And he was a great snogger too."

"Was he?" Rita was surprised to feel a sudden pang of jealousy after all these years.

Abi's eyes glazed over at the thought. "Tom Filmore, the best kisser for miles. In fact," Abi added, "I think I've been secretly looking for another Tom ever since." She closed her eyes, pursed her lips in a dreamy action replay.

"He spoilt it for me with anyone else," she pronounced rather grandly.

Rita laughed "Whatever happened to him?"

"The family moved to Brighton, I think and we lost touch. The usual story."

"Then there was Roy!" Rita teased her.

"Oh, yes I'd forgotten about him. Roy the boy – with the big one!" The two women giggled.

"He was a bit too serious though," Abi declared, "He'd wear those blue Y fronts that showed him off very well I must say. But he had no sense of fun. A right moody bugger. And he thought he was god's gift."

"Yes, I remember us girls had bets as to the size of his todger. Didn't you try and measure it with a ruler once?" Rita enquired smiling mischievously.

Abi laughed, "Yes, that's right. It was in his bedroom when his parents were out at the pictures. But I kept giggling when it went soft. I only did it because Maureen Townsley was banging on about her bloke's dick and how many 'organisms', as she called it, she'd had."

"And what about Terry?" Rita reminded her.

"Terry!" She repeated with a cheer. "Now he *was* the love of my life. My first holiday romance when we went to Clacton."

"Jaywick," Rita corrected her. "Oh yeah," Abi agreed, "that horrible cold, wet week. Our first holiday without our parents."

"Where did he come from?" Rita asked Abi.

"Milton Keynes, new town," Abi remembered. "Oh he had lovely hair, didn't he, blond, just like Brian Jones. And he played guitar in that group. He was gorgeous. He wrote me lovely letters and poems. Do you remember when we went to see his group, The Links, when they played in London that time?"

Rita nodded. "Yes, you were quite smitten weren't you?"

Abi smiled. "I adored him. The music, those times. I can still see that dance hall now."

They reminisced a bit more, including about Abi going off the rails when she was sixteen years old. Make up, music and boys were all she and Rita were keen on. They hung around Hollington Youth Club much against both their parents' orders. Rita's parents were stricter and made her stay in to finish her homework; for all the good it did her. She never fared well in exams whereas Abi seemed to have a natural talent for passing despite, it seemed to Rita, her doing hardly any home work and receiving detention more often than not for larking about and talking back at teachers. The girls had speedily progressed from The Bunty to Jackie and pop weeklies like Fabulous 208 with glossy pictures of their idols, John Leyton, Eden Kane and of course the Beatles and the Stones.

They both finished their drinks as Abi said she needed to get back for Millie.

"How's your day been?" she finally asked Rita as they prepared to leave.

"Oh, you know the usual," now feeling too tired to relate the earlier hospital incident about Dean or her telling off at work, Rita was glad to be heading for home.

"Well at least you've got a job and you're seeing people every day."

"Umm, well, not sure for how long though. There's rumours that Woolies is in trouble."

Abi shook her head in disbelief.

"Anyway," Rita laughed, "Do you know I'm doing this new thing every morning, a kind of mantra to keep in a good mood."

"How's it gone?"

"Terrible! Tomorrow I'm going to begin the day browned off and then things can only get better."

∼ Twenty Five ∼

"Fish fingers and oven chips," Abi replied when Rita asked what Millie usually liked for her tea. Rita was standing by her bedroom door watching Abi get spruced up for her evening date. She was dressed up to the nines. Standing in front of the mirror she was bending her head forward and putting on her long droplet earrings.

"I don't want any of those fake beans," Millie said from the living room. Rita went in to see her. Don't you mean baked beans, auntie?"

"No, they're definitely fake. I heard it on the wireless last week. They're being smuggled in from Europe – Spain I think. You can't tell the difference from the label. But they say they taste awful."

"Where did you hear this, again?"

"On the wireless. They said, be careful, you know, be on your alert."

"Sounds fishy to me," Rita smiled.

"No, not fishy – salty, they said. They're much more salty than Heinz's."

"I brought a nice lasagne over," Rita said.

"What?" Abi asked, preoccupied, turning her head this way and that to see if the earrings looked right. "Lasagne," repeated Rita, "I thought it would be soft for Millie's teeth." Abi nodded in agreement, straightened up and looked at Rita. "Well, what do you think?" Rita had to admire her, she was in good nick for her age. Even feeling envious, but she sometimes had that with Abi who'd always been a looker.

"Yes, lovely dress, but the earrings," she remarked screwing up her face.

"Don't they work?"

Rita shook her head, "A bit tarty," she came in closer to inspect them.

Abi looked again in the mirror. "No, you're right," she agreed and quickly replaced them with a pair of studs. "Oh yes, they're better – more classy,"

Abi smiled. "I've got a good feeling about this date. Look at this Rita." Abi pointed to her horoscope in the newspaper lying open on the dressing table. Rita sat down gently on the edge of the bed and read it out loud.

"You'll meet someone who would like to know you much better!"

"See, it's meant to be, right?" Abi flashed Rita a smile in the mirror.

"So, where's this bloke from?" Rita asked.

"Seaford," Abi replied. "He lives with his mum."

"His mum?" Rita beamed.

"Yes, he's separated from his wife and is living back home with his mum, temporarily."

"Oh, so you're both in the same boat then. You should have a lot in common to talk about."

"And," Abi added enthusiastically, not much liking Rita's remark, "he's got a place in Spain. A villa. Five bedrooms and a pool!" Abi looked smug, trying to impress Rita.

"Oh, that's nice," was all that Rita could muster rather unenthusiastically.

"It sounds gorgeous," Abi glowed. "It's in the Costa del Sol and he goes there several times a year."

"But what about caring for his mum? You just said that he's looking after her," Rita asked, ever the practical one. "Anyway," she reminded Abi, "you haven't even met him yet!" trying to bring her down to earth.

"We've spoken on the phone and we've text," Abi told her.

"He seems a nice man. He's fifty two, got two grown up children. Him and his wife have been separated for years apparently. He likes dogs, country walks and Chinese food," she reeled off the list like a lonely hearts ad.

"So, he's a bit younger than you," Rita mulled it over.

"A little, yes." Abi continued preening herself in front of the mirror.

"Have you told him your age?" Rita asked, teasingly.

"Of course not," Abi replied stiffly.

"I bet you said you were younger," Rita giggled.

Abi didn't rise to the bait and carried on brushing her hair.

"So, what did you tell him, fifty five?" Abi didn't take her eye off the mirror.

"Fifty four … three … two … one … fifty?" Rita prodded gently but got no reply.

"Forty eight … ? Abi, not forty five?" Abi smiled at her. "It was, wasn't it?" Rita asked.

"I'm not saying," Abi said. "Age is immaterial."

"Abi!" Rita sighed, knowing that she was near the truth. "You must be bonkers. I know you look good but not that good. He's bound to rumble you right away, unless he needs glasses. "

"There's nothing wrong with his eyesight."

"Well he should be able to see through you then," Rita laughed.

"Rita!" Abi protested. "Will you stop it please! This is making me nervous." Rita went over and gently tucked Abi's bra strap under her dress for her. "OK, sorry. You look lovely – honestly."

"That's better," Abi sighed with relief.

"Anyway, what's his name?"

"Sherman."

"That's an unusual name. I wonder if it's his real name?"

"What do you mean?" Abi frowned.

"Well, you know some people use different names to make themselves look more attractive."

With both of them looking into the mirror Rita continued to probe, "So, what else did you tell Sherman about yourself. That you've travelled the world?"

"I should have got my hair done," Abi said, still ignoring Rita's remarks and slid her fingers through it.

"Honestly it looks fine," Rita assured her. "But you will be careful won't you?"

"What?" Abi looked surprised.

"You know," Rita said, "this internet dating lark. You hear about some dodgy characters around. You will make sure that you keep yourself safe."

"Rita, I'm not a teenager."

"No, you said, forty something!" and they both burst out laughing.

Hearing their roar, Millie wandered into the bedroom too.

"Oh, you look nice. Where are you going?" she came over and touched Abi's dress; Abi smiled and gave her a hug. "I'm going out to meet a fella, auntie."

"Hanky panky, eh? Is he good looking?" Millie roared.

"Just like Steve McQueen. You liked him didn't you?"

"I did," said Mille, "but I liked Humph better. He was more mean and moody when he was in that film about the lady who lost her passport."

"Do you remember what it was called, auntie?" Abi liked testing her memory whenever she could. Millie closed her eyes tightly, deep in thought. Rita put her hand on her shoulder.

"It's coming," Millie said, "it's coming". She opened up her eyes. "It rhymes with wanker," Millie chimed.

"Auntie Millie!" Rita cried out, shocked, while Abi burst out laughing.

"It's 'Casablanca.' Do you recall the song, auntie?

You must remember this, a kiss is just a kiss, a sigh is just a sigh" …

They all joined in the chorus, humming and singing away while Abi put her shoes on, paraded around the room like a teenager, showing off.

∽ Twenty Six ∽

Abi was running late. She had agreed to meet her date, Sherman, at Mai's, a Thai restaurant in town which he had suggested. The late summer evening was closing in and turning chilly as she hurried to the rendezvous. Passing Debenham's she caught her reflection in the shop window. Abi fluffed up her hair, took out a compact case from her handbag and hastily checked her mascara and lipstick. Arriving at the restaurant, she found it busy. Abi looked out for a single man in a dark blue jacket and wondered if she would recognise him from the photos on his Facebook page. A slim young waitress came up and asked if she had a reservation, but Abi had spotted her date. He stood up at the back and was waving at her. Squinting her eyes, Abi could only just see him. She knew that she should have worn her glasses but these first impressions were all important. Squeezing past the tables to a quieter corner, Sherman was standing smiling. They shook hands.

"Hi Abi."

"Hello Sherman." He helped her off with her coat and she sat down opposite him. Abi was a little disappointed but tried not to show it. He looked older than his photograph; much shorter and stouter. He wore a classic navy blue blazer, open necked white shirt where a St Christopher dangled. Abi spotted that his thinning hair line was battling with the grey tufts over which would win the ageing process first. She wondered if he had his photograph on Facebook air brushed. As he sat down she also noticed that there was a strong whiff of cheap after shave.

"Did you find it here all right?"

"Oh yes, no trouble. Have you been here before?" she asked him.

"No I haven't. I thought it would be good to go somewhere new."

A waiter was soon at their table with menus and he asked them if they would like drinks.

"Oh, yeah," Sherman nodded, "a lager for me and … " he looked at Abi.

"Thanks, a gin and tonic, please."

"Ice and lemon?" the young man checked. Abi nodded, pulling her chair into the table further.

"Got to have ice and lemon, haven't you? It brings out the taste," Sherman quipped.

"Definitely," Abi agreed as they sat for a moment smiling at each other.

"Busy isn't it?" he looked around and Abi nodded. "This credit crunch don't seem to have bothered them yet."

"Cheers!" said Sherman as the drinks soon arrived and they raised their glasses.

He took a long swig, "Ah, that's better."

Sherman began rambling on about his car journey from Seaford, mentioning road works, and how he could never travel on a bus or a train. Abi continued sizing him up, noticing even without her glasses that he had specks of dandruff on the collar of his jacket. He really wasn't anything like the photo. That must have been taken ten years ago.

"Ready to order?" The young waiter had returned. They each fumbled for their menus and as neither of them wished to show to the other that they wore glasses, they each struggled to read the small text. The waiter stood patiently with his pen and pad.

"The Tom Yam Goong is very nice. That's shrimp soup," he suggested, gently pointing at Sherman's menu.

"Is it?" Sherman looked at him, "That sounds OK then, what do you think, Abi?"

Her eyes were screwed up so tightly that she had a little difficulty refocusing but nodded in agreement. "That's number four isn't it?" she asked.

"No, madam, number two for two," the waiter corrected.

"Ah, tea for two," Sherman joked. Abi noticed that he had nearly finished his drink.

"Do you want another?" she pointed to his empty glass.

"No, I'd better not, what with driving."

"So, Sherman," Abi was beginning to feel a little more relaxed with her G&T, "tell me about yourself."

"Which bit?" he sprung back and winked at her, making her think that his silly remarks would really get on her nerves by the end of the evening.

"Well as you know, I live in Seaford. I've been separated from Hilary, my ex now for a few years. It's all been rather ... " he gestured with his hands ... "fraught."

"Oh dear," Abi sympathised.

"Still is as a matter of fact. She's living in our old house and that's why I've had to move back with me mum who's eighty four and a bit of a handful." He looked at Abi in desperation.

She was about to say, 'I know what you mean,' and tell him about Millie but decided not to. Sherman folded his arms.

"I shouldn't say this," he said quietly as though his mum might hear, "but she really is driving me round the bend. She's deaf as a post, refuses to have a hearing aid and treats me like I'm a kid."

Abi wondered if Sherman wore dentures and what the heck that awful aftershave was.

"Take last weekend," he continued. "I cut the lawn and she had a go at me that it wasn't short enough. We had a barney over that and I said, 'Mum, look I'm doing my best here. You know that I hate gardening.' So she then has another poke, saying how much I'm saving by living with her rent free. I mean it's ridiculous. She wants to know what time I'll be home, where I'm going. I tell you I've had it with her. The only time I get any peace and quiet is when I'm at my place in Spain."

Abi brightened up when she heard mention of his place in the sun.

"Who looks after her when you're away?"

"Oh she can sort herself out no problem. She just has a helper to get her shopping in, but I never hear the end of it when I get back. Thank god I've only got my mobile when I'm there or else she'd be trying to contact me all the time. She says it's too expensive to phone," he laughed.

Their food arrived and it smelt very good. Abi was really feeling hungry.

"It's not as if she hasn't got a few bob, but she's so tight it's unbelievable," Sherman started on his soup.

"Ummm. This is very nice isn't it?" Abi said.

He took another mouthful and nodded.

"Yes I love Thai, it's very tasty. Anyway, I'm sorry. I've been rabbiting on about my mum, what about you? What sort of things do you like doing?"

"I like dancing," Abi began, breezily, "Salsa, Latin and all that."

She ate and drank some more and decided to have a bit of fun with him. It was time to gild the lily.

"Although I come from Hastings originally, I've travelled around the world with my work," she said. Sherman's eyebrows raised and he nodded attentively as he tucked into his soup.

"What work's that?"

"Marketing," Abi lied, "wherever the assignments are really. Italy, Australia, New York, you name it."

Sherman looked impressed. "What line are you in?"

"Biscuits!" Abi declared. "From the digestives to The Royals. The world loves a biscuit."

"Yes, I suppose so," he wiped his mouth with his napkin.

"I'm having a career break at present, looking after my

170

aunt," Abi said confidently, "but I'll be off again soon no doubt. Milan, Paris, you know."

Having finished his soup Sherman sat back and looked thoughtful. "I'm a Garibaldi man, myself," he said wiping his mouth on his napkin again.

"Ah, the Garibaldi!" Abi said with an air of authority. "That's a classic that is – shows you've got taste, Sherman."

He looked pleased with himself. "Do you think so? Although, I like Bourbons too. I love dunking them in my tea. What's yours?" Abi put down her spoon and thought for a moment.

"A plate of Cantucci with a glass of Vin Santo and I'm in heaven." Abi even impressed herself with that one.

"Wow," Sherman responded. "You're a lady who really knows her biccies."

Abi shrugged her shoulders. "It's just something I do," she replied with false modesty.

"Sherman, that's an unusual name. It sounds American," Abi drank her G&T.

"You're dead right there. My Dad was in France during the war with the Yanks and he named me after one of their tanks!" he roared.

"So, Sherman, you were saying about your place in Spain," Abi continued.

"Yes, it's brilliant there!" His face lit up and he paused while he asked the waiter for some tap water and another G&T for Abi.

"Los Boliches," he reeled off in pidgin Spanish.

"Oh, I say, you even speak the lingo," Abi giggled.

"Gracias senora," he bowed his head.

"Well that's all really," Sherman admitted. "I've been meaning to learn more but they all speak English there don't they. So why bother?"

"It sounds fun."

"Oh, it's a dream," Sherman enthused. "It's heaven on earth. It's where I feel alive. Everyone's friendly, we all look out for each other. And you can get fish and chips and pie and mash!" he said, feeling sure that this would impress his new date.

"I bet you don't want to come back, Sherman."

"Oh yes, I can't explain it. I feel so relaxed somehow. And I know it's a cliché but I feel really at home there. Mind you," he said, looking rather serious, "the exchange rate now. It's not funny. Everything is so much tighter. Some of the old un's on fixed incomes are feeling the pinch I can tell you."

"What about you, Sherman? Do you think you'll have to sell up?"

"Nah, it'll be fine. I paid for the place outright, years ago. And I'll have a very good index linked pension as it happens. It'll see me through I reckon."

"Oh, that's good," Abi said, looking at her date in a glowing new light. Index linked pension had a very attractive ring to it.

"You see, Abi," Sherman looked at her quite seriously, "you have to make your own luck in this world. I've had to graft hard to get what I've got."

Abi nodded.

"Anyway, I know we've only just met but you'll have to come out with me to Spain. The sunsets – it's a very, very romantic place. And the pool. You'd love the pool!"

Abi was nearly drooling at the thought.

Sherman was on a roll. "We've all got one. You can't live there without it – somewhere to cool off. It's beautiful – drinks in the afternoon, floating around on the water, the smell of the barbeque. You must come over. Will you?"

Sherman almost pleaded.

"Oh, yes please, definitely." Abi sat back in her chair, looking at him. She wondered if he was the sort of bloke that would insist on paying for the meal on a first date. She hoped so.

∼ Twenty Seven ∼

Bill spent the afternoon at the local primary school helping with the children's reading. He had seen the quiet boy, Mustafa, three times so far, but he was not finding it easy. After he collected him from his classroom they went to the school library which was also a corridor for children and staff to get to their classrooms. Mustafa brought along a book to read from his school bag. Without saying a word he opened it where they had left off from the previous week. They sat down on small chairs at a table which Bill still found very uncomfortable as he wound up with back ache. He tried a chatty approach to try and get to know the boy's interests. "Do you like football? What do you like doing at weekends – playing with your mates?"

But Mustafa just shrugged his shoulders gently and smiled. His reading was very slow – often just sitting there staring at the page. Bill tried to be patient though and coaxed him along. Mustafa followed Bill's guidance and gradually things began to click. He got out another book and Mustafa picked out the words from the illustrations that Bill pointed to. Bill also read a little to Mustafa and getting him slowly to pronounce certain words that he found difficult. The boy gradually got them right. Bill felt he was making progress with Mustafa and they were beginning to click.

After school Bill went for a coffee at Rosa's cafe.

"Have you seen anything of Leo?" Bill asked Rosa, when she served him at his table.

"Do you mean Leopoldo?" she asked, putting her tea towel on the table and sitting down opposite him.

"Leopoldo?"

"Yes, that's his full name," Rosa confirmed and added, "but he also goes under Giuseppe or Ferde."

Bill's eyes narrowed, intrigued as Rosa told him more about Leo.

"His dad used to run the ice cream parlour near the pier. During the fifties it was like an ice cream mafia along the south coast," she laughed.

"Leo and my family were pretty close. Quite cliquey in this area. His family expected him to take over the business as he was the eldest son, but he was more interested in girls."

"I can believe that," Bill grinned.

"He had trouble knuckling down to anything. During the sixties he worked for a local promoter putting on pop groups at the pier. There were some amazing shows," she recalled enthusiastically. Bill nodded, having heard something about this. "They started off with some local groups like Tony Delton, The Saints, The Talisman, Southern Sounds," she reeled them off like clockwork. "Then they had The Kinks and The Hollies. They even booked The Rolling Stones and hired an ambulance to get them through the crowd! I know because I was there. Leo even got me Mick Jagger's autograph," she said with some pride. "What a show that was. It was jam packed and we were screaming all night. I was off school the next day, so hoarse, I couldn't speak," she laughed. "Yeah, he did well on the pier. It was a big success, all the kids around here used to go." Bill nodded and listened to her quietly. "But look at the state of it now!" She glanced over to the window.

"Anyway," she said getting back to Leo, "there's always been a few angry women in Hastings on his tail," Rosa smiled and Bill saw that she was enjoying herself, gossiping about Leo. It was a good job that the cafe was empty. "He's a rogue – an old rogue, now!" she laughed, "I don't think that he means to deceive or hurt people, but he can't seem to help himself. Trouble follows him around. He used to be renowned as a romeo all along this stretch of the coast. In the summer, he used to latch on to young women day trippers or holiday makers – chat them up in a cafe or pub. He'd charm 'em. Say that he was a bit short of cash and cadge a few bob off them. He was good at it too!" Rosa declared, smirking. "It was like a hit and run. Apart from wooing the women in Hastings there was Brighton, Bexhill and Eastbourne too. He really did have a girl in every port. And he'd always have some dozy scheme on the go. They were always doomed to collapse and he ended up owing money." Bill nodded and began to bristle again at the thought of their greyhound syndicate.

"But as I said, he did well with the pop groups during the sixties, and he began booking and promoting them. For a while he lived in London when he was managing a pop singer by the name of Tina Laverne. She had a small hit with '*In My Heart.*' Her real name was Margaret Furlong and she came from around here, Queens Road, I think. But," Rosa raised her eyebrows, "it all ended in tears. She returned to hairdressing. From the high life back to highlights!" Rosa shrilled.

"Any idea where I can find Leo?" asked Bill. Rosa went behind the counter and returned with the telephone number of Leo's daughter, Sharon, who lived in Battle. Bill thanked Rosa for her help and went back home.

Later that day Bill phoned Leo's daughter.

"Hello, you don't know me," said Bill, "but I'm trying to get in touch with your dad."

"Which one?" the woman asked, matter of fact, "Giuseppe, Ferde or Leo?"

"Leo."

"Ok," she said, "have you tried his mobile?"

"Aye, yes, I have but no reply." Bill told her the number he already had.

"Does he owe you money?" Sharon asked bluntly.

There was a silence as Bill wondered what to say to her.

"Urm, well … "

"Intuitively she knew that she had guessed right and easing the conversation for Bill, "It's OK I get the picture," she sighed. She gave Bill a different mobile number for Leo.

"Do you have his address by any chance?" Bill asked.

"No, I can't give you that but you might have better luck by dropping into The Crown in Clive Vale, he's usually in there most early evenings."

"Great, that's very helpful," Bill said feeling relieved.

"By the way if you do see him, get him to give me a ring will you? Tell him he can come over for lunch on Sunday. I've forgiven him," she added, laughing. Bill wondered what that was all about.

∼ Twenty Eight ∼

Bill, avoiding the bustle of Queens Road, was standing in front of a shop window wondering if he could afford to buy himself a pair of shoes on a sunny Saturday morning that had an autumnal nip in the air. He felt a tug on his jacket sleeve and looked down to see Mustafa smiling up at him.

"My father is here," the boy pointed to a small Middle Eastern looking man wearing a skull cap and holding a shopping bag.

Bill could not see him at first as the sun was shining so brightly, he was dazzled and put his hand up to shield his eyes.

"I hear that you are helping my son, Mustafa, at school with his reading?" he grinned.

Bill nodded. "Well yes, just once a week, like," glancing down at Mustafa.

"Are you a teacher?"

"Oh no, not me. I'm just a volunteer. You know, I'm helping out."

"Well that is very good. You have many good books here in UK and I want Mustafa to be able to read and get on well with his schooling. But he is a shy boy."

"What do you do?" Bill enquired.

"I am a house decorator here in Hastings and St Leonards."

"Oh aye, that must keep you busy."

"Yes, I work very hard but the pay is not good. Sometimes

you have the work, then you don't. But you know, it is not so bad."

"Where do you come from?"

"Iran. We have been here two years now. Back home in my country, I was a doctor. But here I have to do what I can."

"Can't you get work in the medical profession here?"

"You have different ways and rules. I have tried, but this does not seem possible."

"How do you like it here?" Bill asked him.

"I never thought that I would come to live on an island with sea all around me and such wonderful countryside. I sometimes take my son to the country park woods above the sea just to listen to the trees."

"You listen to them?"

"Why, yes. They make such wonderful sounds in the wind. The rushing and flowing up above you."

Bill had never really thought about that before.

"We have no sea where we lived," he continued, "but here it stretches for miles."

"But you have got a lot of sand!"

"Ah yes, indeed, indeed but your sea sand is very different from my country."

"It's more shingle here. England seems to be built on shingle."

They both laughed.

"Do you miss home?"

"Oh yes, very much but it is very, very unsafe. Some terrible things have happened." He put his hand on Mustafa's head as if to protect him.

"Aye, I can imagine."

"However, we feel safe now in your country and we have this very beautiful seaside weather today. Nothing to complain about, eh?"

"Exactly, it's canny all right."

The man looked at Bill quizzically.

"Excuse me what is this, canny?"

"Oh it just means great, good."

"I see," he smiled.

He put his hand out to shake Bill's. "Well sir, I am very grateful to you for you helping my Mustafa. He is becoming much stronger with your help."

Bill shook his hand. As they walked away with the boy waving back at Bill he strolled up Queens Road to the shopping centre. Feeling a glow inside that he hadn't felt for a long time he decided to treat himself to an M&S cottage pie or maybe a chicken tikka masala.

∼ Twenty Nine ∼

It had been another unsettled night for Bill, tossing and turning, sleeping fitfully. Lying, half dozing, the bedroom somehow seemed bigger in the dark. He strained his eyes to see any chink of light through the heavy curtains – making out the shape of the ceiling rose. He listened to the wind as it whistled down the chimney. Bill resisted glancing at the clock by his bedside, as he reckoned it was about 3am, but dreaded that it might only be one. In the darkened silence, he convinced himself that his heart beat had become irregular. He placed his hand on his chest to confirm his belief and he broke into a cold sweat when he thought it had stopped altogether. However he was then disturbed by the sound of running water, a creaking toilet flush from the upstairs flat where Tomasz, a young Polish man, lived. It was likely that he had worked a late shift or perhaps was due to start early as he was a van driver. Bill became tuned into the rushing flow of the cistern and when the final dripping had subsided, the silence returned. Bill was only on nodding terms with his neighbour. Last weekend he had a girlfriend stay and Bill met them both coming in with shopping as he was going out. Bill smiled and the woman did too. She seemed a lot younger than him. Later that evening they were causing a bit of a racket; heavy bass dance music was spoiling Bill's quiet evening. He was going to complain, but then it stopped. When Bill went to bed he heard the girl's high pitch laugh and clomp of heels running across the floor. It kept him awake for ages. Later he thought he heard them making love.

These sleepless nights seemed to be a regular pattern now for Bill. He reckoned that he was suffering from insomnia. He had tried sleeping pills but they only helped a little. Recurring thoughts about Helen who he still saw everywhere circled around his head like a seabird. It had been a good marriage, more than what a lot of people have. Bill thought of many of their contemporaries who had split up years ago. Bill's old house in Newcastle had finally got too much for him after Helen died. Her rich Geordie twang still echoed around the place – down the hall, the kitchen, bedroom, just as he was going out or coming in: *'Is that you, Billy. Did you remember to bring some milk in with you, pet?'* Her voice seemed to cling to the walls – sometimes it was comforting but more often it made him feel sad because she was now no more. So even this escape to Hastings hadn't cured the incredible numbness that he was feeling.

During the morning, a fresh wind vigorously shook the hawthorn tree outside Bill's flat. A few of its reddened leaves, glowing in the sunshine began to break loose in short bursts flying across the road, spinning in a frenzied dance. He spent the day job searching on the internet and listening to blues albums. Later, as the evening was drawing in, Bill headed off to Clive Vale in search of Leo. He strode up the Old London Road with heavy traffic roaring by, passing the moss covered balustrades of the derelict Clive Vale Hotel, glimpsing at the vista of lights across Hastings. He eventually arrived at The Crown, an inconspicuous looking pub at the top of the hill. Feeling a little nervous in anticipation of confronting Leo, Bill slipped into the pub which was surprisingly quite busy. He quickly scanned the bar for any sign of him. It was about 7pm, maybe still a little early for Leo's apparent regular drop in. After ordering a pint of beer and some crisps, Bill managed to find a small table with a clear vantage point of the door. A welcome open fire was blazing in the grate, throwing out a warm glow across the bar. He thought that he could very easily doze off, still feeling sleepy from the night before. He began reading a Friday Ad paper which was lying around. Bill had one eye on the door, expecting Leo to appear at anytime. If and when he did turn up, he was thinking what he would say. Would they both get angry in the bar? Create a scene? Bill was beginning to doubt the wisdom of his mission; wondering if they could get any of their money back from this crook. In his pocket he had the receipt for his share, but no written agreement between them all. No legal status whatsoever. 'What fools we've been,' thought Bill.

He geared himself up to face the man as soon as he came through the door, but Bill had a long wait. Seven became eight and still no sign. Nursing his pint for as long as he could, he finally decided to get another drink. When he was at the bar Bill asked the barman if he had seen Leo. The man shook his head but then asked another regular sitting on a bar stool nearby.

"Ferde, do you mean?" The man quipped, "He's a smart looking bloke, likes singing Italian songs!"

"Aye, that's him," Bill said. Unmistakably Leo, he thought.

"We haven't seen him since … what?" he looked back at another regular.

"Last Friday," he confirmed. The barman handed Bill his pint and took his money.

"Yeah, that's it, last Friday," the regulars agreed.

"Do you know where I can find him? I've got a message from his daughter," Bill said, suddenly inspired by his recent contact with her which might give him some legitimacy in their eyes.

"Oh, I know they don't get on," the man on the stool mused.

"Can you help me with an address?" Bill asked further.

"Well, no mate, sorry. He's never mentioned where he lives. It's somewhere round here because I've seen him down in town." The barman, now serving a drink to another customer, overhearing the conversation shook his head too. Their chat fizzled out and Bill supped his second pint still hoping that Leo would show. However at about nine he decided to call it a day and left.

Outside the pub Bill felt annoyed about this wasted trip and began walking down Priory Road towards home. The evening had turned brisk and the cold cut through Bill's jacket. He also wished he had gone to the loo before he left the pub. Just as he reached Queens Road, he remembered that he needed to get a pint of milk and headed towards a late night shop. Just stepping into the doorway, Bill was suddenly face to face with Leo, looking rather dishevelled. "Oh, it's you!" Leo said, startled.

Bill was speechless, taken aback by Leo's appearance. Leo stood holding some milk and a loaf of bread. Bill stepped aside as another customer squeezed past them.

"I've been looking for you," Bill said.

"Have you? Well, I'd not gone far," Leo said brusquely and started to walk slowly along the pavement. Bill, suddenly feeling even more desperate for a pee followed him.

"Your daughter, Sharon, gave me your number."

"Oh did she? I thought she might be behind this." Leo stopped walking and looked straight at Bill.

"Well, come out with it. What did you tell her? How I've fiddled you all and run away with the takings?" he spat out. In the cold night air Bill could smell alcohol on Leo's breath or was it his own?

"You know," said Leo, slurring his speech, "the reason that some people don't seem to trust me is that they don't really share my vision. They're locked into their little worlds. Can't see the big picture." Leo gestured with his arms and almost lost the grip on his loaf of bread. Bill was about to let rip about his deceiving them all but seeing Leo in this state, he just stood, listening to him rant. "And also," Leo's eyes narrowed, "I'm fed up with all these questions people have. Questions, questions, questions. Who do they think I am, Brain of Britain?"

"I don't think that," Bill couldn't hide his sniggering at the idea.

"Oh don't you?"

"No," said Bill suddenly remembering that he hadn't bought himself any milk from the shop. Leo staggered on and Bill followed.

"Actually I'm dying to go to the loo, Leo."

"Well you'd better come up to my place, it's just along here. You might as well. See how the other half live."

They soon reached a chemist shop and Leo led Bill to a side door and fumbled for his keys. Inside, the narrow hallway was dark and Bill noticed a damp, musty smell. Leo punched a timer button and a florescent light flickered on illuminating a pile of junk mail, free newspapers and flyers littering the well worn carpet. Clutching his provisions, Leo led Bill upstairs to the first floor but had to take a breather on the landing as he was out of breath.

The flat was pretty small, almost a bedsit and Bill was hit by the raw heat blasting out from a whirling electric fan heater. A line of underpants and socks were drying on a radiator. In the living room there was a television in the corner by the window that Leo had left on which was showing a programme about the current economic crisis.

"Turn this crap off," Leo muttered. He pressed the remote control and put the milk and bread on the table.

"There it is," Leo pointed to the bathroom which Bill was much relieved to use. When he rejoined Leo in the living room Bill also saw that there was an opened suitcase lying on the floor with clothes spilling out as though Leo had been away. On the table there were leftovers of a Chinese take away in cartons and a copy of The Daily Mail opened at the sports page. Bill also saw that it had some race meetings circled in red biro. In careful slow motion Leo cleared a chair of some newspapers, put the milk in the fridge and filled the kettle with water. From the small kitchen, he dished up a couple of mugs from the sink, ran them under the tap and as the kettle began to boil he called over to Bill, "Tea or coffee?"

"Coffee," replied Bill who was still quietly surveying Leo's unkempt flat.

"Take a pew," Leo said, pointing to the chairs around the table. Bill tentatively moved some post and nudged the discarded Chinese take away carton from smelling distance.

"Here," said Leo, hovering. He hurriedly scooped up the left overs into a carrier bag and put them in a waste bin. Bill took his jacket off and sat at the table eyeing the grains of egg fried rice still dotted across the table. Leo brought over two mugs of coffee. Bill noticed that the one placed nearer to him was cracked and so, whilst Leo's back was turned to get some sugar, he quickly changed them round.

Leo slumped down opposite with a groan and made a cursory effort to clear up some stray rice from the table with his hand. There was a restlessness about him that Bill found disquieting. Leo offered Bill some sugar then placed three spoonfuls in his own mug. Stirring it in so rigorously, it spilled on to the table. Bill took a swig of the coffee which was a little too milky for his liking.

"At least you can come and go as you please here, and nobody seems to notice or care even. I think that's what I like about it really – being anonymous." Leo smirked.

"How long have you been here?"

Leo looked around the room as though seeking a clue.

"Just a short while. It's a stopover really before I buy again." He raised a smile. "It reminds me of a bedsit that I once shared with a girlfriend. Well she moved in with me actually."

"Oh aye?"

"She was a beauty, you know, a dolly bird as we used to call them in those days." It was a term which Bill thought made Leo seem very old fashioned.

"But maybe you didn't call them that up north in Geordie land, eh?"

Bill smiled.

"Anyway her name was Caroline. I met her up in London at The Marquee club in Wardour Street where all the top groups were playing. I was managing a group called The Worried Set and she was an art student there. Her parents had quite a bit of money and she'd come down here and crash out. Yes, she was a lovely girl," Leo reflected warmly and sipped his coffee.

"Would you like a little drop of brandy to go with that?" Leo asked Bill.

"Oh no I'm fine with the coffee."

"Come on, Bill," Leo urged him, "it'll keep the cold out." Leo got up, still a little unsteadily, to search for the bottle and found it behind the television. Ignoring Bill's refusal he poured out two glasses.

"Cheers!" Leo raised his glass and Bill quietly accepted.

Leo tipped his drink back in one. Bill took a smaller swig but shook his head when Leo quickly proffered a top up.

"So, Bill, I bet I can guess why you've come here."

Bill looked uneasy and Leo stirred himself. "Come on, you want your money, everyone does!"

"Everyone?" Bill asked, feeling even more off guard by imagining that he had joined a long queue of Leo's creditors.

"You didn't come all this way just to enquire about my health," Leo said, having another slug of brandy.

"Don't you think you should have explained to us what's going on, man?" Bill began. "All we know is that you've tried to palm us off with just a few pounds after that win at the dogs. Then you disappear and I've had to turn detective to track you down."

"Well you've only got yourself to blame. You should have had more trust than that. There was no need to spy on me," Leo looked rather put out.

"I'm not spying on you, man!" Bill was getting riled that Leo was trying to turn things round and evade the point.

"You told us that we'd be due a lot more money when Fly By Knight won a race. And when it did, you did a runner, faster than the dog! That's what happened, Leo. You can't deny that."

"No I didn't do a runner actually. I had some important business to attend to in London as a matter of fact." Leo could see that Bill didn't believe him.

"Look, you'll get your money," he waved his glass at Bill.

"Oh aye," Bill sneered. "Eleven pounds fifty's worth?"

"There you are, you see," Leo protested, "my point exactly."

"What point?" Bill was flush with anger.

"Trust," replied Leo. "Why don't you just have a little more faith in people. That's your trouble Bill, no imagination, if I may say so. That's why you're stuck without a job in Hastings. That's why Rita's still a dead end till girl at Woolies after all these years. And why Abi's tied down to looking after her loopy old aunt, what's-her-name." Leo quickly poured himself another generous measure but was still in full throttle. "You've all lost your nerve. You're *all losers,* the lot of you," he lashed out.

Bill felt himself boiling up at Leo's rant. "That's rich coming from you! Listen Leo, I don't know who you think you are, but you're deluding yourself if you believe that you're better than any of us. As far as I can see you're a cheat and a liar." Bill leant forward across the table to make the point.

"A cheat?" Leo laughed.

"Yes, and a liar," Bill repeated, seething.

"You know what gets me?" said Leo leaning back in his chair. "That you lot all want the gravy but you're not prepared to do the cooking."

"You lot! That's who we are to you is it? Me, Rita and Abi? You've got a very high opinion of yourself, Leo."

"Well what if I have? Some of us have to take the lead." Leo's eyes were almost popping.

Bill shook his head. He'd had enough and stood up, grabbing his jacket, ready to leave.

"I tell you what, Leo. We want our money back. You're not getting away with this. It's theft. And I've got my receipt!" he quickly pulled the crumpled piece of paper out of his jacket and waved it in Leo's face.

"Oh, it's theft now is it? Shall I call the police?" Leo spouted, teasingly, raising his voice higher.

"I'm going," Bill sighed, "I've had enough. You're drunk. Look at the state of you, you're pathetic, man."

"Well you can sling your hook," and Leo got up a bit too sharply, nearly toppling over.

"I'm going all right. But remember, Leo," Bill growled, "we want our money, or else we'll take it further."

Leo lurched over to the door and opened it. "Take it where you like." Holding rigidly on to the door handle, he stood to attention like a sentry. Bill thundered down the darkened stairs.

"You get our money, Leo. You cheat, or else!"

"Get lost," Leo barked after him, slamming the door shut which unexpectedly turned on the hall light. Outside Bill stood on the pavement and put his jacket on. He looked up at the flat and saw the flicker of the television reappear.

∼ Thirty ∼

At Woolies the staff were angry. An announcement had just been made through the media that the firm was going into administration.

"They should have told us first, Rita's friend Pat fumed, slamming shut her locker door in the staff room. Other workers were already besieging the office to try and find out where they stood. Rita, putting on her uniform was trying to be more philosophical.

"Well, when you think about it, these rumours have been flying around for weeks. But maybe this company, Deloitte will sort it out and find a new buyer. Let's face it they can't do much worse than this current lot." Pat looked at her and nodded. "There's been a Woolies in Hastings since the twenties, my nan says. So I can't imagine it'll go, can you?"

*   *   *

After hearing the news on the radio, Bill decided to pop in and see Rita at work. He found her on the upper sales floor in the Homewares Department sorting through some boxes. She stood up pleased to see him.

"I heard the bad news," he smiled sympathetically. He thought that she looked quite pale and drawn as she took a casserole pot out of a box.

"Yeah, it's just suddenly hit me. I'm wondering how we'll manage at home."

Bill moved near to her seeing she was upset and was concerned that she was going to drop the pot which would have been ironic given his own accident in the shop when they both first met.

"Maybe things will be OK when they find a new buyer, what do you think?" Rita asked.

"Aye you could be right there," but in his heart he felt that the store was probably doomed.

"The union is on the case and some of the girls are thinking of getting up a petition. 'Save Woolies!' " Rita laughed and Bill forced a smile.

"You could hold a protest with placards."

"Oh I feel dizzy," Rita suddenly complained. Bill reached out to steady her and took hold of the pot.

"Shall I get someone? Are you OK?"

Rita supported herself against the shelves. "No, I'll be fine in a minute. She took some deep breaths and Bill put the pot carefully up on the shelf.

After a little while Rita recovered, sitting down for a moment on some nearby steps.

"It's good of you to come down, Bill."

"Well it's not easy is it? I know that when our company went to the wall. They don't think of the human cost, families and bills to pay." He put his hand gently on her shoulder and Rita looked up at him and felt good that he was there.

"I also came round to tell you that I saw Leo a few nights back." Rita sat up surprised. "He gave me short shrift about our winnings. To be honest he was paralytic and ranting about us not trusting him." Although Bill was still seething about it he didn't want to upset Rita further.

"Looks like I was wrong then. He really is a bad'un." Rita smiled thinly.

"Looks like it, pet. But I'm not giving up that easily. I'm

going to try and see him again now. Hopefully he'll have sobered up and I can have it out with him."

*   *   *

In daylight, the entrance to Leo's flat looked even shabbier. He peered to see if Leo's name was on the intercom bell, but it wasn't. Bill pushed Flat 1 buzzer and listened closely to hear any response. A minute or so lapsed and Bill pressed the button again, but there was still no reply. Impatiently, he phoned Leo on his mobile feeling disappointed that this element of surprise to catch him was now gone. He only got his voice mail and began to walk away. As he did so, he heard the door open behind him.

"Hello," said Bill, turning back.

"Yes, what do you want?" Bill could hardly see through the crack, but detected that it was an elderly woman.

"Is Leo Moretti in?"

"Are you a relative?" She was peering through the gap.

"Oh no, just a friend."

"They've taken him away," the woman said, her voice barely audible above the noise of the traffic nearby.

"Who have?"

"The ambulance, yesterday."

"What happened?"

"He had a turn."

"A turn?"

"Yes, he collapsed."

"Oh dear. Is he in hospital?"

"Must be, he hasn't come back. Unless … ," she hesitated.

"What?"

"You know. He's conked out!"

"Which hospital is he in?"

"The Conquest I expect." She then abruptly closed the door in Bill's face.

In the afternoon Bill went to the Conquest Hospital just

outside Hastings. He made some enquiries about Leo at the reception and explained that he was a friend. After traipsing through the maze of corridors and getting lost on the way, he eventually arrived at Tressell Ward. Bill smiled to himself that Leo of all people should be placed on a ward named after Bill's socialist hero. Bill quickly looked around to see if he could spot Leo. By the doorway an old man glanced up from his chair. Bill smiled at him, but he continued reading his magazine. Two others were having an afternoon nap, their heads dropped down on their chest. Another was watching TV with headphones on and a fourth was chatting with a visitor. Leo was lying on top of his bed wearing a dressing gown reading a The Daily Mail.

"What's happened to you?"

Leo lowered the newspaper, his face looked quite pale and pinched but he didn't seem surprised to see Bill.

"Oh nothing much, just in here for some tests that's all. Should be out tomorrow probably if they get their act together." He pulled himself up the bed, folded his newspaper and Bill came closer. "I hope so, the food's bloody awful!" Leo grimaced. "Anyway how did you know I was in here?"

"Your neighbour told me after I'd called round. She said you'd collapsed."

"Did she?" Leo looked put out.

"She said you'd come in here by ambulance."

"Well, the nosey cow's exaggerating. She likes a drama."

Bill grabbed a chair, sat down opposite and found that he was looking up at Leo on the bed.

"So, what's happened then. Did you collapse?"

Leo pulled a face. "No, not collapsed exactly, just a bit giddy and you know when your ticker's going ten to the dozen."

"Palpitations?" Bill suggested, nodding that he knew what Leo meant.

"That's it," Leo agreed, "came over quite bad, so I must have panicked and called 999. I just thought they'd send a paramedic, over but before I knew it an ambulance crew were almost knocking my door down, with Mrs Thingy from upstairs looking on. Then after a long wait in A&E they put me in here. Said that they needed to check me over."

"Was it a heart attack?"

Leo shook his head, "No, they reckon it wasn't that. They've taken loads of blood." He rolled up his sleeve to show Bill his arm. "Look I'm like a pin cushion." Bill thought that Leo's arm looked perfectly normal and noticed that he had a faded tattoo of a snake on his left forearm.

They sat in silence awkwardly for a little while not quite knowing what to say given their last encounter. Leo leant over and drank some water which was on his bedside cabinet and Bill saw the headline of the newspaper lying on his bed, *'Unemployment crisis as credit crunch bites'.*

He picked it up. "They're talking about a double dip recession coming," he said to Leo skimming through the main story.

"You know, this credit crunch. It's just like the fairground in Hastings. Your big dipper is the rise and fall – boom and bust of capitalism. The crane grabber takes your savings, but gives you nothing in return. The ghost train has got the frighteners of recession on every corner to make you feel insecure about making ends meet or about your job. You pay your money but you don't know where it's going. It's one big gamble!" Bill smiled, satisfied at his analogy.

"Oh very clever," Leo jeered, "you've missed out 'Knock The Lady Out Of Bed'. My brother and I used to love that as kids in Hastings. Those lovely girls wearing baby doll nighties! I bet that one doesn't fit into your view of the economy, Bill."

"Trust you to bring it all down to sex. But I tell you, Leo, things are going to get a lot worse next year. There's thousands of people unemployed in Hastings already. And those that are working, their wages are among the lowest in the area," Bill added.

Leo put down his glass and raised himself further up the bed. "That's because there's too many foreigners here taking our jobs. I read the papers as well, Bill. They reckon that thousands have arrived in the last six months. There's no controls!"

"People have got every right to come to Britain if they're EU citizens, as we have in going to Europe."

"Yeah but who wants to live in Belarus?"

"I don't think that's a part of the EU, is it?"

"Whatever," Leo raised his eyebrows, "you know what I mean. The fact is that this country's too soft on giving out benefits."

"Well I'd rather have a decent job than be on the dole anytime. Most people come here to find work. Look at the Poles. They're a hard working lot and some of them are going home now because, the work is drying up."

"Exactly, that's my point – taking our jobs and then buggering off," said Leo.

"No, you've got it wrong, man. They're usually doing the jobs people don't want to do here. Mind you, I will say that they're always prepared to work at a lower rate of pay and that keeps the wages down."

"There you are, you see – I'm right!"

"Leo, the point is that there's a credit crunch which is now a recession, caused by the bankers being given a free hand with no restrictions or proper regulation in order for them to make as much profit as they like. Enticing people to have credit well beyond their means and for housing to have become another money making commodity, rather than providing decent homes. That's the problem."

"OK, is the lecture over? I am in hospital you know!" Leo stared at Bill.

"Sorry, well is there anything I can do or get you?" Bill felt guilty about his outburst.

"No, I'm fine, but 'er … " he leant over towards Bill and whispered,

"Could you let me have a tenner on account like? I came in here in such a rush without much cash." Given Leo's recent behaviour with their money Bill was reluctant, but he took out his wallet and pulled out a note, "I've only got twenty, man."

Leo deftly plucked it from Bill's hand like a bird. "That'll do," he said, "thanks, you'll get it back, promise." Leo quickly tucked it in his dressing gown pocket before Bill could protest.

"Is there anything that you want me to bring you from your flat?"

"No, no," Leo was emphatic, "as I say, I should be out tomorrow or the day after."

"Have you told your family? Do they know that you're in here?" Bill asked.

"Oh no I don't want them involved," Leo said looking rather shocked at thethought.

"So, you don't want me to give your daughter, Sharon, a ring?"

"Well no, she and me had a bit of a falling out."

"Oh," Bill raised his eyebrows.

"Well you know how it is," Leo continued, "they think you owe them, don't they?"

"You've got a son as well, haven't you?"

"Dave, yes he lives in Tunbridge Wells. Doing very well for himself too as it happens," Leo smiled with some pride.

"Why don't you give him a ring and tell him what's happened?"

"Oh no, he won't have time to come over. And anyway, his wife, Hazel," Leo mouthed sourly, as though someone might be listening, "she's a bit of a tyrant, and he's under her thumb." Leo pointed his thumb downwards to emphasize the point.

"Is there anyone else that you want me to contact?"

"Well, OK give Sharon a ring if you like. Say that I collapsed and I'm in here."

"But I thought you said you hadn't collapsed?" Bill felt himself getting a bit irritated with Leo's attitude.

Ignoring Bill's question, Leo continued. "Tell her they're doing lots of tests and they're hoping to get to the bottom of it. Oh, and say for her not to worry. I should be OK – eventually."

Bill looked at Leo rather dead pan. "You're making it sound much worse than it appears, Leo! She's going to be worried, surely?"

"Look, you have to lay it on a bit with our Sharon. She won't do anything unless you give her something to think about. Just like her mother. Well, they just think about themselves, don't they? Selfish as they come." Leo looked down at Bill for some agreement.

"Have you got your mobile with you?" Bill asked. Leo nodded that he had.

"Well, give me a ring when you know that you're coming home. I'll pop over and take you back in the car." Bill made a move to leave, looking over at the two men still asleep in their chairs.

"And, you'll give Sharon a ring will you?" Leo's face looked quite expectant.

"OK," Bill agreed, now feeling rather put upon.

As he began to walk to the door, Leo called him back.

"And tell Sharon to tell her mother I'm in here."

"What, your ex?"

"Yeah, that's right."

"Leo, why aren't you doing this, man?"

"Well you did offer," Leo looked hurt. "And anyway it's better coming from you," Leo said, looking rather sorry for himself. "In any case," he added slipping down the bed, "I really do need to get some rest."

∾ Thirty One ∾

There was a ring on Rita's front door. Rain was bouncing hard off the porch roof like tennis balls. The gutter overflowed and water rushed down the drain, flooding the path. Opening the front door, Rita found Gayle standing sodden, with Dean at her side. His hood pulled up, it almost covered his face, with wet dripping off his nose. Gayle was gripping a heavy suitcase in one hand and a bursting bin bag in the other. Her hair, dragged down and flattened by the sudden downpour, plastered her face and neck looking like a cut price wig. Outside the front gate a taxi was waiting to be paid. Rita ushered them both in and dashed out with her purse to settle the fare.

Inside the house and removing their drenched clothes, Gayle was in tears as she explained to Rita that she had just been evicted from her flat. Later she also told Rita that a loan shark was chasing her and getting heavy, demanding repayments.

"I'm taking that fucking landlord to court," Gayle flared up, "he can't do this. I've got a young kid."

Rita put her arms around her daughter.

"Oh Gayle. I think you'll find he can, love. If you hadn't paid your rent, why didn't you say?"

These return trips home had become almost inevitable this past year. With a heavy heart, Rita helped her unpack and move back up into her old room whilst Dean quietly sat down on the sofa drying himself with a towel and watching the telly in the back room.

"We'll go to the Council first thing tomorrow," Rita said, as she went down into the kitchen to prepare some tea.

"There's no hurry," Gayle shouted back. "It'll be Christmas soon."

"Oh yes there is," Rita said, determinedly. She peeked in at Dean, already curled up; he still looked all cuddly and untouched by the big world outside. Rita thought that she'd enjoy having him around, but Gayle was going to be a pain. What would she tell Colin when he got home in order to keep the peace?

The storm had passed and the rain had stopped, leaving trickles of water running down the kitchen window.

∼ Thirty Two ∼

"How's everything?" Bill asked Rita at the checkout. He had popped into Woolies to buy a few household things for the flat.

"It never rains but it pours." My daughter's just moved back home again because she hasn't paid the rent on her flat. She and Colin are at it hammer and tongs already. It couldn't be worse."

"Can't the Council help?"

"I made her an appointment but she didn't keep it. I'll have to get on to them again today. It'll probably end up with me going with her."

"Does she go out to work?"

"No, and the trouble is she's twenty five and never really had a job. She went to college at eighteen to train as a cook but then she met this bloke, Greg, and they both dropped out. She did a little bit of waitressing and they managed to pay the rent on some rooms. Not long after that, she became pregnant with Dean. Colin wouldn't speak to her for ages."

"Well she must have had an interest in cooking to get on the course."

"Yes, she loved cooking as a teenager. In fact she was always mucking around in the kitchen when she was a kid. She got an A for domestic science or whatever it's called these days and she'd always be cooking meals at home: roasts, paella, mousaka,

Chinese. And you should taste her cheesecake! I put on a lot of weight during that time," Rita laughed.

"So what happened to the boyfriend?"

"He was a few years older than her and he had these ideas about them starting a restaurant, but he had no money. When Gayle told him that she was pregnant and she wanted to keep the baby, he was off like a shot."

"And how's it all going here?"

"We're keeping our peckers up but it's not looking good. You can't buy Woolies gift vouchers any longer and customers who've already bought some are asking for their money back because they don't think there'll be anything left worth buying." Rita shook her head in dismay. They've taken back the Lotto machine and other companies are coming in and collecting their sales stands." Bill slowly shook his head too as Rita gave a nervous giggle and continued. "When we make an order, we're getting sent things we don't need. It's a joke because we just had a new stock control system introduced. We've hardly got any Christmas stuff to put out. Christmas will be coming early at Woolies!" Rita waved her hand towards the gaps in the shelves.

"Sounds like you need to meet for a drink soon, take your mind off it?"

"Yes, good idea, definitely. I think I need one. I'll get on to Abi."

∼ Thirty Three ∼

Bill strolled down to the seafront where, walking past recently, he had discovered that Jamal, Mustafa's dad, worked. The group of builders and decorators were renovating a once grand, three storey Victorian house that had fallen into decay. Although the morning was downcast with a light mist beginning to turn to drizzle, the brightness of the newly painted house shone out across the promenade with renewed life. Bill poked his head round the open front door. Upstairs he could hear one of the workers hammering and a distant radio was on. The sound echoed around the empty house. Just along the hallway Jamal was on his hands and knees carefully painting a skirting board.

"Don't take too long over that or you'll get into trouble!" Bill joked as he stood in the doorway.

"Ah it's you, Mr Shields."

"Bill, please," he replied, "it's looking very nice."

"Yes, thank you but we must finish very soon, so I have to rush to get everything done."

"We'll that's the thing isn't it – money! It's all about profit. The bosses are not interested in craftsmanship. Do they get you to water down the paint too?"

Jamal put his brush on top of the paint pot and stood up.

"Anyway I've brought you a present." Bill gave him a carrier bag. Wiping his hands on his overalls, Jamal looked puzzled and opened it, smiling.

"A book!"

"Yes, '*The Ragged Trousered Philanthropists*'," Bill said proudly. It was written by Robert Tressell, or Robert Noonan, his real name and it's about a group of house painters and decorators much like yourself, working in Hastings at the turn of the last century. Except the town's called Mugsborough in the novel."

"Mugsborough?" Jamal queried.

"Yes," Bill beamed, "it's canny isn't it? It means people being taken for mugs, exploited, like."

The man studied the book cover, an illustration of a group of decorators wearing black hats. "The Ragged Trouser Phil … " he struggled with the word.

"Philanthropists," Bill assisted. "It means that the workers are always giving their bosses their labour, skills and craft at far less than what it's really worth. And then the bosses are always demanding that they give even more!"

"Does it end well for them, these house decorators in this story?"

"Ah well, you'll have to see. It's more about the conditions of the workers and their families and how the rich bosses maintain their position in the town of Mugsborough."

Jamal looked at the book cover again and back at Bill.

"I think you'll like it and I don't need it back," Bill hastened to add. "I've got another copy at home. Anyway it's quite a long book so you could take your time reading it."

"That's very kind of you but I had better carry on with my work now." He put the book back in the bag and placed it carefully on the stairs, picking up his paint brush again.

"OK," Bill agreed, "I'd better get off myself. Don't work too hard."

"I will also give you a book of Kurdish poetry, I think you might like that too." Jamal said, returning to his painting.

As Bill sauntered off, he wondered if he had done the right thing giving Jamal the book. He might feel embarrassed or obliged to read it when he didn't want to.

～ Thirty Four ～

Abi was searching Millie's bedroom for a repeat medication prescription; she had looked in all the likely places. She usually kept it in the kitchen, amongst the bills behind the radio but somehow it had gone missing. Millie was in the living room watching a morning TV chat show.

"Auntie, have you seen your prescription?" she called out.

"Me what?" she answered above the sound of the telly.

"Oh nothing, it's all right," Abi sighed heavily, carrying on searching. Then she spotted her aunt's handbag on the bedside table and decided to have a look in there. It was pretty heavy and she pulled out a Kit Kat wrapper, old bus tickets, a packet of mouldy custard creams, some dried up biros, a compact, a 1984 dental appointment card, Millie's tattered birth certificate, a photo of Sam their old B&B cat. "I wondered where that had gone," Abi smiled and continued looking – a dessert spoon, a battered copy of the Highway Code, small packets of ketchup, vinegars, salt, tartar sauce which Abi suspected came from Rosa's cafe. Abi shook her head with amusement about what Millie was carrying around with her. No wonder it was bulging. She looked at the mountain of it now laid out on the bed. "Bingo!" Abi cried out as she unravelled some more crumpled papers including the prescription. Just as she was putting everything back she also came across an envelope addressed to her aunt. It had a Sussex postmark and Abi's curiosity took hold as she opened it and found an official looking letter addressed to Millie. She read the short contents: it described their role as an organisation assisting to reunite families, but Abi was struck by the sentence:... *'Someone has contacted this agency who believes they may be related to you, if you wish to know more, please contact this number ... '*

Abi sat down on the corner of the bed bemused at the letter and wondered who it might be, a distant relation? Millie had always said that she had nobody left in her family. Apart from the letter, photo of their old cat and the prescription, she packed everything else back in the bag.

The TV show in the next room was still in full flow but afterwards Abi told Millie that she had found the prescription and the photo of their old cat. She then asked her quite light heartedly about the letter which she held up for her to see. Millie turned and looked surprised.

"Auntie, why didn't you mention it? Someone's trying to contact you from your past, like they do in that television programme, '*Who Do You Think You Are?*' "

Millie slammed her mug down on the table. The cat squealed, flew off her lap and hid behind the armchair. "You've got no right, that's mine, that's personal!" she spat out. Snatching the letter out of Abi's hand, like a whirlwind, she pushed past her, shot into her room and slammed the door hard, locking it behind.

"What the heck ... " Abi was shaken.

She stood outside Millie's room and knocked gently on the door.

"Auntie, what's up?" There wasn't a murmur from inside and Abi knocked again and tried to open the door. She was annoyed with herself that she hadn't removed the key after the last time Millie had locked herself in.

"Come on, auntie. Look I'm sorry if you're annoyed that I went through your handbag but we need that prescription don't we?" There was still no response. Abi spoke louder, "I was only joking about what I said about the letter. I didn't realise.

Maybe it's a mix up – perhaps they meant to send it to someone else." Abi put her ear to the door again.

"I'm going to make a fresh pot of tea," she said invitingly. "Shall we have it in the kitchen?"

After a little while, as Abi was warming the teapot, she heard the bedroom lock turn and seconds later Millie appeared in the kitchen with the letter still in her hand. She sat down and laid it out on the kitchen table.

Abi looked at Millie, her face was strained and she sat beside her.

"What is it? What's upset you?"

Millie shook her head and remained silent.

Abi re-read it quietly, "*Someone has contacted this agency who believes they may be related to you …* Maybe it's a long lost cousin. Perhaps you've come in to an inheritance, auntie, some money?" Abi's tone was upbeat.

Millie remained silent.

"Don't look so worried, auntie."

Whilst Abi poured the hot water into the tea pot, Millie eventually spoke.

"I know what it's about, but I don't know what to do."

"What do you mean?"

"It's been my secret all these years, even from your mother. Nobody knew."

"What secret?" Abi could see from Millie's troubled face that she was finding it very difficult to talk. A tear began running down her cheek which she wiped away with the back of her hand before the next one appeared. Abi went over and put her arm around her. She hadn't seen Millie cry for years. Not since Dot Cotton in East Enders had disowned her wayward son, Nick. This time it was different – a silent, inner grief, that looked like it was tearing her apart. Millie averted her eyes away from Abi and back to the letter and envelope on the table.

"You're going to think I'm an awful person," she sobbed. "If you knew what I'd done when I was young, it would make your hair curl."

"What is it, silly? It can't be that bad," Abi tried to hold Millie's hand but she had raised it up to her face and was looking tormented.

"Oh, it can, believe me – very bad." She looked away again not bearing to look Abi in the eye.

"Auntie, come on, you're worrying me now, just spit it out, wont you?"

Abi's stomach began turning with anxiety.

Millie closed her eyes but it hadn't stopped the tears flowing.

"Look, you don't have to reply to this letter if it's upsetting you so much. We can just forget about it," Abi smiled, trying to help ease her aunt's obvious fretting.

"No, it won't go away, not now."

"What won't?"

"What I did all that time ago."

"Auntie, you're talking in riddles as though you've committed a murder or something."

"I was bad but I didn't know what to do. I thought it was for the best, see?"

"You're still not making sense, auntie." Abi let out a fluttering laugh.

"The baby!" Millie looked directly at Abi.

"Baby, what baby?"

"Mine."

"Yours?" Abi laughed once again but this time it teetered on the brink of being more of a shriek.

"Yes," Millie sounded almost matter of fact, but her eyes were red and moist.

"You had *a baby?*" Abi's mouth seemed like it had frozen open and time felt suspended until the clatter of the milk being delivered outside shook her out of it.

Leaving her tea untouched on the table, Abi got up and dived over to the kettle, filled it with water and scooped a large teaspoonful of coffee into a mug, her hand was shaking.

As the kettle boiled, Abi lit up a cigarette, whilst momentarily looking out the window, seeing the milkman finishing his round on the landing. She took a long drag on her fag and turned to face Millie.

"Look, auntie, I know this letter is official and all that, but you've just got things a bit confused here, that's all. Maybe you're thinking of your little sister who got killed in the bombing during the war. She was so much younger than you. You've just got things mixed up, eh? Something like that?"

Abi went over and gently rubbed Millie's shoulder, thinking that her confusion was taking a turn for the worse.

Millie spoke as calm and clear as she had for a long time.

"I had a daughter when I was nearly eighteen," she began, wiping her dripping nose with a tissue from up the sleeve of her cardigan, "not long before I'd moved down here again from London. My aunt and parents got me in a mother and baby home for a while, as they decided that the baby should be adopted. It all happened so quickly. I was a mum one minute, then suddenly," she sniffed, "I wasn't … Never saw her after that. I just got on with my life." Millie looked at Abi for a moment for some reassurance but the only sound she could hear was the quiet ticking of the kitchen clock.

"So you think that this is to do with it?" Abi picked the letter up from the table and held it as though it were 'Exhibit A'.

"Yes, I do."

Millie stared at Abi. "What can I do?"

Abi shook her head and took a long drag on her cigarette.

"Look, auntie. You've got this all wrong," Abi said, frowning, firmly holding her hand and trying to take control of the situation. "There's no daughter. You've got mixed up. I'll speak to them myself to clear it up."

Millie shook her head. "I know you think I'm as nutty as a fruit cake, Abi but this is the truth. That's what happened. I had a daughter and I gave her up for adoption." Seeming calmer, Millie was more lucid than she had been in ages.

"OK, auntie," Abi said, still not believing a word of it. "If that's what you think, but we'll see. I'm going to phone them and get to the bottom of it."

∽ Thirty Five ∽

Later that week, Bill, Abi and Rita met up at The Eagle. The place was quite busy as it was darts night and the teams were getting settled in. Bill was munching some crisps and eyeing the activity around the dart board. "I used to love arrows, me – haven't played for years."

"Well you can always come down here and have a go," Rita suggested.

"Oh, I'm out of practice, pet. I'd show myself up."

"We'll all have a game sometime then. We could start a team of our own, couldn't we?"

Bill nodded.

"So, how's our Millie?" Rita asked Abi.

"Great, I left her having her tea in front of the telly. Things seem to have settled down a bit. I'm sleeping a lot better now since the doc's given her those new pills. It's wonderful!"

"That's great news," said Rita. "And what about her wandering around?"

"No, she's seems fine just now, after that escapade with the police. I mean she's still talking crazy, but she always has been!"

"And what about Gayle, Rita, things any better?"

Rita screwed her face up and took a long gulp of white wine before answering.

"Not good," she said, sighing.

"I can't understand why you let her back in with you." Abi shook her head in disapproval.

"Well what else could I do? I had no choice. I couldn't leave her and Dean on the streets."

"But you know she'll take you for a ride – you'll be stuck with her again, just like last time."

"No I won't. She's got an appointment down the housing office in the morning," Rita said rather defensively. Abi shook her head and drank her lager. Bill sitting opposite was preoccupied with watching the darts team begin loosening up, listening to their loud banter and cheer as someone scored a double top.

"Did I tell you that I saw Leo the other day? He's been in hospital," Bill said to Abi.

She bristled at hearing his name.

"He'll be in there again when I get my hands on him."

"He seems to be OK now mind. They reckon it was a touch of angina."

"Shall we send him a card?" Rita asked.

"What I want to know is where's our money?" Abi piped up, then remembered that in her case it had in fact been Rita who had paid.

"You can forget about that, pet. All you'll get is another cock and bull story from him," Bill turned again to look at the darts.

"Well I'm going to give him a mouthful when I see him, angina or not." Abi finished her lager.

"Do you both want another drink?" asked Bill hesitatingly, "It's just that I'm a bit short this week." They nodded and both dipped into their purses for the round. He went to the loo and then up to the bar, looking over at the darts teams, all huddled around. At the far end, he could hear the swift thud of the darts hitting the board. Bringing over their drinks, Bill was surprised to find there was a frosty atmosphere between Rita and Abi.

"Is she going to pay you any keep?" Abi glared at Rita.

"She's only just moved back in," Rita shot back at her.

"Well you remember what happened before," Abi reminded

her. Rita frowned and reached over for the glass of wine from Bill.

"Has she paid you back what she owed you?" Abi barked at Rita.

"None of your business," Rita shouted, rather uncharacteristically.

"I'm just looking out for you, Rita. You let her take advantage and you'll be stuck with her forever."

"Don't be stupid, you've got no idea what it's like."

"I know what *she's* like!" Abi turned her face towards Bill, picking up the lager that he had just bought her and mumbling, "scheming cow."

"What did you say?" Rita snapped.

"Nothing," Abi feigned innocence and supped her drink.

"She's my daughter. You've got no right to run her down."

"Well you've got to face the truth, Rita. I know it hurts but Gayle's got to stand on her own feet sometime."

"Like you, Abi?"

"What do you mean?"

"You know what I mean," Rita continued. "You try to make out you're whiter than white." Rita suddenly stood up and Bill wondered what was coming next.

"We all make mistakes, Abi, and you of all people should know that!"

Before Abi could reply Rita got up, grabbed her bag and coat and made for the door. Bill, completely flummoxed, trying to make head or tail of it all, got up too.

"Just let her stew," Abi shrugged and coolly carried on drinking.

"No, I'll be back." Bill quickly followed Rita outside and saw her going up the road.

"Rita!" he called out, following her.

"What?"

"Are you OK?" he asked, feeling a little breathless when he caught up with her.

She didn't reply and kept walking, looking straight ahead.

"What's this all about between you and Abi. Why are you both getting so het up? It's not like you."

Bill had a sudden urge to put his arms around her and hug her. She looked so sad and vulnerable.

"Look, come back. I'm sure it can be sorted out."

Rita stopped walking and he saw that her eyes were welling up. She wiped them with the back of her hand.

"It's drugs," Rita sniffled, looking down at her feet.

"Pardon?" Bill looked even more confused.

"My daughter, Gayle. That's why she's not been paying her rent. I've known for a while that she'd been spending her money on drugs. I hadn't realised it was so bad." Rita plucked out a tissue from her coat pocket and dabbed her eyes again as she quietly sobbed.

"Oh dear, I see." Bill sighed, holding her arm gently.

"The thing is … with Abi, she used to take drugs herself when she was younger. She became a right handful. We fell out for ages. It's only in the past few years that we've become friends again."

"Does she know about Gayle's drug problem?" Bill asked quietly.

"No!" Rita was startled at the thought. "And please don't tell her."

Bill shook his head.

Rita sniffled.

"She might be able to help you though," suggested Bill, hesitantly, "you know if she's been through it herself."

"Abi doesn't like Gayle … She gets very angry about the way she thinks I've let her have her own way. But she doesn't know what it's like; she's never had kids of her own. She's like one herself sometimes!" Rita dabbed her eyes again.

"Well she is your best friend. What are you going to do?"

"Oh I don't know. I just need to cool down a bit I suppose. I'm going home."

"Can I walk with you?

"No you're OK, you go back and finish your drink with Abi.

She'll be wondering what's happened. But don't tell her what I said though, will you?"

"No, but I think you should talk to her."

"Maybe but not right now. I've got some things to sort out at home." Just as Rita began to walk off she turned back to Bill and gently gave him a kiss on the cheek.

"Goodnight Bill, thank you."

He was touched by her affection.

"Cheerio then, pet. I'll see you soon,"

"Yes, I know." Rita waved and walked off.

*   *   *

When she got back home, Rita made herself some tea. Gayle was in the back room watching television and Dean was asleep upstairs.

"Do you want a cuppa?" Rita poked her head around the door.

"Yeah, go on then," Gayle replied, lounging full length on the sofa, not taking her eyes off the shopping channel presenting a parade of glitzy handbags.

"Where's your dad?"

"Search me," she said, her hand clutching the remote. "Down the club I suppose."

Rita brewed up in the kitchen. She called out, "You haven't forgotten that you've got the appointment with Housing tomorrow at ten?" Rita went back into the room and gave Gayle a mug of tea, whilst supping her own and becoming drawn in by the handbag show.

"Gayle?" Rita prodded for a reply.

Gayle curled her legs up further, putting down the remote and holding her mug with two hands.

"Seeing the Housing tomorrow, you haven't forgotten?" repeated Rita.

"Oh that. It'll be a waste of time."

"What do you mean?" Rita's hackles were rising with Abi's

cutting comments still ringing in her ears.

"They'll just fob me off again."

Both women were now conversing with each other while looking at the television screen.

"Well make sure they don't. Tell them that you're homeless and that you can't stay here any longer. Say that your dad's put his foot down."

"Aren't you coming with me?" Gayle unglued her eyes for a second from the box and glared at Rita.

"No, I can't. I've got to be at work. My manager is on my case. Things are difficult enough as it is."

"But you arranged it all."

"Well you'll have to manage," Rita said tetchily, pointing her finger at her.

"Just make sure you go."

"All right, keep your fucking hair on."

"I mean it, Gayle."

"I said, all right." She began biting her finger nails and dug herself deeper into the sofa.

Alone, upstairs in bed, in the soft glow of her bedside table light, Rita tried reading a crime novel that she'd had on the go for a couple of months. Usually she could manage a few pages before drifting off to sleep but tonight her mind was still racing because of the bust up with Abi. She reached into her bedside cabinet drawer and found a half-full packet of cigarettes that she kept for emergencies. She got up, opened the window and lit up, briefly standing looking out at the lights across to St Leonards. Rita remembered how Abi went off the rails when she was seventeen, hanging out with lads from Silverhill. Rita's parents were much stricter about her being home on time but Abi just ran wild. Rita had always been envious of Abi attracting admirers. Tall and lean Dean with his mohair pullovers. Troublesome Terry, a left-over from the teddy boy era, with his 'brothel creepers'; older than his years, he'd led her astray quite a few times with a penchant for cars that weren't his. Nothing appeared to worry Abi. She seemed game for anything that gave her a thrill. Rita remembered a trip to Brighton with a gang from the youth club when she was sixteen that got out of hand when Terry 'borrowed' a car and they had a spin around town, eventually being chased by the police. They all ended up spending the night in the nick. Rita recalled that she was grounded by her parents and Abi's mum threatened to send her away, if she didn't start behaving herself. They would go down to Hastings Pier every weekend to see the bands, but Rita didn't feel comfortable with some of the people that Abi was hanging around with. Terry was still on the scene and purple hearts were regularly on offer. Abi got in with the Silverhill mob and experimented with drugs. On one occasion, she had a bad reaction to some pills and Rita had to go to the hospital with her. They both managed to keep it quiet from Abi's mum. Later on when Pink Floyd played at The Pier, Abi and Rita went to a party in St Leonards. Abi took some LSD but Rita became frightened and ran out of the house. It only seems like yesterday.

As she got back into bed, Rita also thought about Colin. How did she end up with him? Their loveless marriage trundling on, when they hardly said a word to each other. Was there once a time when she loved him, she wondered? There must have been something, but she had never been very successful with blokes. They were often too bossy and controlling. Now Bill was different, she was comforted by his kindness this evening when she got upset about Abi. She'd not felt that from a man for ages. He was a decent bloke. Not many of them around.

Rita mulled all this over, her head weighed down with the past, present and future. Eventually she fell asleep.

～ Thirty Six ～

The following morning, Gayle remained sullen, got up and made herself some toast, whilst Dean watched cartoons on TV in the back room.

"I don't understand. What made you start taking this stuff?" Rita said to Gayle. She was unable to mention drugs outright.

"Your dad's bound to find out sooner or later. You won't be able to hide it from him."

"I'm not trying to hide *anything*," Gayle retaliated, scowling as she spread jam on her toast.

"You've got to try and get help, Gayle. Can't you see?" Rita pleaded.

"I'll manage," Gayle replied even more determinedly.

"You won't."

"I can, mother. Just don't fucking keep on about it."

"You'll do yourself some damage. Think about Dean."

"Don't be stupid. You don't know what you're talking about."

"Gayle, these drugs are dangerous. I've seen it happen."

"Oh yeah," Gayle grinned cockily, "you've seen it on the fucking telly about the druggies? You're an expert now are you?" she sneered.

"You've got to do something about it," Rita exploded. "You're not bringing this stuff back here."

"Mummy, what's up?" Dean's croaky voice interrupted them.

They both looked down and saw him standing by the kitchen door in his pyjamas.

Gayle turned and ran upstairs to her room crying, "I've had enough of this, I'm gonna have a bath."

"And don't forget the Housing this morning!" Rita shouted up at her before bending down to her grandson.

"Is mummy off on one again?" he whispered, knowingly. Rita smiled.

"She'll be OK. Shall I do you a boiled egg with some soldiers?"

"Yes please, nan," he said. Rita kissed his head and gave him a cuddle.

"Come on then, let's have some breakfast and then we'd better get you to school."

~ Thirty Seven ~

Since his spell in hospital Leo had gone to ground again. Nobody had seen him and Bill had tried calling round to his flat but got no reply. Then out of the blue there was a message on Bill's voice mail.

"He's asked us to meet him at Rosa's on Friday," Bill told Rita on the phone.

"He says it's about the dog."

"Maybe there's going to be a pay out!" she said gleefully.

"I doubt it but you never can tell with Leo. Will you let Abi know?"

Rita hesitated. "I'd rather not," she replied brusquely.

"You two still not speaking to each other?"

There was a silence on the phone and Bill detected that their set-to was still not resolved. "OK," he sighed, "I'll give her a ring."

*   *   *

Bill arranged for everyone to meet up at the cafe. He was the first to arrive. Although it was still not quite December, Rosa had already put their Christmas decorations up. She prided herself on being the first to do so in Hastings. By the counter the aged Christmas tree had been wheeled out again and the big faded Merry Christmas banner hung on the wall. The place felt quite cosy as it was especially cold outside. Abi and Millie turned up soon after.

"I can't stay long," Abi said as they took off their coats and gloves. He asked them if they'd like some drinks. Millie smiled and said that she wanted a hot chocolate.

"It's turned freezing cold," Bill remarked.

"Yes, I've got me socks on," sparkled Millie, putting out her leg to show Bill her red woolly warmers.

"Very nice colour, they must keep you warm."

Soon after, Rita came in and Bill felt uneasy that another spat might ensue between the two women. Rita bent over rather solemn faced and gave Millie a peck on the cheek but ignored Abi altogether. "All right, auntie?"

"Well I've been better. I've been having the dizzies lately."

"Oh dear."

Rita sat down, stiff with the cold whilst Abi sulkily sipped her coffee. You could cut the atmosphere between them with a knife. Bill ordered Rita a coffee and took out a flyer about a Christmas do at the community centre. He showed it to Abi and Millie looked over her shoulder.

"What's this?" asked Millie.

"A Christmas Dance."

"Will they be doing the foxtrot? I love that."

"I expect so," Bill smiled.

"And the tango," Millie continued, "I was always very good at that as well."

"Were you?"

"Oh yes, wasn't I, Abi?"

"So I hear," she replied, pouting.

"What do you think? Bill asked.

"I'll come!" Millie was enthusiastic.

"No you won't," Abi glared at her.

"Why not?" Millie asked, her eyes widening.

"Because you'll make a scene and get us all chucked out."

"No I won't," Millie looked hurt.

"We could all help keep an eye, couldn't we, Rita?" Bill suggested.

"Yes of course we could," agreed Rita drinking her coffee. "You'd be no trouble, auntie, would you?"

"Oh no, not me," Millie replied sweetly.

For a little while they all sat in silence, except Millie who noisily supped her mug of hot chocolate, eyeing everyone as she did so.

"Now come on you two," Bill said looking across at Abi and Rita. "This is really silly – you both not talking."

His plea was quite heartfelt and it struck a chord with Millie.

"You just want to knock their heads together," she joked. "That's what I used to do. Crack!" She clapped her hands together and laughed out loud.

"Anyway, I'm off to the loo," she stood up and pushed past Abi.

"Will she make it?" Rita asked, looking over her shoulder as Millie almost broke into a sprint for the toilet.

"She's been pretty good lately, those pills help," replied Abi.

"That's good," said Rita.

"She's not a bad old stick," Abi said.

"Oh she's a lovely person," agreed Rita, "I suppose it's what old age can do to you."

"She's the same old Auntie Millie underneath though," Abi said. "She'd do anything for you if she could."

Bill looked on rather relieved that the two women were talking again.

"More coffee?" he asked, thinking that their delicate reconciliation needed supporting.

"I'd better just check if she's OK," Abi sighed, going off to the toilet.

Rita smiled at Bill. "I don't know how Abi copes sometimes. It's constant, twenty-four seven."

Bill nodded, "Yes, it must be difficult not to have a life of your own."

Just then through the cafe window, they spotted Leo arriving. After his usual sing-song entrance and hug for Rosa, he swaggered over to their table, removing his scarf, he left his overcoat on and sat down with them.

"Hello all."

"So you've recovered then. We heard that you'd been in hospital," Rita enquired.

"Me? Yeah, I'm as fit as a fiddle now."

"So was it what you said?" Bill asked.

"Yeah, angina. So they gave me some pills and this." He pulled out a puffer from his coat pocket to show them in case they didn't believe him.

Abi and Millie returned from the toilet. Millie was singing to herself, '*I'm In The Mood For Love.*'

"Oh look what the cat dragged in," Abi jeered, ready to have a go at Leo about the money.

"Well it's a dog actually," smiled Leo.

"What do you mean?" asked Bill.

"Come and have a look," urged Leo and pointed over to the window overlooking the seafront. Just outside the cafe and tied to a lamp post was their greyhound. They all got up to see.

"Is that Fly By Knight?" asked Bill.

"Hasn't he got long legs," said Millie. "Poor thing, he must be cold out there."

"Ah, isn't he lovely," cooed Rita.

"Don't tell me, you've brought him down here for a holiday?" quipped Bill.

"Well not exactly. More retirement really," Leo began to explain. "You see that business with the prize money." He began to sound a bit shifty again and he noticed that they were all looking at him rather po-faced. "Well it really wasn't my fault. Terry the trainer took more than his fair share and said that it was expenses – vet bills what have you." Bill shook his head despondently.

"I tried to press him," continued Leo, "but he disappeared and now he's in the nick, on remand."

"In prison?" Rita looked shocked.

"Yes, fraud," Leo confirmed. He was involved in some money laundering racket."

"I might have guessed it," Bill said, folding his arms and feeling justified about his scepticism all along. "So that's the end of us seeing our money back then."

"But does that mean that he's all ours now as we're the co-owners?" Abi asked with renewed interest, peering at the dog tethered to the post.

"That's exactly right," Leo nodded.

"Well we can race him ourselves then and take *all* the profit," she added, her eyes lighting up.

"Ah, unfortunately not at the moment," Leo pulled up a chair and they all sat down again, except Millie, still concerned that the dog was out in the cold.

"You see, he's had to be temporarily retired from racing."

"Retired?" they echoed.

"Yes I'm afraid so. He's got something wrong with his back legs."

"Oh sod it, I knew there'd be a catch," Abi cursed.

"So what are you going to do with him?" Bill asked.

"Well that's it you see," said Leo, "technically he's ours but we can't afford to put him in kennels, so I was going to take him to one of those animal rescue places. Then I thought, no, I'd better let you all decide. You never know, he might recover and then we can try and race him again. Although he'll need some treatment and to be honest, I haven't got the cash at the moment."

Abi got up and joined Millie looking out of the window. The dog seemed quite content, staring back at them.

"We could take him home with us," Millie suggested to Abi.

"No we can't, remember we've got a cat," Abi said firmly. "Anyway I've got enough to contend with looking after you without a greyhound as well."

"It would be company," Millie said.

"No!" Abi repeated.

"Oh, he's so sweet. Our Dean would love him," Rita said, tilting her head coyly on one side, "but," she sighed, "Colin would go potty if I turned up with him, what with our Gayle being with us."

"It's a shame isn't it," said Leo, "and he's such a nice dog. So good natured."

"Well why don't you have him then?" Bill asked bluntly.

"Ah, I'm afraid I can't, matey. I'm allergic to dogs. I start wheezing and coughing. It's the same with cats. They just set me off."

"Oh aye?" Bill looked at him suspiciously. "That's very convenient."

"It's absolutely true, honest." Leo gave one of his little nervous laughs.

"I could have one of my attacks at any time," he said slightly coughing as if to demonstrate. And anyway, you've seen the size of my flat."

"What about you, Bill?" asked Rita finally. "Could you take him in?"

"Me? No way. I'm not taking responsibility. He'll have to go to the rescue home or something."

"But look," Rita implored "we can't just dump him."

"We won't be," Bill argued, "they'll look after him. They'll find him a good home. You're all getting daft and sentimental. It's not practical to take him on."

"We could take him for walks," Millie offered, "couldn't we, Abi?"

"I suppose so. Yeah, we could."

"And Bill, we could all chip in towards the costs," Rita proposed.

Bill felt that he was being pressed into a corner.

"I'm not really a dog person and look at the size of him, my flat's not very big you know."

"But you're on your own, Bill," Leo chipped in.

"You can keep quiet, this was all your mess in the first place," Bill hit back.

"I was just saying … " Leo started,

"Well don't!"

Rita, even more determined, tried a softer approach. "Bill,

what about a trial period with him staying with you? We'll all share the costs of food, vet bills and everything. Don't let's put him away," she pleaded.

"Come on Billy boy," Millie joined in. "A dog's a man's best friend. Isn't that right, Abi?"

"In some cases their only friend," Abi smiled.

Leo got up. "Look, this is rather unfair on Bill. He's said that he doesn't want to take on the dog and we should respect his decision. Maybe I shouldn't have come here and caused this problem. So why don't I just take him down to that rescue place?" Leo got up, made a move to leave and Bill was confused as to why he was defending his position.

"Oh dear," Rita sighed, "that's such a shame."

"OK, Ok," said Bill reluctantly, "I'll take him in and give it a go. But only for a little while, mind," holding up his hand to emphasise the point.

Rita leant over and gave him a kiss and Millie came over and hugged him.

"You're a lovely man you are," she said, "a lovely man."

"But I want it all sorted out properly, mind – everyone paying towards his keep, all right, including any vet bills?"

"Absolutely matey, no question." Leo quickly sat down again.

They all went outside the cafe and Leo undid Fly By Knight's lead from the lamp post and handed him over to Bill. The dog seemed to be enjoying all the attention that he was getting from everyone, as Rita and Millie bent down and stroked him.

"We'll have to give him a proper name," suggested Rita.

"He's got one already, Fly By Knight," said Abi.

"No, that's his racing name. Let's give him a new one, a personal one, now that he's ours."

"Won't he get confused?" asked Abi.

"We don't have to do it now. Let's all think about it shall we?" suggested Bill.

"I'm very excited. I've never owned a dog before," enthused Rita.

"We did once," said Abi, "and it pooed everywhere."

"Oh thanks," Bill, said glumly.

"Well I'd better be off," Leo made a move to leave. "When shall we meet up again to sort things out?"

"There's a Christmas Dance coming up at the community centre soon. We're all going," said Rita.

"I'm coming!" Millie chipped in.

"No you're not," Abi reminded her.

"A dance. Great. I'll be there," said Leo.

As they all waved each other goodbye and headed off. Bill was left with the dog. He gripped the lead tightly and he and the greyhound looked at each other. It had been a long time since he'd had a dog; in fact not since he was a child. "Redundant – on the scrapheap like me, eh?" he spoke to the animal.

"Come on then, let's take you home." They walked together along the seafront and surprisingly Bill felt in a good mood.

～ Thirty Eight ～

Bill sparked awake, startled by a noise as though someone had broken in, but then realised it was just the ancient central heating system, knocking and creaking into action, sounding like an old river boat at high tide. He got up, had a quick shower and drank some coffee. Fly had been living with him for a little while now and they were getting used to each other. Bill had wondered how the racer would settle down to being a house dog. He still felt resentful towards Leo about taking him in, particularly when he realised that the dog was not fully house trained; sometimes he would return home to find little puddles on the floor. However with Fly's endearing, docile manner – constantly sniffing around him and lifting his head up for attention – it was not difficult for Bill to feel anything but a growing affection for his new companion. In a corner of the living room Bill had made up a bed for him from an old duvet. The dog had also commandeered a rolled up pair of his socks to chew.

After breakfast, Bill took Fly for a walk. It was a cold morning and he tightened his scarf as they left the house. Fly pulled his lead gently towards Alexandra Park. With winter starting to set in, there were widening gaps between the branches of the trees and the sun came bursting through, bouncing playfully over the rooftops of the houses in Lower Road. The silvery carpet of frost spread out across the grass. 'What a wonderful park this is,' Bill thought.

Later Bill went to the school. On his way to Mustafa's classroom he was amused by a sign stuck on a gigantic piece of cardboard packaging '*2 R needs this to build a rocket!*' Collecting Mustafa from class they settled down to read, '*Horrid Henry's Birthday Party.*' Mustafa was not progressing very quickly but did like the character of Henry.

"What have you been doing in class this week?" asked Bill.

The boy shrugged his shoulders as usual, but then suddenly enthused,

"We saw lots of fossils from thousands of years ago." his eyes lit up.

"That's good," said Bill, "we can learn a lot from them about what kind of creatures existed in prehistoric times."

"Our teacher is taking us down to the beach soon to look for some near the cliffs." They carried on reading together whilst a class upstairs were practising a performance of the song, '*Food Glorious Food.*'

"My father is reading the book that you gave him," he said.

"It's a very big book," Bill said.

"Yes, he reads it in the evening when I have gone to bed."

Bill sat back after their session, pleasantly surprised that Mustafa had read through several pages without much prompting from Bill. At the end of the session, Mustafa stood by the table and grinned at Bill. He drew something out of his trouser pocket holding it in his clenched fist.

"Shall I show you a magic trick?" his eyes twinkled.

Bill smiled, "Go on then."

He opened up his right hand and disclosed a small white ball.

"I can make this disappear and reappear in my left hand," he said confidently.

Mustafa then shuffled his hands in front of Bill and opened them to reveal that the ball had vanished. Another deft shuffle and sure enough the ball reappeared in his left hand.

"How did you do that?" Bill was genuinely impressed.

"My father showed me, he does magic at home."

"Your dad's very clever."

"Yes I know. He can do many tricks and he is going to teach me all of them."

"So you'll become a magician?"

"Maybe, if I am good enough one day."

Bill smiled as Mustafa went back to his class.

∼ Thirty Nine ∼

At work Rita had just gone for a break when one of the regular customers burst into the store, jabbering, "Have you heard? I've just seen it on the telly. Woolies! They're finished! All the stores are closing down!" His face flushed with excitement, his eyes almost popping out of his head, it sounded like a desperate call to abandon ship – shoppers and children first.

"What?" Rita looked at him in disbelief.

"That's what they said on the news. They can't find a buyer and its £385 million in debt, they reckon."

Rita and her workmate Pat stood there stunned at the news, holding some packs of stationery. Everyone was shocked, still expecting some takeover to eventually save the day. Pat was seething. Again, management had not told the staff what was going on. They both went straight up to the office to get an explanation, but found it locked. They asked Tony the deputy manager where Kate was and he said that she had not turned up today. Rita grilled him about the announcement, but he was none the wiser. During the afternoon, Rita was relieved to see Dennis, their old manager, arrive. He announced that Kate would not be back. She had left the company suddenly for personal reasons. Dennis held a staff meeting and confirmed that Woolworths, now almost a hundred years old, would be closing and that the Hastings branch's last day of business would be 3rd January 2009. There was a gasp from everyone. Dennis handled it as well as he could; he was very aware of the impact it would have on everyone's lives. Feelings ran high and there was a lot of anger and tears as to why the company had kept them all in the dark. A few wanted to walk out there and then. "Why didn't they have the guts to tell us what was happening?" "What a thing to do to us and just before Christmas." "I've been working here for over thirty years," one old hand said.

The next day they were all still reeling from the shock that their jobs were to go. The eighty-year old Hastings branch received a stream of older customers and their families coming in to share their sorrow for the staff. "I've been coming here since I was a child," cried an elderly woman. As the end of an era, dawned an even greater sense of camaraderie grew amongst the workers. It was also strengthened in adversity when a few customers, relishing in the store's downfall, jibed, snidely, "I've heard you're going to lose your job."

At home Rita watched the news on the telly and it was confirmed that 27,000 Woolworths staff across Britain were to be made redundant. The figures shocked her and made her blood boil that nothing further could have been done to save the high street store. She had worked there since 1983. Despite her moans, it had been like a second family. She was furious too at the store's critics, those that claimed it was just a giant out-dated sweet shop and failed to keep up with the times. So far Rita had hardly given a second thought to what she would do next. Would she be able to get another job? She hoped so; going to work kept her sane from family life.

Rita bumped into Bill in town. He offered his sympathies and having been through the mill of redundancy himself he tried to be positive for Rita's sake. The local council were providing job advice and support, but Rita was not yet ready to do anything about her future. "They're closing, hundreds of branches by the New Year," she told him.

"We're in a recession, Rita," Bill reminded her, matter of

fact. "It was MFI the other week and there'll be more to come I'm afraid," he said, sounding like a prophet of doom. "But don't worry, pet. Look you've got all this experience and years in retail. You'll get something for sure. It's people like me who are the problem. Too qualified that's my trouble. I don't fit in."

Bill had Fly with him and they looked content in each others company.

"How's it going?" Rita asked as she patted the dogs head; its long tongue hanging down from his mouth, looking up at her.

"Aye, we're doing OK, like. Aren't we pal?" Fly turned his attention to Bill. "We're just off to the beach for a walk. It's good exercise for me too."

Rita nodded and continued to stroke Fly's smooth coat.

"I've discovered he likes sardines," Bill smiled. "And I've also bought him some greyhound nuts. Getting him off that racing diet that they give them for speed."

"We'll club together soon to help out, Bill."

"Aye, the sooner the better. I can't afford to be out of pocket. Things are tight enough as it is."

∼ Forty ∼

A couple of days later Bill was walking Fly along the seafront at Hastings near Rock-a-Nore, by the fishing huts. The smell of the sea and the fish market nearby reminded him of when he was a small child during the 1950s. The regular Sunday morning outings along the coast at Sea Houses, Northumberland, with his father and elder brother were a welcome respitefor his dad after a gruelling week down the pit that forever punished his lungs and would eventually finish him off.

They strolled further along the esplanade towards the pier. Bill looked up at the leaden clouds racing across the sky. The bracing wind took his breath away and buffeted them like a punch bag. As they stepped down to the beach, Fly seemed tentative, almost holding back; his spindly legs were awkwardly off balance on the pebbles until they reached a patch of sand. Bill wondered if it might be too early to do so, but he let him off his lead and the dog bobbed down to the sea edge. Fly keenly watched the waves pound the shingle and then he backed off as the foam rose and crashed before him. Bill looked on nervously, not knowing what he'd do if the creature just made a dog track bolt for it. Suddenly a bigger wave struck the shore and chased after Fly. He yelped and Bill laughed as the dog retreated back behind him for protection, eyeing the unpredictable surge.

Bill shivered in the December cold, "Come on boy, let's get moving. That's enough for today." He re-attached the dog's lead and they headed for the promenade. Walking along the top, the wind still pushing hard against them, Bill faintly heard his name being called from across the road. It was Mustafa's father, Jamal, leaning out of the first floor open window, waving to attract his attention. Bill crossed the road, went over to the house and stood just below the window.

"I really enjoyed your book, the '*Ragged Trousered Philanthropists*.' It is similar to today with building work," he said, laughing and gesturing into the house where he was working. "Our boss is another Hunter," he said, referring to one of the characters in the novel. "He is always cutting down our materials and making us go faster." Bill had trouble hearing him due to the wind and the noise of the traffic, so Jamal had to speak up and repeat some of what he said.

"That's it!" Bill smiled and agreed. "You've got the picture."

"I see that you have a new friend," Jamal said, looking at the greyhound.

"Yes, my new companion, for a while at least," Bill nodded.

"What's he called?"

"Fly By Knight," said Bill and stroked the dog's head.

"I will tell Mustafa, he loves dogs. He wants me to get him one but they are not animals we usually have as pets and are very expensive to keep."

"Too true," Bill agreed, reminding him that he must arrange to collect money from the others for his keep.

"Well, maybe Mustafa can help me take this one for a walk sometime."

"Oh yes he would enjoy that."

"Is he reading much at home?" Bill asked.

"A little," Jamal said, raising his eyebrows.

"I'll see him next week and I'll try and persuade him to do more."

"He likes coming to see you at school, Bill. I am sure that he will improve."

"Let's hope so," Bill agreed.

"Well, I'd better be off," bracing himself for the walk back home.

The two men bid each other farewell and Bill and the dog headed off along the seafront.

∼ Forty One ∼

"There's a few bargains here," Bill saw Rita at the checkout.

He had just found a blues compilation CD in the Woolies £5 closing down sale and although chuffed at the surprise discovery, he was also feeling slightly guilty and disloyal in benefiting from the situation, given what was happening to Rita and her workmates.

"It's getting worse down at the Job Centre with this recession," Bill said.

"There are more people now chasing fewer jobs. I've given up thinking that I'll get anything in my line. It's the youngsters though, that are hit worse. They'll have to leave the area to get work, just like it was in Newcastle when the pits and ship building went. Even the local language schools down here are feeling the pinch."

"Do you fancy a coffee, Bill? I'm just going for my break – my treat!"

It was cold outside and they nipped over to a café near the store. They sat on bar stools by the window overlooking the shoppers ambling along the street.

"Won't your husband mind, you and me, having a coffee together?" Bill grinned.

"Oh him, we're like ships in the night. He don't ask about me and I don't ask about him." Rita curled her hands around her cup for warmth. "So, you were saying there's still nothing going on the job front?"

Bill shook his head in resignation. "It's funny really. I've felt quite guilty not going out to work and earning money. I've worked all my life."

"Well it's hardly your fault is it? Anyway I don't know why you don't just drop out, like they did in the sixties, Bill. Especially now that we're nearly all reaching our own sixties," Rita chuckled at the thought.

"What do you mean?"

"Well you know, stop chasing these duff jobs that must be driving you mad. All this pressure you put yourself through – you should be enjoying yourself. Take it easy."

"Lazing around, you mean?" He looked hurt.

"No not at all. Having a bit of fun – let your hair down."

"I'm not ready for that, man. I've still got work in me. I still feel I'm in my prime. And I need the money!"

"Yes, me too, I suppose," Rita sighed, feeling that she had defeated her own case. "If I didn't get out of the house every day, I'd go up the wall. But I must admit the thought of another ten years on a checkout makes my stomach turn. Anyway, Bill, you're free and more your own man. Don't you think you've done your bit – paid your dues?"

"I may have paid my way but when I get it, my work pension will be nothing like they said it would be. In any case are you saying I should just give up?" Bill looked rattled again.

"No, Bill, but there's more to life. Anyway I know what you mean."

"When I think about it, I've worked since I was sixteen apart from a short break after having our Gayle," Rita mused. "What would I do if I didn't have a job? It's frightening really." she said shrugging her shoulders. "It'll be the first time I've been on the dole."

"Tell me about it. But could you afford not to work?"

"No way!" Rita was alarmed at the thought. "I'm not doing it just for pin money. Colin spends cash like there's no tomorrow and Gayle ... well!"

Rita lowered her voice. "To be honest we've got debts. Lots of them."

"So, you'll have to start looking around soon enough then. Anyway, how's things going at work?"

"Some of the girls have already been poached by a new firm opening up but they didn't want me! Woolies have set up support for people to take exams in maths and English to help them get new jobs – they're good like that."

Bill nodded but he wasn't impressed with the situation that the staff were in. Rita continued. "Deliveries have stopped altogether. As you can see we've closed the upper sales floor. But we've still got shoplifters. There won't be anything worth nicking soon! Pat at work reckons we could both get a job at Iceland just along the way, but I don't know what it is ... I just can't seem to get motivated."

"Aye, it's not easy," Bill commiserated, "particularly if you've been working at the same place for so long."

"That's it really. I don't think I can still quite believe it's happening. I'm thinking that at the last minute someone's going to come along and save Woolies and we'll just carry on as usual."

Bill looked at her rather pitifully, but managed to restrain himself from launching into another anti-capitalist tirade.

"And you'll miss your mates too I suppose?" he said softly.

"Yes, I will. We all have a moan, but they're a great crowd."

Beginning to relax and taking another sip of coffee, Rita looked up at the clock, suddenly startled.

"Blimey look at the time," she quickly grabbed her bag. "I'd better get back or else they'll give me the boot even before Woolies goes down the pan."

∼ Forty Two ∼

On a chilly walk back from another fruitless visit to the Job Centre, Bill thought he would try some charity shops for a new overcoat. His present coat really wasn't warm enough and was looking worn. He meandered along Queens Road but had no luck. He also popped into Oxfam to see if there were any interesting books on the history shelves. A little further along the road outside a toy and model shop, he saw a small group of children. The two boys were about seven or eight and glued to the shop window with the older girl about twelve – perhaps their sister as she looked in charge of them. As Bill got nearer he heard the boys arguing between themselves. They were almost coming to blows as they tried to shove each other out of the way, scrambling for a better view of the Christmas display. Bill slowed down and looked at some of the model kits in the window, recalling how his own sons used to enjoy window shopping and making model planes.

"I saw it first," said the bigger one, pointing to the Combat Robot.

"No you didn't. It's mine," said the smaller of the two boys, his puffa jacket a size too big.

"It ain't fair. Tell him Kylie, he always wants what I've got."

The girl, busy texting, broke off, irritated by her brothers behaviour. "Look just shut up will 'yer. You're both getting on my nerves."

"But I've got to have it," he whined again.

"We'll have to see what Father Christmas says," the girl sighed, putting her hands gently on his shoulders. "It's up to him isn't it?" she spoke softly.

The boy quietened down. It was all there in front of him, but for the window, almost in his reach. "I've got to have it. I've got to," he groaned with frustration, his reddened face seemed on the verge of tears.

"Well you'll have to be patient. Mum's doing all she can for Christmas," the girl tried to comfort him again.

Bill had no idea of their family situation but was immediately reminded of a passage in 'The Ragged Trousered Philanthropists' where the character, Barrington, a key socialist figure in the novel, comes across a group of children of the men he works with, similarly ogling a Christmas window display in Mugsborough. In their case, the families were poverty stricken and the children were dreaming Santa Claus may bring them the expensive toys that they spotted. Bill was always moved by this episode in the book where Barrington, an independent and relatively wealthy young man, who champions justice for the working class magically comes to their rescue. He told them that it was lucky that he had bumped into them because as Father Christmas was getting old, he had appointed him as one of his helpers and that he had on him a list of what toys each child in front of him should get as a present which coincided with what he had overheard the children saying. The children were amazed as Barrington took them inside the shop and purchased each toy that they had longingly been drooling over. Bill thought to himself, still standing by the shop window, that this group of 21st Century Hastings kids had a similar ring about it. Bill thought that modern day consumerism could make kids feel that they must have everything but for many poor families it was just as out of reach as it was in Edwardian times, unless you got yourself into debt.

A moments silence was broken by the smaller boy taking a

swipe at the other as he was teased and he almost fell onto Bill.

"Stop it you two," their sister shrieked, grabbing their arms and hauling them off in another direction.

Bill walked down to the Reference Library at the Brassey Institute in Claremont to have a look through the local newspapers for a job. With Tressell's novel still ringing in his mind, he was thinking that the author himself probably tramped these streets and used the reading room, for researching his book or perhaps just to keep warm.

Today the place was busy, all the computers were taken up. Bill loosened his coat and scarf and settled into a corner. He began scanning the vacancies section of the local papers. Nothing doing. The slim pages of employment opportunities only contained positions that were well out of Bill's league. 'Get Christmas over with,' he thought, 'and see what the New Year brings.' A national newspaper headline was less optimistic: *'Mass Unemployment Forecast as Economy Plunges.'* Looking around the reading room, Bill observed mainly older people sitting in their regular seats huddled over newspapers at the table. Some looked as though they were in a similar position to him, searching for jobs but others were reading obituaries, gasping at the news of fuel bill rises or whiling away time doing crosswords before lunch. On the computers, youngsters were facebooking, googling, job searching or perhaps home sick and e-mailing their girlfriends and boyfriends back home in Warsaw, Turin, or Belgrade.

Bill put the Hastings Observer back on the rack with a heavy heart about whether he would ever work again. He looked out of the window down to Claremont and thought, 'Maybe it was time to move back home to Newcastle.' Why did he ever think that Hastings could be the promised land and where he would find a new life? He shrugged off the thought with his dead wife, Helen's voice cracking in with 'Away, Bill, man. You've made some good friends here. Just get on with it.'

It was lunchtime but Bill was trying to skip having a meal, partly to help lose some weight and also to save money. So, maybe an apple would do. He hurried down the stairs as he needed to get home for Fly and take him for a walk, particularly as he'd now got him more house trained. On the way he wondered whether he should give a Christmas card to Mustafa at school. 'Do you give Christmas cards to Muslims?' he wondered.

∼ Forty Three ∼

The Cliff End Community Centre Christmas dance; the usual suspects were there – the middle aged singles, groups of older women out for fun and a few families. Rita and Abi arrived early and bagged a small table at the back of the hall near the bar. Abi eventually conceded, and brought Millie along and she was there, proudly wearing her pearl necklace that unknown to her, Abi had nearly flogged.

Bob Marley's '*Jammin*' was playing loudly as they arrived but nobody was dancing yet. They each had to speak up to be heard and Rita was curious when Abi told her that she had finished with 'Spanish Villa,' Sherman.

"So what happened?"

"I just cried off on a date. Then I sent him a don't-call-me-I'll-call-you sort of text," Abi said casually. "I'm trying to cool it. I think he's got the message."

"But I thought you were keen on seeing his place in Spain and you said he was quite a bit of fun."

"Yeah I know but he does go on a lot about his mum."

"A mummy's boy?"

"I suppose so. Don't get me wrong I admire a man who looks after his old mum but, well you know it's all got a bit too much. It's as though she is always with us," Abi said.

"And there's his after shave. Urgh!" Abi squirmed. "It stinks to high heaven. I keep telling him, Sherman, it's too much. It's really overpowering."

"Maybe he's trying to bowl you over so he can have his wicked way with you," Rita grinned.

"I can still smell it now, talk about pungent, agh!" she shivered at the thought.

Rita smiled wryly, "Anybody else on the horizon, Abi?"

She shook her head, "Well I've been looking again on the dating web site, even in the local rag – lonely hearts. I must be desperate! Most of them look either like they're sixth formers or well past it."

"I thought you liked them young?" Rita laughed.

"I do, but you can't beat a bit of maturity, do you know what I mean? Someone you can have a good banter with and be on the same wavelength. It's much more relaxing. Most of the younger blokes I've been out with don't seem to have much up here." Abi tapped her forehead.

"But all right down below?" Rita grinned.

"You could say that!" They both giggled.

"What you two gabbling about?" Millie asked, sipping her drink and watching people getting up to dance.

"Men, auntie," Rita laughed.

"Oh them!" Millie raised her eyebrows. "They can be trouble they can, what with their train sets."

"Train sets?" Abi gave Rita a look.

"Yes," said Millie, "they don't know when to stop," she said and carried on looking at the dancers.

"So, what about your Gayle then? Things any better?"

"Not really," Rita sighed, "she's still in a full time strop and, well I've discovered something about her." Rita hesitated and with a serious look on her face, nudged forward to make herself heard, "Now don't fly off the handle, Abi but I think she's taking cocaine."

"Oh no," Abi cried, "are you sure?"

"Yes, that's where all her money has been going."

"Have you talked to her about it?"

"She just clams up and denies it's a problem but it's getting worse. I'm worried about her and I know it's costing her a bomb and me too for that matter."

"Do you mean the money that you won on the scratch card?"

"Yes, that's all gone now on bailing her out from this loan shark," Rita sighed. "I know that she'll be up to her eyes in debt again soon. I'm also worried about Dean?"

"Maybe I can help."

"I don't see how, Abi. You and her have never really hit it off have you?"

"No, I know that," Abi agreed, "but something's got to be done. Does Colin know anything about it?" Rita drank some wine and shook her head.

"No way, at least not yet. He'll hit the roof if he finds out. It's like walking on eggshells at home."

"Don't worry, Rita. We'll find a way somehow," Abi tried to reassure her.

Rita smiled and noticed from the corner of her eye that Bill had just arrived and was looking around for them.

"Bill!" Rita shouted out, standing up and waving to him over the sound of the Stones' 'Get Off My Cloud' which everyone was singing along to.

"Hello there. My, it's lively isn't it. What you all drinking?" asked Bill when he came over but hoping he wouldn't have to buy a full round.

"We're OK," said Rita.

"I'll have a thingy, young man," said Millie showing that her glass was empty.

"What's that?" Bill smiled.

"You know."

"I don't."

"Yes you do,"

"I don't." It was like a pantomime act.

"Auntie," Rita broke in, "it's got bubbles," she said giving her a clue.

"Martini," Millie said. Rita shook her head.

"Urm, rum – no I mean brandy!"

"When did brandy have bubbles in it?" Abi asked her.

"Cider."

"Auntie, you know that you're not allowed alcohol,"

"Aren't I?" Millie said all innocent.

"No," Abi said firmly. Millie was still holding up her empty glass to give to Bill but had now run out of ideas.

"It's orange with lemonade and a dash of ice, isn't it?" Rita reminded her.

"That's it. I'll have one of them."

"On the rocks, eh?" said Bill taking her glass up to the bar.

"Well I still like Martini," Millie mused. I used to like the adverts when the man used to climb through the window and leave a bottle in the young woman's bedroom while she was asleep."

"That was Milk Tray, auntie – the lady loves Milk Tray," Abi said gently.

"*Hands that do dishes can feel as soft as your face,*" Millie sang out spontaneously.

"Well you can't drink that either, it was for Fairy, washing up liquid."

"Yes, I know." Millie carried on gazing at the growing crowd on the dance floor, and despite the loud music, hummed to herself other themes from TV adverts.

When Bill returned with the drinks, Abi was already up dancing. Millie pointed her out on the dance floor with a couple of others gyrating to '*I'm In The Mood For Dancing.*'

"Look at her," Millie cried out, hoarsely, "making a spectacle of herself as usual."

Bill leaned forward, "Anyway, I thought you weren't allowed to come tonight."

Millie roared loudly, "I've been behaving myself," she winked.

Bill sat down next to Rita.

"Cheers," he said lifting up his pint of lager.

"She's a girl, isn't she?" Rita remarked above the music, watching Abi in full swing.

"She certainly knows how to enjoy herself," said Bill, looking at her strut around, eyes closed, moving hypnotically to the disco beat as more people piled onto the floor.

"You going to have a dance?" Bill asked Rita having to raise his voice above the music.

"Later, when I've had a few more of these," she said, pointing to her wine.

"How's things at home with your daughter?"

"Oh much the same. It's lovely having Dean there, but Gayle's a nightmare. I know that she's my daughter and I shouldn't say it but she is. She's just so self-centred. She gets it from her dad."

"What about Woolies," Bill asked, "how's it all going?"

"It's quite depressing really. The stock's run down even more and we're having a hard time with some customers, because they think we should be just giving things away for free. I had a go at one the other day – what have I got to lose? And do you know, we heard that with the closing down and selling up, Woolworths are making nearly £30 million a day!"

Bill nodded, "Well, it doesn't surprise me one bit, pet. When it comes down to it, the bosses have no loyalty to their workers. They'll drop you like a stone!"

"But we're like a family."

"Oh aye, when it suits them you are," Bill argued, "but now they're abandoning you all – on the streets. Sink or swim!"

"Anyway, I don't want to talk about work tonight. We're here to enjoy ourselves."

A new disc came on, Gloria Gaynor's '*I Will Survive*' and Abi with a group of other women on the dance floor began acting out the song in theatrical manner, mouthing the words.

Millie laughed, pointing her out again to Rita and Bill. They smiled and Bill asked Rita, "You and Abi OK now?"

"Yeah, we're fine. We're mates aren't we? We look after each other."

"That's good."

They just sat for a while with Millie looking around the hall.

"So, how you finding Hastings, Bill?"

"Aye, OK."

"Have you made many friends?"

"Well I've always been a bit of a loner, me. I like company but you know I like my own space too. Anyway I've got Fly now, he's become good company and he gets me out." Rita nodded and they both continued looking at the dancers.

"Well Bill," Rita beamed, "you've got all of us now, we're your mates."

Quiet unexpectedly, she leant over and gave him a kiss on his cheek. It was a nice surprise and Bill realised that since Helen had gone how much he missed a woman's company.

"Yes, I suppose I have." He began to blush and quickly finished the rest of his lager. Feeling a bit awkward, he asked Rita if she wanted another drink.

"Go on then," she said and he trotted over to the bar.

"What's his name?" Millie asked Rita, looking at Bill waiting to be served.

"Bill, that's Bill, you know we all meet up."

"Is he your bloke?" Millie asked.

"No, my husband's Colin. That's Bill, he's our pal."

"Your bit on the side, you mean!" Millie shrilled, "Does he light your fire?"

"Auntie Millie," Rita feigned outrage and laughed too.

When Bill returned with the drinks he was put out to see that Leo had arrived and was sitting in his seat at the table talking to Rita.

"Hello matey," he grinned at Bill, spotting his rather glum look. "It's OK, you don't need to get me one in. I've already bought my own pint," Leo said, raising it up from the table.

Abi had just returned from the dance floor and Bill was annoyed that he had to put his drink down and hunt for another chair for himself.

Leo was chatting quite merrily with Millie and she was roaring with laughter. With her high heels off, Abi was having a rest. Fanning herself with a beer mat with one hand, she was rubbing the underside of her foot with the other.

"What's up? Is it painful?" Rita asked.

"Yes, it is a bit. I think I might have a bunion. Maybe I should go to see a chiropodist."

"Podiatrist," Rita corrected her.

"What?"

"They call themselves podiatrists these days. You should go. They make you feel like you are walking on air."

"Ooo," said Mille.

"So, how's our dog – boy wonder?" Leo asked Bill.

"Fly's OK now, but you didn't tell me that he wasn't house trained!"

"Fly? Leo smiled, ignoring Bill's remark, "Are you sticking with that name then?

"I think it's a nice name," said Rita. "It has a certain ring about it. What do you think, Abi?"

"Whatever," Abi replied, still attending to her foot.

"I'd have preferred Clint myself," Leo remarked.

"Oh that's a good one," Millie chipped in, "like that actor, Clint Eastman, on the films."

"Eastwood," Abi corrected her.

"It's a bit posey," Bill remarked. "In any case as I seem to have been lumbered looking after him, it's simpler. It's what he knows, like."

"I agree," said Rita, "it's only fair. And we did say that we'd all chip in towards the food and help take him for walks."

"Who, Bill?" Leo joked.

"Don't be silly," Rita said. "So, Bill how do you want to do this? Weekly pay up from each of us and that could go towards the vet bills too?"

"Aye, OK, that seems all right. I've had to buy him a new lead, bowl and I think we should get some pet insurance. You never know."

"Yeah, fine" said Leo. Abi nodded too, putting her shoe back on.

"OK," said Rita, pleased that her business like manner had

got things sorted out. "I could do a couple of evening walks during the week."

"We could take him for bit of a run," offered Millie, "I love dogs."

"Alright," Abi sighed, "we'll do a turn together too."

"What about you, Leo?" asked Rita but he was distracted by spotting a young woman at the next table who he knew from art classes and was smiling back at him.

"Oh yes, walking the dog," he replied rather preoccupied, "whatever fits in with Bill, just let me know and I'll pop round."

"When do you think we'll be able to race him again?" asked Abi.

"We should get him checked out by the vet first to see if he's fit enough," suggested Rita.

"Well there's no hurry," replied Bill. "I think we should wait a while and let him get settled in. All this change, he's had a traumatic time of it."

"Traumatic!" Leo jeered, suddenly paying more attention. "Don't make me laugh, the dog's a racer. He can't wait to be back on the track. We should get him going again as soon as he's fit enough. We're losing money."

"You were all for taking him down to the animal rescue the other week! He needs time," snapped Bill. "He's been pushed from pillar to post lately."

Rita nodded in agreement. Sensing he was losing the argument, Leo turned to Millie.

"Come on then, auntie, let's have a dance." Before she could reply, Leo grabbed her hand and led her on to the dance floor for Rod Stewart's 'Do You Think I'm Sexy.'

"He really fancies himself," Bill jibed, still seething at his attitude over Fly.

"He's OK," Abi said, "look, Millie's happy."

"He's just doing that for effect when he doesn't get his own way. I tell you, we've still got to watch him."

"Oh come on, Bill, don't get yourself in a state. Let's all have another drink," Rita offered and went to the bar.

"Look at her," Abi said to Bill watching Millie dancing away and enjoying herself.

"Has she always been so good humoured?" Bill asked.

"Yes but she has her moments now, poor love, when she gets really confused and frustrated. Wanting to say something but not knowing what. It's always worse first thing in the morning in getting her washed and dressed. Trying to persuade her to have a shower is murder! She screams the flat down. People in the flats must think I'm mistreating her. It's very upsetting."

"But you're getting help now aren't you?" asked Bill.

"No, not really. We've got good neighbours and Rita helps out when she can."

"Don't you think that you should ask social services for support?"

"That's what everyone is telling me, especially after she went missing."

"She always seems fine when she's out with us," Bill remarked.

"Yeah, it's funny isn't it? Maybe it's more stimulating for her than hanging around the flat – keeps her occupied and amused or something. Perhaps it's Leo's captivating charm!" she giggled.

"Oh that!" Bill supped the rest of his pint.

Rita came back from the bar with a tray of drinks and put them on the table.

"Well this is fun," she said, sitting down, "all of us out together and Millie enjoying herself too." She lifted her glass up as a toast and Abi and Bill joined in.

"Had a dance yet, Bill?" Abi asked.

"No fear!" he replied firmly, appearing to dig himself further into his chair.

The evening carried on, they all drank some more and Rita and Abi danced together. Leo moved on from dancing with Millie to the younger set who had been sitting at the next table. They all made a circle and each person took it in turn, including Leo, to show off their dancing skills. Bill looked on contemptuously. "What a dick head," he muttered to himself.

But Leo certainly was in his element. Rita returned to the table for a drink, panting.

"Oh, that's better," she gulped, wiping her brow. "Come on, Bill, we're all having fun."

"No, I'm OK, really."

"Are you sure?"

"Oh yes, don't mind me."

The evening carried on, the raffle was called and Rita was soon back on the dance floor. As Bill looked on she blew him a kiss and without thinking he returned it. The tunes were hotting up for the finale with *'Ring My Bell'* and Marvin Gaye's *'Sexual Healing.'* Then Rita wouldn't take no for an answer from Bill. She tugged him up from his chair on to the dance floor and clutched him close.

Bill was surprised at feeling quite dizzy and held on to Rita, more to stop himself falling over. He felt very hot and wished he had taken his jacket off. Rita moved closer to him and her head rested gently on his chest. Bill could smell a touch of lavender perfume. His chin was now resting lightly on top of her head as they moved around in a slow circle until the song finished. Then the DJ called on everyone for the final dance of the evening. The familiar fanfare of The Beatles' *'All You Need Is Love'* drew an unruly surge on to the dance floor.

Before he could escape, Bill was grabbed by Rita and Abi and they pulled him forward towards a wide circle of dancers. As he reached the centre he felt even more wobbly. He hazily recognised Leo and Millie but it was a good job Rita and Abi still had hold of him. Now they were moving into the circle and back again to the sing along chorus:

"All You Need Is Love
Dah, dah, dah – dah – dah
All You Need Is Love
Dah, dah, dah – dah – dah"

On the second round Bill spontaneously introduced his own lyrics as his head just spun and spun.

"All You Need Is Love

BOLLOCKS!
All You Need Is Love
BOLLOCKS!"

The gang cheered at his loud drunken outburst.

Then things went wobbly for Bill. The flashing disco lights seemed to phase into each other. The Beatles became more psychedelic and disjointed. Bill found himself on the floor looking up at Rita, Abi, Millie and Leo who were peering down at him.

"I think he's passed out," said Rita.

"I'm not surprised," said Abi.

"Blimey, he's well and truly pissed," laughed Leo.

All Bill remembered next was being outside and Leo holding him up.

"This makes a change," Bill slurred.

Leo smiled. "Yeah, OK matey. We just need to get you home now."

Bill suddenly rushed over to a handrail facing the sea and then threw up in the gutter.

Leo looked on quite passively and trying to take Bill's mind off things he asked him if he'd seen the piece on the TV News about a teacher being sacked for telling her class that Santa Claus didn't exist.

"Agh," Bill wretched again. "This is end of the world … "

"No it's not Bill, it's Hastings," Leo chuckled.

"Oh dear," Rita said, seeing Bill bent over.

"He's had a real skinful, hasn't he?"

" 'Fraid so," Leo agreed. "Bill did you drive down here?" he asked.

Sitting on a bench overlooking the sea and wiping his lips with some tissues that Rita had just given him, Bill nodded and pointed to the nearby car park.

"OK, give me your keys and I'll drop you home." Bill was about to protest but as another wave of nausea welled up he handed the keys to Leo. Rita helped him over to the car. She got in the back seat as Leo said he'd drop her off home too. Bill, still bleary eyed, sat uneasily in the front seat with the window wide open and Leo's erratic driving through town made him feel even sicker.

"How have Abi and Millie got home?" asked Leo.

"Cab," replied Rita, tightly, "like I should have done," feeling frozen from the open window and jittery at the speed that Leo was doing.

Bill suddenly awoke from his brief slumber and began singing heartily:

"*Oh me lads, ye should have seen us gannin'*
Passin' the foaks upon the road just as they wor stannin';
Thor wes lots o' lads an' lasses there, aal wi' smilin' faces,
Gannin' alang the Scotswood Road, to see the Blaydon Races."

Leo laughed at his drunken Geordie twang.

"Are you OK, Bill?" Rita giggled, reaching forward and putting her hand on his shoulder. He nodded and continued singing as the car sped through town.

They soon dropped Rita at her house.

"Hope you're feeling better tomorrow, Bill," she said as she got out of the car and bent down closer to see how he looked. His eyes were shut and his singing now was more a mumble:

"*We flew across the Chain Bridge reet into Blaydon toon. The bellman he was caalin' there – they caal him Jacky Broon. Aw saw him talking to sum cheps, an' them he was persuading ... *"

"See him safely home, won't you," Rita laughed and waved to Leo.

"Of course I will, don't worry."

Back at his flat, Bill rallied round enough to let Fly out to do his business while Leo made some coffee for both of them, despite complaining loudly that it was cheap instant. Bill then sat in an armchair stroking Fly, now lying sprawled out in front of him with his tail drumming gently on the carpet. The dog's calmness helped to settle Bill.

Handing him a mug of black coffee, Leo sat opposite him. "He's taken a real shine to you, Bill."

"Oh aye, he's a good dog all right, aren't you?" He bent over again and patted Fly. The dog responded by lifting his head up, whilst Bill sat back in the chair, his head still spinning.

"Yeah, he's settled down very well with you," Leo smiled, sipping his coffee.

"But somehow, what with his gammy leg, I don't think we'll see him on the track again. I reckon I got a bit carried away when I said how much money we'd make." Turning to Bill he saw that he'd dozed off again. He too closed his eyes.

A little while later they both came round.

"Feeling any better?" Leo asked.

"Kind of. I'm not feeling sick at least," he drank some more coffee. "Thanks for getting me back."

"No problem. You've got a nice pad here I must say," Leo was looking at the tidy bookshelves compared to his own place.

"Yes it's home," Bill agreed.

"But don't you still miss the Tyneside?"

"Yes I do sometimes, but funnily enough I'm feeling more settled down here now."

"Well I admire you starting a new life. It's very brave. Every time that I've tried it's gone belly up," he laughed.

"Oh aye?" Bill was struck by Leo's candidness.

"Yeah, one thing or another has scuttled it and I've ended up back where I've started. It's a bit like snakes and ladders really."

"Well it's not a bad place – Hastings," Bill said.

"No I suppose not, but you know when you're young and you've got plans –big plans!" Leo paused as though he was reflecting on it all and he slowly sipped his coffee. "You think that the world's at your finger tips. I know I was headstrong and was full of ideas – still am really. And then things just seem to slip away, people let you down then you let yourself down." Leo seemed to look rather sorry for himself.

"You haven't got any brandy by any chance have you, Bill? This coffee's gone cold."

"Yeah," Bill tried getting up too quickly.

"No, you stay there, matey. I'll do the honours," Leo said

springing to his feet.

"It's in that cupboard, second shelf and the glasses are in the kitchen," Bill slumped down again.

Leo brought in two glasses. "Hair of the dog?" Leo held up the bottle, looking at the label, "Um, good brandy too. You've got better taste than I thought." Even though it was probably unwise, Bill nodded, "Ok, just a small one."

Taking a swig, Leo gazed around the flat. "All these books. I've never had the patience to read. My missus did. She was mad keen on crime. Anything with blood and gore," he chuckled.

"But as I was saying, Bill," Leo continued, "Hastings. It's always drawn me back. Maybe it's the sea, or the people. I don't know. But I think I'll probably end my days here. Fate I suppose!"

"Would that be such a bad thing? I really like it here. The locals are friendly, it's got a good feel to it and there's the countryside."

Leo nodded in agreement. "Yes, you're probably right. The grass always seems greener somewhere else, doesn't it?"

As the evening mellowed with the drink Bill surprised himself by saying to Leo, "I was getting quite jealous of you tonight."

"Me?" Leo looked baffled at Bill's remark and helped himself, without asking to another shot of brandy.

"Aye, dancing with those women. I don't know why. People just seem to be drawn to you. You have an allure."

"An allure! I don't know about that. All I can say is that I just like enjoying myself. It's as simple as that."

"Oh aye, I know. Maybe that's what I'm envious of. You seem to find everything so easy."

Leo drank some more, bemused by Bill's flattery and still mildly suspicious that it was a ploy to somehow wrong foot him.

"Yes, it's true, I do like the ladies," Leo laughed. "That's probably it. I've still got, you know, that drive."

Bill gently sipped his brandy and Fly raised his head up

slightly but soon settled down again, yawning and stretching. Seeing Bill still looking rather maudlin, Leo leaned forward in his chair.

"But look, I don't see why you should be envious of me. It gets me into all sorts of trouble, always has done: misunderstandings, arguments, being chased by women, their fathers, boyfriends, husbands. And that's without even mentioning the money troubles," Leo reeled off. "It's not an easy life, you know," he said relaxing back again, shaking his head.

"I suppose not," Bill was beginning to feel almost sorry for him.

"Do you want another?" Leo raised his empty glass and Bill shook his head, feeling quite sleepy now.

"You know, if I could swap places … " Leo said, pouring himself another generous measure and looking around again at Bill's spacious flat, … "I wouldn't mind. And I tell you another thing, Bill, you've got a lot going for you

around here even though you have crap dress sense."

"What?" Bill looked startled.

"Well," Leo laughed, "who'd wear navy blue trousers and a green pullover to a dance? I ask you."

"What's the matter with that?" Bill asked, looking down at himself.

"My point exactly," replied Leo.

There was a pause in the conversation as Leo drank some more brandy and Bill closed his eyes.

"Anyway you do have one admirer," Leo burst out laughing.

"What?" Bill's opened his eyelids a little and wondered if he had heard right.

"An admirer!"

"Who?"

"Rita of course! You must know, she thinks that you're the bees knees. Apparently her old man's a bit of a tyrant but according to Abi, she's got a soft spot for you, matey!" Leo nodded, grinning, his face flushed with the brandy which made Bill want to dismiss this rambling.

"Anyway, you can see it in her eyes," Leo said wistfully.

"Don't be daft, man." Bill looked uncomfortable and was blushing.

"It's true. She said to me tonight, 'that Bill, he's such a gentleman it's a pity he's on his own.'"

"Did she? But that doesn't mean … " Bill began but Leo dismissed him with a wave of his hand.

"Take it from me, from one who knows" Leo interrupted. "You have an admirer."

Bill closed his eyes again and wanted to go to bed.

"There you are you see, that's put lead in your pencil," Leo laughed helping himself to another nip of brandy. "One more for the road and then I'd better get going."

∾ Forty Four ∾

The mid-Sunday morning sun had yet to warm up the Old Town's sleepy, wintry streets; its higgledy-piggledy houses lay silent in the chilly shade of the brilliant blue sky. The light was just beginning to pick off the glint of an odd window and spread a promising glow over the terracotta chimney pots. Bill was sitting at his favourite spot on a bench by the West Hill cafe just as the shutters were removed for the day's business. Nearby, Fly bobbed contentedly around almost in a circle across the neatly cut grass – sniffing and stretching; off the lead this had now become his home patch. Another regular morning walker with a half pint dog sized up to Fly, making him jump and he retreated back to Bill for some reassurance. Way down on the beach, fishing boats lined up by the seashore looked like they had been sellotaped on to the Hastings shingle, ready for the off. Despite the season, the gentle shimmering sea was calm and pancake flat with a single fishing catch returning home. The only movement in the sky was from a lone gull gently gliding down on to the cliff tops.

That afternoon the group arranged to meet up at the entrance of Hastings Pier. It was still a lovely crisp, sunny day and it sharply silhouetted East Hill and the castle. On the promenade people were strolling along enjoying the fine weather. The old pier remained silent with its gates firmly locked whilst the owners, the local council and the town's people were still debating its future.

"Isn't it a shame?" Rita moaned to Abi, pulling up her scarf and leaning against a handrail wondering if their teenage haunt would finally be abandoned and sink into the sea.

"Your mum and I used to go dancing," recalled Millie, peeking through the bars of the gates out to the ballroom.

"What here, auntie?" Abi looked, surprised.

"Oh now, you've got me there," Millie paused. "I do remember that there were some Americans."

"You would have been too young during the war," said Rita.

"I don't think it was down here, auntie, probably back in London."

"Yes it might have been," she agreed rather whimsically. "I've not been there for years. They do a lot of dancing up there after dark."

"Do they?" Rita laughed

"Yes, there's a lot of it going on. It gets very noisy."

"Oh look here comes Bill," Abi spotted Bill walking with Fly towards them.

"My, it's a canny day isn't it? It's like being at home this weather – rugged."

"It's that all right," Millie patted Fly.

Abi and Rita had their hands deep in their coat pockets, shivering in the cold with their backs to the sea.

"You're still in the land of living then, Bill?" Rita smiled.

"Oh aye," he looked a little embarrassed. Did I make a chump of myself the other night at the dance?" Abi and Rita looked at each other and smirked mischievously.

"Oh no, man. Don't tell me. Did I do something really stupid?" Frowning hard, Bill's face looked a picture as the women giggled.

"Was it on the dance floor? I remember dancing, I think and I don't really do that kind of thing." Abi and Rita kept up the silence. "What? Come on, man, tell us what happened!"

"You were very good – great entertainment," Abi roared.

"Wasn't he, Rita?

All the right moves," she continued, "you had me going I can tell you. Here you are if you don't believe us." Removing her gloves, Abi took her mobile out of her handbag. Zipping through the pictures she showed Rita first.

"What is it, man?" Bill was getting anxious and passed Fly's lead to Millie. Finally Abi gave Bill the phone.

He stared at the hazy picture. "It's you in your all together," cried Abi.

The photo was from the back. It was difficult to see on the small screen because of the harsh sunlight if it was his backside or not. Bill squinted then put on his glasses for a closer look, trying to hold the phone away from the sunlight.

"It can't be!"

"I tell you what, Bill, you've got a few fans down at Woolies now," said Rita, stifling a laugh. "They'll be all over you next time you're in."

Bill looked horrified at the thought, as he gave the phone back to Abi who showed it to Millie.

"Who's that?" she asked.

"It's Bill," Abi said laughing.

"I wouldn't have recognised him."

"I hope not" said Rita giggling some more

Bill shook his head. "No," he said firmly. "You're having me on. I remember getting back to the flat and that I still had my clothes on."

"Of course you did," Abi continued. "Before Leo drove you home he helped you get your kit back on," she said rather coyly. "In fact we all helped you with your clothes, didn't we Rita?"

"That's right, you were a star attraction last Saturday, people are still talking about it."

Bill just shook his head in disbelief.

"What's all this then?" Leo turned up rubbing his hands together to keep warm.

"It's the picture of Bill. You know the other night, when he did that strip," said Abi showing him on her phone.

"Look, why don't you just show all the passers by?" Bill protested.

Leo laughed, "I'm going to have my work cut out with the ladies now in this town."

"By the way, are you still signing on at the Job Centre, Bill?" asked Leo still looking at the picture.

"Yes, why?"

"Because I reckon you could get a job as a life model, like me, at the college. They're always on the look out for new people."

"Very funny."

"Don't knock it. It's not bad pay."

"No thanks." They all had a giggle at the thought of Bill in a classroom posing.

"Anyway, Bill," said Rita, taking his arm, "you know we've been having you on don't you?"

"Well I was a bit out of it and didn't really recover until Tuesday. It's flattering I suppose."

"I wouldn't go that far," said Abi, laughing and lighting up a cigarette.

"The old pier's looking very sad and ropey isn't it?" Leo remarked, moving a little nearer to the gates."

"Yeah, we were just saying all our teenage years are locked up in there." Abi said, puffing on her cigarette.

"Mine too. Had some right old times out there," Leo smiled and pointed towards the abandoned dance hall stranded up at the end, its windows boarded and the rushing waves smashing against the rusty pillars below.

"But you can't get sentimental about these things. I reckon they should pull it down. It's an eyesore, puts the tourists off and makes the town look grubby. This pier represents all that's wrong with Hastings. It's a crumbling old wreck and if I had my way I would put it out of its misery and blow it up. It's like us – redundant. We should be looking forward not backwards."

"No way," Rita trumped up. "There's nothing but a good lick of paint wouldn't sort out."

"It'll take a bit more than that, darling. It's unsafe, that's why it's closed!" Leo laughed.

"Well OK," Abi joined in. "The council should take it over. Compulsory purchase or something. You can't just let it rot, the pier should be the centrepiece of the town."

"That's right," Bill agreed. "The same thing happened to the Spanish City in Whitley Bay, near where I come from. You should preserve the past as well as look to the future."

Leo bristled and shook his head, "Well I still think it's like throwing money in the sea. You could get a good price from salvage to help build a nice marina. Now that would be great. You'd attract a better class to the town I reckon."

Rita came forward and Bill thought that by the look on her face she was going to hit him. "You ever touch this pier, Leo, and I'll flatten you."

"I was only saying … " Leo chuckled. "Don't get so worked up, darling."

"It may be an old wreck to you but it means a lot to people round here. It's continuity, passed down to generations. My gran used to have her afternoon tea in the restaurant, my mum used to go ballroom dancing in the thirties, my older brother went jiving to the jazz bands, and me and Abi had our first snogs there with boyfriends." Rita paused for thought and Abi smiled. "And I hope my little grandson will be able enjoy going on it in the future."

"Ok, Rita, I get your point but it still doesn't make it a commercial proposition does it?"

"Money isn't everything, Leo." Bill piped up.

"Oh here we go, I can see I'm on me own again," Leo raised his hands in despair.

"Well you've touched a raw nerve. Hastings Pier it's iconic, like Brighton," Rita said.

"Yeah, well they've lost one of theirs as it happens. Look shall we go for a cuppa or something? It's freezing," Leo made a move to go, using his mouth spray to help with his angina.

They strolled towards the town with Millie up front with

the greyhound. Fly's slight limp made them all realise that his race track days might now be over.

"I see you've bought him a new collar too, Bill." Then addressing the group Rita continued, "So, as we all agreed the other night. We're going to give Bill a tenner each now for looking after Fly. And we'll do a rota to help him with walking the dog." Everyone nodded in agreement. As Abi and Rita drew out their money to give to Bill, Leo looked surprised. "Oh, we're doing it now are we?"

"Yes, Leo we said, didn't we, the other evening?" Rita was getting tired of his dodges.

"Ok, it's just that I've not had time to go to the cash point and I've left my cards at home."

"How convenient," Bill mumbled.

"Well look, let me just take him off your hands now for a couple of hours." Leo leant over to grab the dog's lead from Millie but Bill pulled him back.

"No you won't! I'm not letting you loose with him."

"But I thought we were going to take it in turns?"

"Yes, well," Bill hesitated, "let's just get him settled in first. It's still early days. He's only just getting to know me. He might run off at any time."

"He knows me," Millie said, still stroking the dog, "don't you, Fly, baby?"

"Yes he loves you, doesn't he, auntie," agreed Rita.

They all walked slowly along the front. The late afternoon sun washed over the grand Victorian terraces making them shine pastel-like out towards the sea. Bill spotted the one that Jamal had been working on and wondered how he was getting on.

Rita pulled out some bananas from her bag and offered them around.

"No thanks," said Leo, laughing, "I was born during the war, bananas frighten me."

Bill and Leo stopped and looked over at a boarded up furniture shop.

"There's a sign of the times." Bill nodded over at a 'closing down sale' poster fluttering in the wind.

"Well it's not all bad around here is it? I read this week that there's a new ASDA planned in Silverhill and a Tesco's at Hollington."

"Oh aye, but how many staff will they be employing? Woolworths has over seventy. I'll bet that these new places will be operating with just a handful. That's the thing you see. Keep the labour costs down and you make much more profit."

Leo shook his head, "Well what's wrong with that? I'm a businessman. I'm not going to work for the sake of keeping others in jobs. I invest time and money into my ventures, so why shouldn't I make a reasonable profit?"

"Nobody's saying that you shouldn't but we've got to have social responsibility too or else we wouldn't have a civil society."

"Some civil society this is! You go into any town on Saturday night. Outside the bars it's like the wild west with all the fighting and drunken yobs."

Before Bill could get a word in, Leo continued at a pace, "And what about Hastings having one of the highest rates of teenage pregnancy in the area?"

"Well from what I've heard, Leo, you were no angel yourself when you were a youngster." Bill scoffed.

"I didn't carry on like they do now," said Leo. "Kids can get away with almost anything they like."

"No wonder. They're Thatcher's children aren't they?" Bill continued, "them and their parents have been brought up believing in individualism, consumerism and there's less state control. That's another reason why we're in this economic mess today."

"State control – you're talking bollocks!" Leo cried, their walking pace sped up as they disagreed. "You ask any Hastings fisherman about what he thinks about the government and the EU's new quotas on fishing – they're on their knees as it is."

As the men strode and argued Rita and Abi lagged behind. "I've got some really good news," Rita said excitedly. "Gayle told me last night that she is going back to college. She's got herself on a short catering course starting in January."

"Well that's great. It might help turn things around."

"Exactly. I don't know what's happened to her but this past week she's suddenly started cooking again at home. Even Colin's impressed. She did us a risotto last night – one of his favourites."

"What's caused this?" Abi looked very pleased for Rita.

"I don't know really but we've had rows at home and Colin put his foot down. He said that either she gets out and do something or she'd be on her own."

"Does he know about the drugs problem?"

"Oh, god no. He'd really go mental. I'm just hoping it'll get sorted."

"One step at a time, eh?"

"Exactly. Anyway it's made me feel a bit better and I've not had one of those dizzy spells for a while either."

As they walked on, Rita glanced back at the pier, and with the sea lapping around it, for a moment seemed like it was floating.

"And what about Woolies?" Abi asked.

"I'm trying not to think about it. In a few weeks I'll be out of a job and me and Colin will have had even more blow-ups at home about money. Anyway, for the moment I've still got my staff discount." Rita took a deep breath and closed her eyes momentarily. "I expect I'll find something else in town. I could do with trying something new."

∼ Forty Five ∼

"Where are we going again?" Millie asked Abi who was just finishing putting on some face cream in the bedroom.

"Over to Leo's place. He's cooking us all a Christmas meal. Rita and Bill will be there too."

"Oh I don't know," Millie sat in the kitchen, mulling it over, looking disgruntled with her hat and coat on – the cat sitting on her lap. "I'll miss me telly programme," she moaned.

"Come on," Abi said tetchily as she quickly checked that she had put her mobile in her handbag and got the bottle of wine she had bought earlier.

"You'll enjoy it when we get there. He's cooking Italian. You like that."

"Do I?"

"Yes, you like my spaghetti bolognese and Leo comes from an Italian family, so it's bound to be good."

"As long as it's not liver and bacon," Millie pulled a face. "It doesn't agree with me and it makes me blow off."

"Don't worry, auntie, it won't be that. It's hardly Italian is it? Anyway there's our cab, come on."

The taxi driver who collected them was a bit surly. As soon as they had got inthe back of the car and even before they could get their seat belts on, he was whizzing through the town centre.

"I'm going to complain about him, he tried to overcharge

us. He must be new," Abi moaned after he dropped them and the car roared off along Queens Road. She rang Leo's bell but they didn't have to wait long before he appeared at the door, all smiles, wearing a snazzy purple waistcoat and a kitchen apron.

"Ladies!" he greeted them and gave them each a kiss on the cheek

"Benvenuto!"

"Ooo, I say, Italiana!" laughed Millie.

"Come on up." Leo led the way and inside everything was snug and warm. Bill was already settled in, sitting on the sofa with a glass of red wine. He was glad to see that Leo's flat had been tidily transformed since his last visit. He stood up to greet them when they came in and Abi gave Leo the bottle of wine.

"Chianti, excellent." He took their coats. The cosy atmosphere was topped by the alluring smell of Italian sauces wafting from the kitchen and the windows nicely steamed up from Leo's cooking.

"This is lovely," Abi said seeing the dinner table all set up for them.

"Something smells … " Millie smiled, poking her head round the kitchen door and pausing.

"Nice, the word's nice, auntie," Abi quickly jumped in.

"I was just going to say. It's not liver and bacon is it?" she looked at Leo quizzically. "Because it makes me … "

"No, Auntie," Abi again swiftly interrupted her, "I told you we're having Italian."

Leo laughed, "That's right, it's Ravioli for starters, followed by Risotto." Leo said with a heavy Italian accent, taking their coats into the bedroom.

"I'm hungry. When are we going to eat?" moaned Mille.

"Auntie, stop it." Millie sat at the dinner table where there was a bowl of olives to nibble.

"Rita not here yet?" Abi asked.

"No," Bill replied whilst Leo busied himself in the kitchen preparing the meal. "I expect she's got tied up at work. They've never been busier since Woolies announced they're closing down." Abi sat next to Bill on the sofa.

"She's going to find it hard when that place goes – they all will. Who'd have thought?"

"Here we are then." Leo breezed in with two large glasses of red. Handing one to Abi he was just about to give the other to Millie.

"Agh! No, not for her, she's not allowed." Leo froze, the glass suspended in mid air and Millie's hand too, reaching out.

"Just one, surely?" Leo tried to insist.

"I'm sorry, she can't, it'll play havoc with her pills. She'll be up all night."

Leo straightened up and looked back at Millie whose face had suddenly sunk with disappointment. "It's not fair, you've all got one."

"I know what you'll like!" Leo grinned, having an inspired thought.

He returned quickly with a glass that still looked like red wine.

"Leo!" Abi protested again.

"No, don't worry, Abi it's perfectly safe. You'll like this, auntie. A unique Christmas concoction especially for you."

"Oh it looks very nice," she smiled, "is it a cocktail?"

"It certainly is. Christmas Ribena punch. It's got the zing and the ping!"

Millie laughed and took a sip. Abi still looked apprehensive that Leo may have slipped in some booze.

"I guarantee you'll get merry on that before we do."

"Mmm, yeah, it's got ping all right – lovely," Millie rolled her eyes in delight and grabbed another olive. Abi leant over to have a sip. "Mmm not bad, what is it?"

"Not saying," Leo chuckled slipping back into the kitchen to see to the food.

Abi looked at her watch again. "Rita's late. I wonder what's happened. I hope that Gayle's not playing her up again."

"Well how's things with you?" Bill asked her. "Have you been able to get out much yourself lately?"

"Only around town. To tell you the truth I'm too skint to go gadding about these days."

"Aye, we could all do with a bit more cash all right."

"Still no luck in getting a job?" Abi enquired enjoying the Chianti.

"Not yet, pet. The only vacancies round here seems to be shop work and that's hardly me. The trouble is I still see myself as an engineer and there's just not the jobs, like. I seem to have suddenly become an old codger! Bill chuckled at himself. Abi smiled and looked at Millie still enjoying her drink.

"You know, he's got the right idea," Bill pointed to Leo in the kitchen. "He's a survivor, ducking and diving. I couldn't do it myself, like. But I have to admit he's very resourceful even though sometimes it's at other people's expense."

"Have you thought about going back home to Newcastle?" Abi took another sip of wine.

"Things are no better there. Engineering has gone to the wall. There's just as many of them on the dole queue. At least down here in the summer, it's like being on the Riviera!"

"The Riviera!" Abi roared. "You've got a good imagination, Bill, I'll give you that. This is dear old Hastings we're talking about. Day trippers, amusement arcades, hot dogs, burgers, bars and crazy golf," she giggled.

"Don't forget the bingo," chipped in Millie happily sipping her Ribena punch and munching olives.

"Ah, you're forgetting the beauty of the place, man." Bill's face lit up with enthusiasm. "What about the Old Town, that's steeped in history? There's the country park for walking and the seaside. It's a grand place Hastings – you don't know how lucky you are."

"Maybe I've lived here too long. It isn't what it used to be. We've got our share of problems with drugs, down and outs and crime." Abi reached over to the table for an olive.

"Aye well, I canna deny that, but that's a sign of the times of almost anywhere in Britain."

"Hastings has become a dump," Abi insisted.

"Nah, I couldn't agree with you there, pet. It's far from that."

Leo poked his head out from the kitchen, a glass of red wine in hand, hearing raised voices.

"What are you two bickering about?"

"Hastings." Millie spoke up. "Bill thinks it's lovely and she doesn't. What do you think?" He thought for a moment and drank some more wine.

"Depends on how I'm doing I suppose. It's not a bad place and also it's where I was born! If I'm earning some dosh and the sun's out you can't beat Hastings. And it's become more cosmopolitan now with all the eating places – a café culture. Saturday afternoon in the summer; a stroll along the front, late breakfast in Rosa's, bet at the bookies and a pint in the High Street. It's great! But on a bad day when you're up against it and people are being so small minded then I'd rather be up in the smoke."

"What, London?" Abi looked at him horrified at the thought.

"Yeah why not? There's always something going on up the west end. No two days the same there."

"Urgh, no" Abi dismissed the idea with a wave of her hand. "The place is a cess pit. Noisy, congested, dirty, expensive and mean too."

"It's like anywhere, Abi. It depends where you go and who you know. It's been a second home to me," Leo said fondly.

"I lived in London once, I think." Millie trilled.

"But I must admit a few things do get my goat in the Old Town," Leo continued. "Those arty types swanning around with their long straggly hair like seaweed. And that mob dressed up and posing in 17th century gear. It's like walking onto a film set. What's that all about?"

"Do you mean the Jack in the Green Festival? It's a Celtic tradition; an historical part of Hastings charm," Bill reminded him.

"Nah, you can keep it. It's just fancy middle class twaddle." Leo dived back into the kitchen to attend to their meal.

The door bell rang; Rita had arrived. Bill went down to let

her in. Rita looked quite tired and after climbing the stairs and taking off her coat she collapsedonto the sofa. "Ooo it's lovely and warm in here. Hi Leo," she called out to him in the kitchen. "Smells nice!"

"It's not liver and bacon," Millie told her, finishing off the olives. Rita smiled at her.

"What a day I've just had at work – awful. I tell you it's been an eye opener how people can behave. The place is being ripped apart and the customers are running amok. We've even got to taking off our name badges because of the abuse we're getting from some of them. For a joke, me and Pat have got to calling each other Pollyanna when we're on the tills!"

Bill put a glass of red in her hand and she took a long gulp.

"Ah, that's better. I needed that."

"Rita, we were just talking about whether we liked living in Hastings or not," Abi told her. "What do you think?"

"At the moment what I'd like is to be as far away from here as possible," she sighed, taking another sip of wine.

"Somewhere nice and warm?" Abi asked.

"Oh yesss," Rita purred, closing her eyes momentarily with exhaustion to indulge in a dream-like fantasy, "I'd sleep for a week."

"You could visit me in Costa Del Sol when I stay at Sherman's villa, if you like," Abi nudged her, checking her phone for any messages.

Rita suddenly perked up, opening her sleepy eyes.

"Hang on a minute. I thought you'd packed him in?"

"Well, we're back on again. He took me out for a meal last week," Abi said rather slyly.

"So, will you get a pay-out Rita, when you all get the boot?" Abi enquired, putting her phone back in her bag.

"Yeah, we've just had a meeting about our redundancy. I'll get some dosh but it's hardly a fortune based on what I earn. I expect I'll have to join you down at the Job Centre in the New Year, Bill," still having second thoughts about whether she should have got another job sorted a lot earlier.

"Well good luck, pet. The queue's getting longer all the time and the way things are going I'm sure there's worse to come. Aye, these bankers have got a lot to answer for. It's all based on greed you know, downright greed. And you'll see, they'll get their bonuses as normal," he ranted. "I say we should nationalise all the banks with all these loans that the government's giving them and put the bankers on a flat-rate wage like the rest of us."

"Up the revolution, eh, Bill?" Leo shouted out from the kitchen.

"Where's our dinner? I'm hungry," Millie complained again. She was still the only one sitting up at the table. On cue, Leo tripped in with their starters.

"Here we are, Ravioli di spinaci e ricotta," showing off again his Italian.

"Come on then, shifty, shifty. It's a bit of a squeeze but I think you'll fit in." They all sat together around the table almost shoulder to shoulder. Leo pulled up a kitchen stool which made him a bit higher than the others whilst Bill's chair was much lower and he felt a little awkward.

Leo raised his glass. "Happy Christmas, one and all." Everyone clinked their glasses.

"Parmesan anyone?"

"This looks lovely," Rita said as she unfolded her napkin.

"Mmm, not bad," said Abi as she began eating, "I love Italian. It's my favourite next to Chinese ... and Greek."

"Aye, I'm fond of Italian too," agreed Bill, "I bought a tin of Ravioli last week for me tea."

Leo frowned at him. "A tin?" he put his fork down and looked quite insulted.

"I hope you're not going to compare this dish I have been preparing for hours to one of your cut price buys?"

Bill had his mouth full and couldn't answer. Narrowing his eyes, Leo continued. "I mean this meal was created from scratch, all fresh ingredients." Bill glanced around at the others, feeling a bit embarrassed.

"Yes, it must have taken you ages," said Rita, "it's very nice."

"Well yes, you have to make these little parcels very carefully and just the right measure of everything, it's a real art," Leo continued.

"You couldn't get *this* flavour out of a *tin*, Bill."

"Is there anymore?" Millie asked. She was the first to finish.

"Auntie!" Abi frowned at her, "Don't be rude, you've got your main meal to come yet."

"No, that's OK." Leo quickly got up and gave her some of the left over portion from the kitchen. "It'll only go to the cat," he said dishing it on to her plate, "she's fond of Italian too."

"You've got a cat?" Millie sparkled.

"Yeah, Sunday, she's around somewhere. Probably hiding under the bed."

"I love cats."

"Why is she called Sunday?" Abi asked.

"It was the day she just turned up out of the blue, on the doorstep."

"I thought that you were allergic to cats and dogs," Bill said.

"Ah, dogs more than cats." Bill recognised Leo's usual shifty look as he offered round some bread.

"So, how does this compare to your *tin*, Bill?" Leo sniped.

"Aye, it's canny."

"Canny," Leo muttered sourly while clearing up the plates, "I suppose that's a compliment of sorts."

"Top up anybody?" Abi asked, leaning over with another bottle of red that Rita had brought, refilling Bill and Leo's glass. Millie held up her empty glass.

"I'll get you some more of that punch," said Abi.

Leo reappeared from the kitchen with a large bowl of steaming Risotto and placed it carefully in the middle of the table.

"This looks lovely," Abi smiled.

"Risotto alla marinara," Leo beamed "Sea food to you. I got the fish fresh from the market at Rock-a-Nore this morning. Buon appetito!"

He began dishing up and the group eagerly tucked into their

main meal. There was a whoop of delight as they tasted more of Leo's fine cuisine.

"What's for afters?" asked Millie, eagerly, whilst she was eating and attracted another steely glare from Abi.

"Ah, something rather special," replied Leo.

After they had finished, Leo popped into the kitchen while Bill gave a hand in clearing away the plates from the table. Leo soon reappeared with small cut glass dessert bowls.

"These are nice," said Rita holding one of the dishes up to the light.

"Yes, family heirloom. Used to be my mum's." Leo then brought in a large bowl.

"Ice cream!" they all cheered.

"Not just ice cream," Leo informed them, handing out the spoons. "This is *very special*, once manufactured here in Hastings by my dear old dad during the fifties at our shop in Robertson Street."

"We must have gone there," Rita turned to Abi. "Mmm, it's gorgeous," she said, being the first to taste it and licking her lips, "What's in it?"

Leo smiled, "It's a secret family recipe. My dad got offers from the big companies at the time for the copyright. If he had sold it he could have been pretty rich."

"What stopped him?" asked Bill.

"Oh he was very suspicious of them and protective of his little empire in Hastings. We sold tons of the stuff. On a hot summer's day they'd be queuing round the corner to the seafront."

"Nice and creamy." Millie had finished hers already. "Can I have some more?"

Leo took her bowl and scooped up another portion. "It's one of those things in life. My dad made a decent living but he was frightened to expand his business. His brothers were just the same. They also had ice cream parlours along the south coast." As he handed Millie some more he looked quite sad.

"Pity really, what might have been. As immigrants to this

country they worked very hard all their lives, my parents, but what did they have to show for it? My dad had come here just before the war and he was interned for a while on the Isle of Man as an enemy alien."

"So, who owns the rights on the ice cream now?" asked Rita.

"My eldest brother, Carl," Leo said rather offhand, quickly changing the subject.

"Anymore, anybody?" Abi shook her head as he gave Bill another helping.

"No love lost there then," Abi whispered to Rita, behind her napkin.

"I can't see any Christmas cards, Leo," Rita observed looking around the room. "Oh and that reminds me," she leant over and plucked some envelopes from her bag and gave them out.

"Thanks," said Abi. "We're still doing ours."

Bill opened his and was quite touched by Rita's gesture.

"A card," Leo sat back down on the stool and smiled. "It's just like Christmas! Well I'm afraid I don't do cards, never have done. I'm eco friendly, me."

Abi took a call on her mobile and winking at Rita she got up and slipped into the kitchen. "Hi babe, … yeah … yeah … yeah. No that's OK. We can meet whenever. Let me give you a buzz later this evening … .yeah of course. Loveya!"

She came back in the room and winked at Rita who looked very amused, suspecting that it was Sherman calling her.

"Coffee and brandies?" asked Leo.

"Just coffee for me," Rita held up her hand "I've had enough booze. I've got an early start tomorrow, we're visiting Colin's mum over at Eastbourne." The thought of it made her toes curl with Colin shouting at her during the trip about her anxiety over his driving.

Leo and Bill cleared the table again and Leo got the coffee on the go. Millie was beginning to doze.

Leo lifted up the brandy bottle.

Abi nodded and smiled, "Oh go on then. It's been a lovely evening, Leo. The meal was delicious. There's more to you than meets the eye," she twinkled.

"Well it's nice to push the boat out when you can," he said, pouring out the drinks." This'll keep us warm. And in fact it's by courtesy of the government, all paid for by my winter fuel payment," he laughed.

"What's that?" Rita asked.

"It's the money that the government give to people over sixty to help with heating bills. Your Colin should get it," Abi explained.

"He's never said."

"Anyway, we'll all get it soon when we hit the big Six-O."

"I thought you were putting off being sixty," Rita joked.

Bill was eager to jump in. "Aye well, if the government paid a proper state pension rate in this country like they do in Europe, then we wouldn't need these patronising handouts. The old age pension is a disgrace, man. It should be doubled."

"I'll drink to that," said Leo, sipping his brandy. "But in the meantime let's raise a toast to the Department of Work and Pensions for a wonderful Christmas!"

"I'll not do that," Bill protested, "the way they've treated me, bugger man."

"Oh come on, Bill," Abi chided him, "It is Christmas."

She turned to Leo, "So, what are you doing over the holiday?"

"Not sure yet. Probably stay here with the cat. My daughter has asked me to go over to their place, but her ex mother-in-law will be there and anyway I don't know if I can be bothered, to be honest. What about you?"

"We'll be at home as usual, won't we auntie?"

Millie had dozed off. Abi looked at Rita who was finishing her coffee.

"Yeah, I'll be at home too, slaving over the cooker but Dean will love it. We're getting him some new computer game that he's been on about. What about you, Bill?"

"Me? I haven't decided yet, hen. My son and his girlfriend have just been in contact and asked me up there but there's Fly to think about now."

"Well we could look after him for a few days," Rita offered. "Dean would love it and it would be good for you to see your family."

"Oh, I don't know. He's still settling down at my place."

The party began to break up. Abi phoned for a cab and Rita got their coats together to share the journey home. Bill began collecting up the remaining dishes and glasses even though Leo insisted that he would sort it all out in the morning.

Their taxi arrived promptly.

"Lovely evening, Leo." Abi gave him a peck on the cheek then to Bill. Rita did the same. "Nice ice cream," Millie said, suddenly sparking back to life.

"You know, you remind me of a boy that I used to be friendly with," Millie said to Leo up close as he helped her on with her coat.

"Oh yeah?" Leo smiled and she held his hand quite tightly, suddenly looking wide eyed and back on the ball.

"Yes, he was a charmer just like you. He had all the women chasing after him."

"Is that what you think I'm like, auntie?"

"Maybe, but after tonight I reckon you'd be better off settling down with some nice woman who'd enjoy your home cooking."

"Is that right?" Leo was feeling a bit cornered.

"Come on, auntie, that's enough, the cab's waiting," Abi called out.

"What about her?" Millie quipped, letting go of his hand and pointing her finger. "She needs taking in hand."

They continued saying their goodbyes as Leo put the unpredictable hall light timer on and they headed rather rowdily down the stairs with Leo and Bill at the top waving.

"Leave that, Bill," Leo said, inside the flat as he lolled on the sofa watching him stacking dishes in the kitchen.

"Do you fancy another brandy?"

"OK, just the one, mind, then I'd better get back; Fly needs taking for a walk."

Bill lay back in the armchair, both of them feeling nicely soporific by the booze and the good food.

"Well that were a grand meal, Leo. I wish I could cook like that."

"What's stopping you? You could do it if you put your mind to it."

"Maybe. Well it's just that Helen, my wife, used to do it all see."

"Ok, but you're your own man now aren't you? Get yourself a recipe book and have a bash. You'll soon get the hang of it. I did when my wife chucked me out."

"What, you mean all this cooking, you've learnt to do fairly recent?" Bill pointed to the remains of their fine banquet lying in the kitchen.

"Yeah, not long. But one thing I've learnt, if you want to attract a bird, then cooking definitely helps to swing it."

"I'd be quite happy to knock up a pasta, me." Bill mused.

They sat quietly drinking their brandies and mulling over the evening.

"I've been invited for a meal with a Kurdish family in town," said Bill laying his head back on the armchair. Leo was stretched full length on the sofa and looked at him blankly.

"You see, I've been helping this Kurdish boy at school, Mustafa, with his reading and I've just recently discovered that he's from Iran. His dad's a doctor and has been working as a decorator in one of those big houses on the front near the pier."

"They shouldn't be here – there's too many of them," Leo remarked gruffly.

"But they need sanctuary and they work and pay their taxes."

"Not all of them."

"Only because the government doesn't always allow them to work." Bill began to get vexed with Leo. "Anyway what about your parents when they came here in the thirties to escape the fascists. You just told us that your dad was classed as an alien."

"That was different. It was during the war," Leo shrugged. "It was a state of emergency. Churchill said 'collar the lot' in case there were fifth columnists coming in." Leo leant over, emphasising his point.

"Isn't this an emergency when people face a serious threat to their lives? Alien, asylum seeker, illegal immigrant – they're all miserable labels often given to decent people who are just trying to keep themselves and their families safe."

"You missed out spongers and benefit cheats," Leo hit back. "And you've forgotten to mention all these bloody Eastern Europeans coming over to do the jobs that by rights British people should be doing. Some of them come all the way from fucking Bulgaria to do our fruit picking."

"Well aye and can you blame them? For what they get, five to seven pounds an hour it takes them a day to earn that kind of money back home."

"But it ain't right, it should be done by British people," Leo argued.

"Well nobody's stopping them but they don't want it, man. It doesn't pay enough. When people come and do that kind of seasonal work here from Europe they live in caravans. It keeps the costs down. They're often students back home, studying medicine, engineering, psychology and whatever."

"So what happened to the hard working British working class then, Bill?"

"Well people here struggle to pay their bills on five pound an hour."

"We've gone soft if you ask me," Leo huffed, raising himself up, taking another swig of his drink and collapsing back down again.

"Well I don't know what you're complaining about. As a Thatcherite, you believe in the free market economy and all that crap don't you?" Bill's voice raised higher.

"Within reason, yeah. But the world's gone mad. There's just too many of e'm here."

"Anyway you must have taken on some migrant labour on

your own property developments?"

"Not if I could help it."

"Come off it, man. I don't believe you haven't used a cut price Polish plasterer or plumber to help keep the costs down."

"I always try and use local labour. There's more than enough who need the work around here. Anyway I've had my fill of it. They come here, all live in one room in St Leonards, charge half the going rate for doing a conversion and bugger off back home until the next one."

"Aye, well, that's the free economy for you," Bill smiled.

"Don't get all bleedin' sanctimonious with me, Bill." Leo took another nip of brandy. "It's the likes of them and the sodding banks that's got me in this mess."

"Well I dare say you'll bounce back as soon as these so called green roots of recovery start appearing. The banks will be lending again and the … "

"Not to me they won't," Leo cut in sharply.

"What?"

"Not to me, I said." Leo lifted himself up on one elbow. "I'm bankrupt!" He almost shouted it across the room as though it were a public announcement.

Bill looked at him gob smacked.

"Liquidation. Lost my business, properties, money, nice house and company car. Now look at me living in this hovel whilst my fucking ex is wallowing in luxury over at Robertsbridge on the proceeds of all my hard work." Leo sunk back down on the sofa again. "She won't even give me the time of day," he muttered under his breath. There was a moment of silence. Bill was stunned but felt he had to ask, "How much did you lose?"

Leo looked at him coldly, "Five hundred grand." There was a further pause only interrupted by the clug, clug of the old plumbing from upstairs.

"Well, now you know," Leo looked at Bill, "You don't think I live in this dump for fun do you? Not after what I've been used to?"

"It's not that bad," Bill gazed around the room. He was still feeling a glow from Leo's Christmas meal and the brandy; the place had taken on a more convivial feel.

"Come off it. It's the pits. I've gone from a plush six bedroom, detached over at Fairlight with remote control gates and sea views, to *this!*"

"I've heard that you can get dismissed from bankruptcy after a while," Bill piped up, trying hard to help lighten Leo's mood.

"Yeah, a year in Britain. But how can I start again? I'm rock bottom. I can't even organise a decent return on a racing greyhound. A fucking gammy leg, I ask you!" Leo chuckled to himself.

Bill leant forward in his chair, "Look you're the sort of bloke who picks himself up – you'll not be down for long. I dare say you'll find another venture."

"Not this time, matey. I've made too many enemies in Hastings with suppliers and what not. It seems that I owe everybody."

Bill sat back again and drank his brandy and while thinking of something positive to say, it all fell into place why Leo had been so shifty, avoiding people around town.

"Well at least you've got your health," Bill finally said.

Leo stared at the ceiling and mulled things over. "Have I?" He pulled out his angina puffer. "But, yeah, you're right, I've just got to think of it as a bad patch I suppose. Be positive. Things'll move on. In fact I was reading an advert in the local rag the other day about selling property abroad. It looks ideal. I just need a bit of capital to buy into it." Bill was aghast as he realised it was the same advert he'd replied to when he went to Bexhill. Leo raised his head up from the sofa again.

"I don't suppose you've got some spare cash, Bill to come in with me. We could split the profits, you know – fifty fifty?"

Bill, looking at Leo in horror with the thought of using his depleted redundancy savings, shook his head slowly.

Leo made a move to get up. "Do you want a coffee?"

"No, I'd better get back, Fly will be wanting his pee."

"By the way did I tell you about these anonymous gifts and things that I've been getting through the post for about a year?" Leo appeared to suddenly cheer up and went over to the mantelpiece.

"Yeah, you did mention it," Bill said, yawning, stretching his arms and starting to put on his overcoat. Leo picked up a Christmas card and an envelope.

"Read it, go on," he urged Bill, handing it to him.

"*Look forward to seeing you in 2009,*" Bill shrugged his shoulders.

"I reckon it's from this French woman, Adele. I went out with her a few times. We met down at The Regal but her husband found out and, well, it got a bit hairy to be honest. I had to lay low – he sounds a nasty bit of work." Leo then pulled out a birthday card. "Look, see, same handwriting! I only came across it again the other day under the bed. She gave me that when we were meeting up. It matches right?" Leo searched Bill's face for confirmation.

Bill looked at the two and nodded that it did look similar.

"It's been her sending me these gifts and things all this time." Leo's face, all alight was delighted at his discovery. Bill slowly began putting on his scarf.

"I reckon she's a bit kinky," Leo fizzed. Bill stopped tying his scarf and gave him a funny look, wondering how much of this was the drink talking.

"I think she's still after me," he chuckled with self satisfaction. "She's one of those birds who likes to keep you dangling, you know, a bit of a tease, build up the tension." The two of them stood stock still and Bill suddenly felt Leo's cat, Sunday, leaning, warm up against his leg. He bent down and gave it a stroke and the cat twirled around again, its tail up high.

"Leo," Bill said very deadpan, backing towards the door, "I think you should have a lie down, man. Just take it easy, OK?"

"But what do you think then, it could be her, couldn't it? It all adds up – doesn't it?"

Bill opened the door to Leo's flat and began to descend the

stairs with the cat eager to follow him out.

"I'll be seeing you then, Leo. Thanks again for a great meal."

Quite unexpectedly Leo lurched forward to hug Bill and nearly tipped him over. Bill was startled and reacted awkwardly, overpowered by the smell of brandy on Leo's breath.

"Remember Bill, if you're on your own on Christmas Day, you're welcome to share a cracker here with me."

Untangling himself and moving downstairs, Bill looked up at Leo standing on the landing.

"Ok, thanks, that's nice, we'll see eh?"

"Oh yeah, exactly. Let's just see how things pan out."

~ Forty Six ~

Millie found herself alone on the upper deck of a bus with just a packet of chocolate digestive biscuits in her handbag. She had on her thick winter coat – a good thing too, as outside the sleety rain lashed the front window where she was sitting. Millie had no idea of the time of day but this didn't matter to her. A few passengers had got on and one or two had come upstairs, but they had got off at Rye. That was a long way back and now this winding road, passing forlorn looking pylons stretching across the flat grey fields; it could be anywhere but in fact it was Romney Marsh which she once knew well. As the bus slowed down, negotiating the sharp ditch–lined bends, Millie gently swayed from side to side, a feeling that she quite liked. In fact it made her smile as she put her hand in her bag and plucked out a milky biscuit. This was as much of a treat as she liked. All the upstairs windows were masked with condensation making Millie feel nicely enclosed and undisturbed by all the interruptions she had to put up with lately. She leaned forward, wiped her hand lightly across the window and gazed out at the rain soaked marshes and misty horizon. The bus dipped here and there and pulled back to allow other vehicles to squeeze by when the road became too narrow. A group of starlings rose up in front, shrieking from a hedgerow and neatly resettled on a nearby telegraph wire one by one. She thought that she recognised the next town by its church, was it New Romney? She remembered hearing during the war that a couple of Nazi spies had landed nearby but were caught and later executed.

Now this long bus journey had a sea view. The old Martello towers, looking just like steak and kidney puddings, dotted along the winding shoreline, watching the wayward sea. Was this Dymchurch? Millie recalled her old friend Dot, who ran a B&B in the area. Just before she died they used to meet up for a game of bingo in Hastings and she would be forever complaining about her house guests and their 'nasty little habits'. This place had a small fun fair. All shut up today of course. 'No buckets and spades in this weather,' thought Millie. Then she must have dozed off. The gentle rhythm of the bus along this straighter roadway as it buzzed through Hythe without her even noticing. She dreamt that she was in Victoria Park, Bethnal Green feeding the ducks. Her mum was standing behind her when she suddenly slipped and fell into the freezing water. Her clothes were soaked and she started crying. Did this really happen?

When Millie awoke it had turned dark, the bus was no longer travelling through countryside but was in a town. It passed by some old tenement buildings and a lot of 'To Let' signs. The traffic was congested. Eventually it stopped at what looked like a bus station. A man behind her who she hadn't noticed got up and made his way to the stairs.

"Where are we?" Mille asked.

"Folkestone," he looked surprised that she didn't know.

"Folkestone," Millie repeated under her breath to herself. "Where the heck is that?"

Millie followed him and gingerly stepped off the bus. The doors whooshed closed behind her. She stood for a moment staring at the timetable at the bus stop and dug in her bag for her specs, eventually finding them buried under the biscuits. She couldn't make head or tail of the schedule.

"Folkestone – that's near what's name, Southend, I think."

She looked at the old people sitting on a bench opposite

waiting for buses and was about to ask them, but thought better of it.

Millie wandered into the town. The rain had not reached there. The pavements were as dry as a bone, but heavy clouds threatened. It was nearly tea time and teenage school kids were spreading themselves like jam across the pavements and roads. Takeaways were doing good trade it seemed. Millie wandered along casually looking into shop windows. Jewellers, dry cleaners, fish & chips, estate agents, charity shop (cats), health food shop, Polish shop. She stopped at the Tasty Burger Bite. It smelt good and Millie was very hungry. She didn't realise that apart from the biscuits, she hadn't eaten anything since breakfast.

Millie peered into the window and saw that there were plenty of tables to sit at. There was a line of people queuing and Millie joined them. She put her specs on to see the menu above the counter, cheesy egg, mega smokey bacon. None of it made much sense to her. Two schoolgirls, probably about fourteen, were standing in front of her. They were both quite lanky and one had her mobile phone on the go – texting whilst they chatted to each other.

"Oh my God!" shrieked one, "Tracey's back with Mark," her friend looked over her shoulder at the message.

"No! What after the way he treated her? The girl stupid or something?"

"She must need her head testing." The mobile phone girl agreed and was already replying. I'll ask her what she's playing at."

"Yeah, tell her she's a right doormat. That'll get her going." They both laughed and were then suddenly head of the queue to be served.

"Two veggies, fries and cokes, please."

The young man about twenty smiled at them from behind the counter.

"Takeaway or dining here, girls?"

They giggled. "Takeaway, like always."

"Salt and vinegar?" he asked as he turned his back and made

up their order.

He started a high pitched whistling which sounded rather manic.

The girls looked at each other. "He really fancies himself doesn't he?" one whispered to the other.

Behind them Millie was trying to make sense of the menu which was lit up over the counter.

"Paying together?" the boy asked, beaming, putting their order in a bag.

"No, separate." They dived into their school uniform jackets for change.

"There we are, special price for two beautiful young ladies," his eyes shone at them, but they were well used to his usual corny lines and they hurriedly turned to leave. "Bye."

Millie hesitated for a moment before moving forward to the counter.

"And what can I do for you, young lady?"

"Can I have a cheese and tomato sandwich, please?" Millie looked straight faced, ignoring his patronising address.

He shook his head and suddenly appeared very bored. "Only what's up on the menu, mum," pointing behind him.

Millie squinted her eyes looking at the board again, flummoxed.

"We're a burger bar," he smiled at her pityingly, looking at the other customers behind for some acknowledgment of this simple fact.

"We only sell burgers, see?"

"Well what can I have then?" she felt stumped and was irritated as to why he was speaking so fast, or was it her hearing?

"What about a cheese burger?" He pointed to a picture on the menu with his biro. She looked unimpressed.

"Is that lettuce?" Millie screwed up her nose and cocked an ear ready for his reply,

"Garnish, they all come with garnish and fries."

"I can't have lettuce. It gets under my dentures." She paused for a moment and looked at him earnestly. "You haven't got baked beans on toast have you?"

The young man shook his head again and was close to losing patience with her.

"No scrambled eggs either?" she asked quite meekly.

"Just the burgers," he jumped in, beginning to look agitated.

Behind Millie, the queue was almost to the door, and he was tapping his pen nervously on the counter top.

"Ok then, I'll have one of them cheese thingy's. But no lettuce."

"Takeaway or eat here?" he asked.

"What?"

"Takeaway with you or eat it here?" he almost spelt it out.

"Here of course. Where else would I eat it?" She shook her head in disbelief.

"Drink?" he bellowed across to Millie as she ambled over to a table near the window. She hadn't heard him and one of the women customers in the queue came over and relayed back. "Tea, strong with two sugars."

"She's starting to get to me, man," he grumbled to his assistant as he dealt with his next customer.

Millie looked out of the window at passers–by, laden with Christmas shopping.

Her meal was delivered with the minimum of courtesy and she just sat and stared at it for a while, sipping her tea. She saw that the garnish had not been removed but Millie carefully picked it out and put it aside on the plate. Finally she took a bite of the burger and was surprised that it didn't taste half bad.

She must have sat there for the best part of an hour nursing her mug of tea. She had left most of the fries because she thought that they weren't real chips at all. The queue had quietened down and the young man came over to collect the plates, not saying a word or making any eye contact. He left the bill on the table.

Millie stared at the piece of paper. "What's this?" she held it up. He turned, not quite making it back to the counter.

"It's your bill. Four pounds twenty pence."

"What for?"

He came back over, his face slightly reddening. "It's for your cheese burger," he replied sharply, leaning against a chair. Millie looked thoughtful but still surprised, and half got up and half sat down in a nervous manner, opening up her handbag. To the further annoyance of the young man she started emptying the contents on to the table – searching for her purse. Combs, biscuits, photos – her usual collection began to emerge. Searching through the contents, Millie peered into the bottom of the bag and then up at him and gave a playful chuckle.

"How much did you say, again?"

"Four pounds twenty." He was now holding the bill tightly as though his life depended on it and the cafe was beginning to get busy again.

"Well?" he asked impatiently.

"Well what?" Millie really seemed none the wiser.

"Are you going to pay or what?"

"What for?"

"Christ," he sighed, "Are you trying to wind me up? You're the third one this week," pointing to her as though Millie were part of some conspiracy. Turning on his heels, towards the counter he served a few customers and then got on his mobile.

"Dad, we've got another one … elderly, non-payer. Cheese burger and chips." Staring hard at Millie from across the room, "I'm gonna call the police, they can sort it out. We can't keep having this. She's a batty old woman." He then made another call and strode over to Millie's table.

"Ok, now listen, right." Millie still looked a bit vacant but could see that he was angry.

"I've called the police,"

"Is something up?" she gasped.

"Look, you just stay there lady, that's all." He raised his voice, "They're coming to sort you out."

"But I haven't done anything wrong. I've never been in trouble with the police."

"Well if you won't pay up for what you've had!"

"What have I had then?" she looked at him quite innocently.

"A cheese burger – you know you have."

"But I just wanted a cheese sandwich."

"Yes, but you had a cheese burger. Anyway, lady, I'm not going to argue. The cops will see to you." He headed back to the counter.

"Excuse me," Millie called over. "Can I use the loo, please?"

"Help yourself," he pointed to a door nearby.

"I'm bursting," Millie muttered to herself and slipped into the rather small toilet. She loosened her coat and sat down on the toilet seat. She was feeling upset. 'The cops are coming. Where was Abi when you needed her?' She had to get home, but how?

Returning to her table, she noticed that the queue to the counter was long and the young man and his assistant had their backs turned dealing with orders. Millie simply slipped out the front door without them seeing her. A little way up the road, she noticed a police car cruising towards the cafe. Millie quickened her pace and went into a shopping mall. The place was busy with shoppers. Millie found a bench, sat down and began watching passers-by, some of whom she smiled at. The mall was bedecked with Christmas decorations and a tall Christmas tree in the middle – its lights twinkling grandly. Millie dozed off for a little while and when she awoke she felt hungry again. Reaching for her bag she saw it wasn't there. She was sure she had it. Where did she leave it? Had it been stolen? Perhaps in the cafe, but she couldn't go back there again.

Millie got up and decided to go home. Outdoors the evening air had got much colder and she pulled up the collar of her coat. Her feet felt frozen through and she wished she had brought a scarf too. How could she get home? She came here by bus she recalled. She stopped a young man who looked like he was returning from work.

"Excuse me, I'm a bit lost. Where can I get a bus?"

He smiled at her. "Where do you want to go?" He had a Polish or maybe Russian accent.

"I'm not sure."

He laughed a little. "You don't know where you want to go?"

"Home I suppose," Millie said rather casually.

"Well, where's that?"

"Ah, that's it you see, it's moved."

"Your home has moved?" he laughed politely and Millie noticed what nice teeth he had.

"Perhaps you should go to the bus station and remember, eh?"

Millie smiled. That seemed like a good idea.

"You turn right and right again and it's a little way down there."

Under her breath, Millie repeated the instruction, rote.

"Will you be OK?"

"Oh yes, I'll be fine, thank you."

"You are very welcome, take care."

Suddenly with the dark and the cold everything seemed quite menacing. Millie really did need to be home and in the warm. She quickened her pace along the street muttering the directions over and over again. But then she spotted the bus station and as though by magic a bus was drawing in with Hastings on the front.

"That's it, that's me," Millie yelped with relief.

A small crowd gathered to get on and Millie realised that she had lost her bus pass along with her handbag. As a group of foreign students with enormous back packs in front of her were trying to buy tickets, Millie skilfully bypassed the driver and found a seat at the back of the bus. She sank down out of sight and was feeling quite hungry. She began fretting about her lost handbag, the biscuits, her glasses and all her personal things. That letter about her daughter, that was in it too. What will happen about that now, she wondered?

Millie dozed off during the long journey home. She woke up feeling shivery and all she could see outside was the pitch black countryside, broken up by the reflection of the headlights from passing traffic. The two girls before in the cafe came to mind and it made Millie think about the letter regarding her daughter. What would she have been like at their age? She couldn't even recall her name now. Jane, Janet, something like that. How old was she? Must be sixty, easily. All those years wasted, not knowing where she was, who she was, but always hoping that she was happy. Millie still remembered her birthday, 14th March, but the year that she was born – that seemed to have gone completely. On that day Millie used to sing happy birthday to her. Once or twice she was, caught out by Abi's mum who thought it a bit odd. Millie wondered if her daughter looked much like her when she was younger. She wouldn't recognise her now, how could she?

All in the past, Millie thought, and maybe best left there.

The bus pulled up sharply and interrupted her thoughts. Students with their back packs scrambled heavily downstairs and got off.

"Where's this?" Millie muttered to herself. She was almost alone again as the bus swept along the highway, dipping here and there and along the way illuminating trees, throwing ghostly shapes across the marsh. Millie fell into a slumber again, passing along the coast line.

When the bus finally pulled into Hastings railway station, Millie had awoken. She thought it must be the last one, as there was hardly anyone around.

As she got off, the cold cut through her, but at least this time she remembered where she lived and swiftly made her way home.

Tired and hungry, she rang the doorbell of the flat. Abi opened the door and looked very relieved to see her. Sherman was standing behind her smiling, Millie suddenly remembered that they all had a row earlier or was it yesterday? That was why she had skedaddled.

"Millie!" Where the hell have you been?"

"I've come home for Christmas," she said rather snootily as she brushed Abi aside. "Put the kettle on and I need something to eat."

* * *

A few days later Abi was still trying to get things into perspective. Millie's recent disappearance had given her a shock. The police had turned up today to return Millie's handbag, saying that it had been found in a cafe in Folkestone. Also worryingly, Millie was said to have left without paying the bill for her meal. When Abi looked, Millie had enough money stashed in her purse. Could Millie have made her way to Folkestone and back on her own? Abi wondered. Millie couldn't remember a thing about her journey. On some days now, she could hardly work out who she was and on others she was as bright as a button. On the day that she had vanished, Abi and Sherman searched frantically around all the likely places. At least this time she didn't go missing in her night clothes, although Abi saw that when she came in, she was still wearing her well-worn carpet slippers.

Abi noticed that Millie had been unusually quiet since her disappearing act. After a while, she asked Sherman to go home and give them a bit of space. He hadn't taken the hint at first so Abi had to spell it out. She thought that he being around the flat, may have contributed to Millie going off. He'd been kind to her – making cups of teas and chatting, but nowadays you could never tell with Millie, how she felt about things. Sherman did tend to make a song and dance which may have upset her. Perhaps, thought Abi, that's where things started to go a bit haywire for auntie. He could have put her nose out of joint. Sherman could be a bit larger than life. Also he's not so fond of cats and she would have noticed that with their Tiggy. Also this whole thing about Millie's granddaughter and family being in touch, maybe that has been preying on her mind.

During the past month, things between Abi and Sherman had got more serious and Abi was not sure why, because he wasn't really her type of bloke. She had come to rely on him being around – he had grown on her. For all of Sherman's brashness and swagger, she had become very fond of him and he was someone, apart from Rita with whom she could let off steam. Even so there were things that she thought needed sorting. For example there was his personal hygiene: a) foot odour b) dandruff c) going on about his mum d) naff blazer, dress style etc. etc.

However there had also been the regular sex of course. From early on Abi made it clear that is what she expected. Sherman was taken aback by her forthright manner and insatiable appetite for lovemaking. Her spontaneous, lustful and imaginative repertoire had caught him off guard at times to the point where he thought he should get himself some Viagra. Also given their individual circumstances – each having elderly charges at home – meant a lack of privacy. Sometimes they had to resort to the back seat of Sherman's car, which was not ideal for him, as he was so fussy about its polished interior. Also there was the odd fumble in a bus shelter along the seafront which did not bother Abi who always enjoyed an edge to her nights of passion.

"You're a lady who could give a bloke a heart attack," he said one evening, hot under the collar as she disrobed playfully for him in his front room whilst his mum was still preparing for bed upstairs.

"Ooo, Sherman," Abi cried out, moving closer, gently pulling at what little hair he had left on his head and breathing heavily in his ear.

"Keep it down for gawd sake, mum'll hear," signalling to her bedroom just above them.

They fell on the sofa and Abi already had her hands down his trousers, unbuckling his belt.

"I thought you said she was deaf," she panted as their bodies swiftly entwined.

"Only when she wants to be."

"Oh, fuck!" Abi's voice rose with the excitement of his touch.

"Mum," Sherman pleaded to her again; his body stiff with tension.

"Oh fuck mum," Abi aroused and wanting more.

"Fuck mum?" his eyes jutted out like propellers.

"Yes, oh, yes, fuck, fuck, fuck!" she gasped even louder as they both reached a climax.

They rolled on to the carpet, caressing each other, outstretched in front of the telly. Upstairs they heard Sherman's mum go into the bathroom.

"Are you one of those feminists?" Sherman asked Abi, stroking her arm as they relaxed.

"What do you mean?"

"Well you seem to like taking charge."

"Don't be daft, that's not feminism – I'm spontaneous. I just like to grab the moment, that's all. It's me! Don't you like it?"

"Oh yes, I'm not complaining. I like being your sex slave." He grinned although the romp had caused the sciatica in his legs to play up again.

Going back to today. After the police had left, Abi concluded that she wasn't really coping. The officers both had a cup of tea and Millie amused them with her tales of her days running the B&B. Then the female PC took Abi aside and gave her a telephone number of a local carers support group. She said that her own grandmother was suffering from what Millie probably had got, although she didn't say what.

"You know, forgetting all sorts of stuff and often turning up on the other side of town. And she's not the only one! We get calls like this all the time." Abi thought that the young woman made Hastings sound as though it was the twilight zone.

Later that day, Abi felt quite depressed as she watched Millie continually go through bits and pieces from her handbag. Things had got worse for auntie and she hadn't even noticed. Millie's behaviour was becoming more unpredictable. However she couldn't lock her indoors when she went out, so where would she disappear to next? Millie could have a fatal accident crossing the road as she seemed to be losing all common sense.

Lighting up a cigarette in the kitchen, Abi was feeling very resentful. It was though she had become a prisoner, looking after Millie twenty-four seven. Abi wanted to spend more time alone with Sherman and she needed her own space too. Why did this make her feel so guilty? Maybe a day centre was the answer after all, or a care worker at home but that would cost. She couldn't keep asking Rita. And that was another thing, she hadn't told her yet about any of this. Rita had been right all along about getting help. Well maybe now she really had to do something about it. Abi looked out of the kitchen window. Her hands were shaking and she felt sick.

∼ Forty Seven ∼

Abi phoned Rita at one in the morning – howling and hardly making much sense at all. Between Abi's wailing she could just hear her say, Millie walking out, carers, Sherman, money and knickers!

They met up the next day in an out of the way small café near the town centre. Rita could see why Abi felt in such turmoil, it was a crisis. She wasn't surprised to hear about Millie's latest disappearance – that seemed inevitable. In a way as Millie had made her own way back home from Folkestone, she thought it was a kind of improvement from the last time she went walkabout. It was quite a surprise though for Rita to hear that Abi and Sherman had become an item. Rita had to do a lot of hand holding with Abi and listen to her cry for help. They went over again how Abi might get some proper support now for auntie. Rita told her that she couldn't go on like this and totally agreed that she should have more of a life of her own.

"It feels like everything is crashing down on me at the moment," Abi moaned.

"And there's this letter of Millie's too. I've wanted to burn it." Rita was reading through the letter for the third time. "Auntie let me contact them eventually on her behalf. It turns out that she not only has a daughter but a granddaughter who is the one who wants to get in touch."

"Who'd have thought it?" Rita lifted her cup of coffee without drinking any, still not taking her eyes off the letter. It was a revelation.

"I wonder who it was, the bloke I mean," Rita chewed it over, "she'd never spoken about him had she?"

Abi shook her head and drawing breath said, "Her daughter could be just a bit older than us."

"I hadn't thought of that." Rita's eyes widened and she gulped her coffee which had gone cold. "I'd always reckoned auntie being, well, a single lady, a spinster I suppose, in the old term."

"I know what you mean. At home when I was a kid she was always there, just dear old auntie. But this sort of changes everything about the past. All the while she was with us, she had a sprog being brought up by someone else and we never knew. I can't get my head around it. I don't know whether I feel angry or what."

"Well we don't know the big picture do we?" Rita chipped in, wistfully.

"Who's to say what the circumstances were and she was just in her teens herself. It wasn't easy in those days bringing up a kid and on your own if that was the case."

"Maybe that's why she was so good to me when I became pregnant and had that miscarriage … well you know." Abi said, looking very thoughtful.

Rita nodded, they hadn't spoken about it for years.

"I always remember she'd come in and sit down on my bed and put her hand on my stomach. 'How you doing?' she'd say. Not that you could really feel anything at that stage. If only I'd known that she'd been through it all herself." They were both becoming weepy now.

"It's very sad really – it must have been hard for her at the time and this has brought it all back," Rita frowned and raised a gentle smile.

"Yeah, must have. And you know what, Rita? I think that's what's getting to me. When I lost mine I reckon that I'd got over it, but now it's all been churned up again somehow. Me and auntie, we've both been in the same boat – losing our kids. But now hers has turned up. And where's that leave me?" Abi looked confused and Rita noticed that she had let her coffee get cold too.

They both held hands for a while in silence and Abi rubbed her eyes.

"Millie wasn't keen on me contacting them but I persuaded her we should find out. Now I feel like her. I just want it all to go away. It's a nightmare."

"But look at it this way," Rita suggested, trying to be positive. "If they meet and it works out, this granddaughter and maybe her own daughter might be able to help with looking after her. You'd have more freedom with Sherman."

Abi threw Rita a look of horror, "But she doesn't know Millie and auntie doesn't know *this woman*," she blurted out, feeling exasperated. "Anyway what if it's a mistake? They may have all got their wires crossed. It will be really upsetting for her. Things are confusing enough for her as it is." Abi looked ahead in a daze. Rita folded the letter carefully and put it back in its envelope.

"I know that, Abi, but this might be a relief for her. She's probably been bottling it up for years. Meeting up with her family could be very good for her. In any case," Rita added. "It may not be up to you."

"What do you mean?" Abi wiped her eyes and looked a bit confused.

"Well you know, in the end Millie may want contact with her. You won't be able to stand in her way. I mean, you haven't got any legal responsibility have you – Power of Attorney or whatever it's called? " Abi felt her stomach tighten as Rita's question hung in the air.

"I could speak to them again and explain the situation more, to say that it would make Millie even worse. All this change, new people in her life. It could cause her a lot of distress."

"You don't know that, Abi, I think you need to get some advice."

"But where do *I* fit in then, Rita?" Abi raised her voice, folding her arms and leant back rigidly in her chair. "I've been looking after her for years and this woman who she never knew and claims to be family can just swan in and take over. It isn't right – it really isn't." Abi suddenly got up from her chair and hurried outside the café. Rita watched her through the window. She turned her face from the wind, her red hair blowing wildly as she pulled out a packet of cigarettes, her hand shielding the spark of the lighter. When Rita joined her on the pavement, she saw that Abi still had a frightened look in her eyes, afraid of what was to become of Millie and her. Abi took a long draw of her cigarette and the smoke vanished down the street in a puff.

"Are you OK?" Rita asked putting her hand softly on Abi's shoulder.

"She's all I've got, Abi sobbed, resting her head against Rita.

"I know love," Rita comforted her with a gentle hug. "It'll be all right, really, you won't lose her. What would she do without you, eh? Come on let me have a drag of that ciggie."

They huddled together in the doorway, sheltering from the icy blast.

"So, this Sherman. He makes you happy does he?"

Abi smiled through the tears and gave Rita a coy look.

～ Forty Eight ～

On her way to work during the last week, Rita was appalled to see in the window of a nearby DIY shop, a poster advertising *'Buy Here – now that Woolworths is closing down!'* Rita was livid. She nearly stormed into the shop to give them a mouthful. How could they have no respect, cashing in on what was happening to the town's store?

The final week at Woolworths was mayhem. Posters filled the store's window-front announcing: *'70% Off,'* before it rocketed to 90% and on the door, a countdown of the days left. Woolies legendary January sales had turned into a final bonanza for diehard bargain hunters attracting those as pushy as they come. Staff were demoralised further and emotions ran high when more 'vultures' arrived, complaining that the left over goods were not going cheap enough. Each day, the shop area became smaller and smaller. It was like the Alamo! After all the shelves were stripped bare, they too were flogged off, along with other fixtures and fittings, making the place look like a shell. Rita even spotted the staff lockers being wheeled out of the store and she wondered if hers still had her picture of Tom Jones pasted up on the inside. Rita looked again at a letter that they had all just received from the Job Centre to say that they were opening over the weekend, especially for all the redundant Woolies staff to attend and sign on.

Then suddenly it was all over: Saturday 3rd January 2009.

Rita gathered outside the store with her work mates as the shutters were rolled down on the shop for the very last time. A biting cold coastal wind snapped at their ankles. A few of the regulars turned up too including the elderly lady with the canvas shoes, crying. Where would she go now to while away her days? Rita wondered.

Unemployed at fifty seven, Rita thought to herself – what now? She could almost consider herself a pensioner. She wasn't ready for that yet. She certainly wasn't as badly off as some. Her mate Pat was just forty-five, a single mum with three hungry young teenagers to support. Rita felt very emotional as the shop lights were switched off and they gathered together in the darkness and gaze of West Hill. Rita thought for a moment about how many generations of Hastings families had shopped at Woolworths. She had a sudden pang of nostalgia, remembering her mother bringing her to the store as a child to buy sweets. Now the building looked like it had been ransacked, desecrating those intimate memories. Woolies had played a part in her growing up and it was also the longest job that she'd ever had. It didn't seem fair. Rita felt that she still had work in her and she wasn't going to give up.

Shivering in the cold, the workers chatted about their prospects; a few had got jobs already at Iceland and in Priory Meadow Centre shops. Young Michael had secured a position at WH Smith, but some, like Rita, were going to sign on. There was a jovial mood and even a chorus or two of Pink Floyd's 'Money' with high kicks from a group of young women who had quickly opened a few cans to celebrate getting their redundancy pay. A couple of bottles of bubbly were also produced and eventually, with tearful goodbyes and embracing each other, things began to gradually break up. Everyone began drifting off in different directions.

Rita hugged Pat and some of the others, looked up at the store sign, and turned towards the town centre heading for home, when she spotted Millie with Fly walking towards her. And just nearby, sitting on a bench was Abi, Leo, and Bill singing 'Auld Lang Syne' to her. 'Should auld acquaintance be forgot, and never brought to mind … ' Rita's face lit up, surprised and touched by them all turning up together for her last day.

"All over?" Abi asked, putting her arm around her.

"Yes, all finished," Rita gasped, shivering with the cold and inside feeling a sudden wave of panic about her future.

"Well let's all go and have a nice drink then," Leo suggested.

Fly led the way to The Eagle.

"You'll find something else," said Bill, sounding unusually optimistic.

Abi linked her arm through Rita's as they strolled along.

"Yes, I know. Something will turn up I dare say. Anyway I've got me P45 and they've paid me off – so the first round's on me!"

"Only the first?" cut in Leo, "You mean I've come out in this freezing cold to help cheer you up for just one measly pint?"

"Does this mean that you didn't do too well at the bookies this afternoon, Leo?" Abi asked.

"Let's just say that it could have been better."

"Don't worry, Leo you won't go thirsty. Anyway I feel like having a celebration. It's an end of an era and it's a New Year," Rita laughed.

Millie was now walking out in front with Fly. "Is this the way?" she called back to them.

"Yes, auntie, just follow the dog. He knows where we're going," Leo cried out.

"I'm glad somebody does."

Abi and Rita stopped walking for a moment.

"I've phoned up about Millie's family being in contact with her."

"Have you?"

"Yes, it's for the best isn't it?" Abi looked at her for some reassurance.

Rita nodded, even though she was wondering whether it was.

"But you know, Millie, she's her own person. If she doesn't want to do something, nobody's going to force her."

"Absolutely," Rita agreed and gently squeezed her arm.

"Don't worry, love, you're not going to lose her, you'll see."

"And what about Sherman?"

"I'm keeping him at bay at the moment, until this gets sorted."

They walked on to catch up with the others.

"So, this New Year is gonna be a lot of change for both of us." Rita said, pulling up the collar of her coat and glimpsing up at the stars in the clear winter sky. "I reckon we might even get a bit of snow before long."